Angel's Triumph

HUGH A. FLOWERS

Paperback-Press
an imprint of A & S Publishing
A & S Holmes, Inc.

ISBN: 978-0692333341
ISBN-13: 0692333347

TABLE OF CONTENTS

ACKNOWLEDGMENTS i
CHAPTER ONE...3
CHAPTER TWO...10
CHAPTER THREE...17
CHAPTER FOUR 24
CHAPTER FIVE 31
CHAPTER SIX 39
CHAPTER SEVEN 45
CHAPTER EIGHT 50
CHAPTER NINE 56
CHAPTER TEN 64
CHAPTER ELEVEN 68
CHAPTER TWELVE..74
CHAPTER THIRTEEN...82
CHAPTER FOURTEEN 89
CHAPTER FIFTEEN 96
CHAPTER SIXTEEN 103
CHAPTER SEVENTEEN 111
CHAPTER EIGHTEEN 117
CHAPTER NINETEEN 125
CHAPTER TWENTY 132
CHAPTER TWENTY-ONE...140
CHAPTER TWENTY-TWO 144
CHAPTER TWENTY-THREE...152
CHAPTER TWENTY-FOUR...159
CHAPTER TWENTY-FIVE 164
CHAPTER TWENTY-SIX...169
CHAPTER TWENTY-SEVEN...176
CHAPTER TWENTY-EIGHT 183
CHAPTER TWENTY-NINE..190
CHAPTER THIRTY 196
CHAPTER THIRTY-ONE 205
CHAPTER THIRTY-TWO 213
ABOUT THE AUTHOR 220

.

ACKNOWLEDGMENTS

I'd like to give a special thank you to Nathalie Kelley for once again painting the perfect cover art for this book. You did a wonderful job.

My thanks also goes out to Tina Vyborny for her help. Your time is appreciated

.

CHAPTER ONE

Lilly and I were walking back to the MU campus. It was late for us to be out, but we treated ourselves to the movie to celebrate finishing our finals for the end of this semester. We walked three blocks before I became aware that two men were following us and who were now almost upon us.

"Lilly, let's cross the street! There's two men behind us."

Lilly looked behind us at the men as we crossed the street and saw that they were running toward us. A street light cast our long shadows toward them as we stopped in the street and faced them.

"Aw Pete'y they didn't run," said the larger of the two men as they now slowly approached us. We separated so that we had room to act as they stopped in front of us and gave us evil smiles of anticipation.

"Pete'y I want the skinny white girl, you can have the black one." The two men made their move then by reaching out for us. We surprised them by taking their outreaching arms and twisting them as we threw them over our heads in a classic judo move. They fell on their back's with broken arms screaming in pain. We walked to our attackers and as mine tried to stand, I kicked his broken arm silencing his cries of pain as he passed out. Lilly's attacker was still screaming, so I kicked his broken arm too, causing him to pass out.

I used my cell to summon the police and EMT's. While we waited we dragged the two men to the side of the road in case of traffic. I asked, "How do you feel?"

"Angel! Crap a 'doddle. I'm still shaking, look at my hand. It's a good thing you taught me some judo moves, it sure saved my ass. Why did you kick them?"

"I didn't want him to run off and their screams got on my nerves. Besides, they needed a lesson on what happens when they attack women."

It wasn't long before the police arrived closely followed by a EMT wagon. We gave our report to the pair of officers. The female officer gave us a slight smile before saying, "good for you. What kind of martial art moves did you use on them?"

"Judo. I'm a black belt and I taught Lilly enough moves to get the job done."

"You two both students at MU?"

"Yeah, we were walking back after seeing a movie in town and these jokers tried to assault us. I think from their conversation that they wanted to rape us, but we changed their minds."

"Okay, I've got your statements. Come by the station tomorrow and sign them. If we need to talk to you again we know how to reach you."

Two weeks later we were in Kansas City, Missouri visiting my parents on semester break. Lilly urged me to join her in visiting her parents in Hannibal.

"Angel, please come with me. I'm not sure I can take any more of my father's hellfire and brimstone preaching. I might just break with him and never come home again. Mom is caught between us and if I leave home I may never see her another time."

She looked ready to cry with eyes glassy and bright with unshed tears, so I knew she was serious and really needed my help. I placed my arm around her and gave her a hug and agreed to go home with her for the remainder of our break from Missouri University at Columbia. Lilly's father is the head of the black Baptist Church in Hannibal, Missouri, who raised her on a diet of the wrath of God coming down on all those who didn't follow His word.

My name is Angel Pearson and many remember me as the

little white-haired girl who could heal people by direct contact, or by a ill person touching a picture of me. Recently, God took away the healing power of my touch, but my pictures still have healing power. He instead gave me the ability to diagnose medical problems to replace the power to heal. Aunt Barbara, who is a messenger angel from God, informed me that I needed to learn how to make better use of this power through medical training. My ambition now is to go to medical school.

Lilly's goal when she left home for college on a basketball scholarship, was to get away from what she considered her father's excessive control of her life. Religion under his tutelage smothered her to a point that she was ready to leave by any means she could find. When we met as dorm roommates, Lilly initially thought that God played a terrible trick on her by matching us up. However, when Lilly heard my story we came to an understanding. The deal was, I wouldn't preach at her and she would help and protect me, a fifteen year-old home schooled innocent girl, and show me how to survive the ways of the world.

Lilly now wanted me to protect her from her father's excessive religious attacks while home on her break. She much preferred my Aunt Barbara's love from God, rather than her father's fire and brimstone preaching.

As we approached Hannibal, I asked Lilly where her father's church was located in the town, and she smiled and said, "I don't want to spoil your surprise. Just wait and see."

Lilly drove down Front Street near the Mississippi River, past Becky Thatcher's house and a block later stopped in front of the white steeple Baptist Church. It appeared to be the same church I saw in illustrations from Mark Twain's books. "Really! This is it?"

"Yes, it's been a black church since the original white congregation built a larger church over fifty years ago."

"How far away is your home?"

"Not far. Dad walks to the church every day." She said as we left the beautiful old church behind.

"We get a lot of tourist traffic to the church and their donations help with the maintenance. Members couldn't maintain this old church without that help."

Lilly drove about six blocks and pulled into a driveway sitting between two older two-story homes that looked as if they were constructed using the same plans. Lilly's home was painted white with blue shutters and trim. The adjacent house was painted gray with white trim. Other than the color, the two houses appeared identical. The whole block of homes appeared to have been built at least 100 years ago.

We pulled our luggage out of the her car and I followed Lilly around to the back door where we entered the house. Lilly yelled, "Mom, I'm home and I brought company."

Lilly's mother hurried to meet us as we entered the kitchen. "Lilly! You scared me out of my wits, and you brought Angel with you. Welcome, welcome, welcome! Oh my Lord, why didn't you tell me you were coming today, so I could prepare a proper welcome?"

Lilly hugged her mother and kissed her cheek. "That's why I didn't tell you, because you work too hard keeping this old house up. We can help you now that we are here, and do I need to go get some more groceries since we're going to be here for a few days?"

June looked at her daughter and smiled as tears ran down her cheek. "Maybe, does Angel want something special."

"Mother, trust me. Angel doesn't have any special needs. She eats the same foods we do, although, unless its pizza, not as much as a bird."

June looked at me in surprise. "You're putting me on. She's skinny, but doesn't look like she's missed any meals."

I said. "Don't believe everything she says. I just don't eat as much as she does. She needs to eat more because of the exercise she gets playing basketball."

"Lilly, quit making fun of how little Angel eats. Looking at you I'd say you need to cut back or your behind is going to be as big as your mouth."

My mouth hung open in surprise because I never expected such a retort coming from Lilly's mother. "Mom! Angel, is my butt getting bigger?"

I hid my grin, then replied, "Better go look in a mirror, don't take my word for it."

Lilly fled the kitchen looking for the closest full length mirror. I looked at June and said, "That was a good one. That's one area of her body that she's the most critical of. We haven't exercised enough while on break. Maybe I can get her to jog with me to burn off those extra calories she's been eating."

We suddenly heard a scream from upstairs and then loud groans as she returned. "Angel, my butt is getting humongous! Let's go for a quick run before we do anything else."

I winked at June before we gathered our luggage and headed upstairs to change. Lilly showed me the spare room next to hers that would be mine during my stay. "Don't dally. I want to get my butt back to the size I want it to be."

Lilly led the way and I followed a step or two behind and to her right. Since the sidewalks were buckled we ran in the street facing the traffic. We eventually arrived at an overlook of Hannibal and the Mississippi River. It was quite a sight with the barge traffic on the river and I would have liked to stay and watch it for awhile, but Lilly soon took off again at a slightly slower pace. Thirty minutes later we were back at her house where we each took a shower, changed clothes, and returned to the kitchen.

June gave Lilly a grocery list and some money and told us to hurry and return so she could start supper. Soon we were back and started helping put together a meal following June's directions. Ten minutes later I heard the back door shut and looked up, seeing Reverend Williamson standing in the doorway staring at Lilly.

"Daughter! I'm happy to see that you have decided to grace our home with your presence."

Apparently, he hadn't seen me until I moved and approached him, causing him to flinch. "I came with Lilly. I hope you don't mind?"

"No, I don't mind at all. I'm happy to see you again and from my daughter's letters you appear to be close friends at school."

"Yes, we're very close friends now. She stayed with me and my family in Kansas City before coming here. While we were there, I introduced her to my Aunt Barbara after Lilly asked about her painting's history."

The Reverend appeared confused. Lilly interrupted, "Dad, I met and talked to an actual angel. Barbara stepped out of her painting and stood before me, which gave me quite a start, as you might imagine. I asked her about God and how you preach about the wrath of God if you don't follow his commandments, whereas this angel's message is God's love of mankind."

"How did the angel respond?"

"She asked me what I thought after being exposed to my father's teachings and her message. I replied that both were probably true, but I preferred His love over His wrath, which I needn't fear as long as I was with Angel and followed Jesus' teachings."

"Daughter, you don't like my sermons of fire and brimstone?"

"No. You should show both sides of God, not just the vengeful side. Show him as a loving God as well."

Lilly's father turned to me and asked, "You have been talking to my daughter about my teachings?"

"No. The very first day in the dorm we made a pact. I wouldn't preach at her and she would help me fit in with other people. You do her a disservice by your actions and came close to losing her to the forces of evil in her attempt to distance herself from your preaching."

"You're saying she needs the love of God in her life, not just the fear of His wrath."

He turned to his daughter and held out his arms to her. "Come here daughter, so that I can hug you and show you my love for you."

Lilly ran into his arms with tears of happiness in her eyes. Lilly was a powerfully built young woman and nearly bowled her father over, who didn't outweigh her by much. June came up from behind Lilly and hugged both her loves, all three with tears in their eyes. Eventually, they broke apart and Lilly smiled at me in gratitude.

June said, "Back to work if we're ever going to get this meal finished."

Reverend Williamson came up behind me and gave my shoulder a squeeze before leaving the kitchen. I watched him leave and thought his steps looked like they had a little more spring to them than when he came in. June winked at me and then pointed at the carrots I was supposed to be cutting.

June was a great cook and that night, I ate the best fried chicken I ever tasted. However, her apple pie didn't match Grandmother's, but it was close. When Lilly started to take seconds I cleared my throat, and when she looked at me I shook my head and rubbed my bottom. She rolled her eyes at me, but dropped the chicken leg back onto the platter.

Later, she helped me make the bed in my assigned room and when we finished we sat on it and talked. "Angel, I don't know how I can ever repay you for what you did for me and my father's relationship. I think we may have a chance for a normal father/daughter relationship now. If you hadn't come home with me this might not have happened."

I hugged her against me and we leaned towards each other until our heads touched. "That's what friends are for. We watch out for each other."

She got up and wiped her eyes before saying, "Good night," and shutting the door behind her. Wiping my own eyes and finding a tissue, I blew my nose. Later, lying in bed, I kept remembering Lilly's face as she rushed into her father's arms, causing me to remember my own last departure from my family's apartment and the loss on my parents' faces as they watched their only child leave. Vowing to give them a call tomorrow, I finally fell asleep.

CHAPTER TWO

I awoke to the smell of frying bacon, which got me out of bed and into my clothes in record time, and after hurrying downstairs, I found June in the kitchen cooking breakfast. She pointed to the toaster where I began my part in this production. Ten minutes later Lilly showed up and received a (where have you been) look from her mother, which caused her to ask what she could do to help.

Reverend Williamson arrived shortly thereafter and taking in all the women working in the kitchen, quietly sat down at the table with a newspaper. June brought him his coffee, which he sampled before adding cream and sugar. He sat there sipping his hot coffee watching us work together for a few minutes before opening his newspaper and looking at the headlines.

It wasn't long before we were all seated at the table, ready to eat. Reverend Williamson said a brief prayer before we began our meal. I noticed that he looked at me several times with a thoughtful expression on his face, before he seemed to reach a decision.

"Angel, would you mind if I used you as an example of God's love for my flock. Lilly wants me to show His love as well as His displeasure when people don't follow His commandments. I think His gift to you of healing powers would make an excellent example."

"You do remember that he took away that gift."

"I remember, but that gift is still working for your photograph and he gave you another gift that will personally benefit you in the future and all those that you treat."

I nodded my head in agreement and thought for a moment. "You don't think I'm too controversial for your church?"

June spoke up. "We need to shake people up sometimes so that they pay attention to what's going on around them."

Lilly said, "Do it! I can even give testimony that there are angels from my own personal experience."

Reverend Williamson looked at his daughter with pride and a hint of tears in his eyes, before saying, "How about it? It should make an interesting experience for you."

"That's what I'm afraid of. I've been keeping a low profile at MU and this may put the spotlight back on me."

Reverend Williamson smiled at me, before saying, "You've never been shy before. I still remember those news programs where you stepped up and told your story. It should be no different today."

I looked at him and gave a crooked smile of defeat. "Okay. I'll do as you ask. What time do you want me there? June, you're going to have to help me get the wrinkles out of my best dress."

Sunday morning found me sitting up front with June and Lilly, waiting for the services to start. Reverend Williamson stood and stepped up to the pulpit and raised his arms above his head loudly saying, "Hallelujah, I say Hallelujah!"

This caused the congregation to repeat his words several more times before he lowered his arms and looked over his people. "Today we all are going to bear witness to a miracle. I'm going to present to you God's gift to mankind, Angel Pearson. She was given the power of healing when she was only a eight year old child. She is now a sixteen year-old teenager attending Missouri University with my daughter, Lilly. Angel, come up here and tell your story."

I stood and made my way to the stage, where Reverend Williamson ushered me to the mic at the pulpit. I repeated the story of my initial discovery of my healing powers and how my parents devised a way for my powers to reach the masses of sick and injured people throughout the world. I then told them of my loss of this gift and God's replacement with another power and my new goal of becoming a medical doctor to use this new power properly.

"I met Lilly at MU when I moved into the dorm. She was my roommate and we became best friends, and I acquired an older sister. Lilly, come up here and tell them what you have experienced since meeting me."

Lilly took my place at the pulpit and smiled at me. "She says I became her older sister. I didn't know what to make of her, this fifteen year-old, whose parents were helping move her into the dorm. After they left, she sat on her bed trying hard not to cry. This was her first time out on her own, because she had been home schooled from the time her healing powers became known. I was mad at her at first because she was so different from me. She was so young and innocent, and white. Even her hair was white and her name was Angel. Who would name their child Angel? When I asked her that she looked at me in surprise."

I interrupted. "I couldn't believe she didn't know who I was, and when I told her she acted like God was conspiring against her because of her temporary loss of faith. We made a pact where I wouldn't preach at her and she would watch over me and teach me how to blend in with the other students."

Lilly continued, "Despite myself, we became friends and confidents, telling each other our secrets and fears. She's very smart and helped me with my studies. I took her home to Kansas City on Spring Break and met her parents. I also met her aunt, Barbara Powers. On their mantel were two self portraits, one was her Aunt Barbara, who died shortly after painting it, and the other was of Barbara Messing. The Messing portrait was of a eight year old, who reportedly looked just like Barbara Powers at that age. The Messing girl had stayed with the Pearson's for a time after her last relative died while at their law offices and had become enamored with the Powers' painting."

I interrupted Lilly. "I told Lilly that I had carried on conversations with my Aunt several times before, but she thought maybe I was pulling her leg."

"Exactly. When I looked at the painting I could feel something I hadn't felt before. It was a powerful force I couldn't describe. Angel wanted to know if I had a question to ask her, and I was considering what to ask, when Barbara stepped out of the painting and stood before me. It scared me so much that I took a step back, but then the force of her power hit me hard. The angel asked me if I had a question. I knew then what that force was. It was love, God's love. I asked about my father's sermons preaching fire and brimstone as opposed to her message of God's love. She asked me what I thought it was. I realized that it was both, his love for us and his wrath if we don't follow his teaching. Barbara smiled at me and said she was sure I would make the right decisions in the future, then she returned to the painting. I still feel that love, even now."

The silence of the congregation was broken by their enthusiastic shouting of "Hallelujah", over and over again, each time louder than the last. Several women fainted and had to be tended to until finally, Reverend Williamson called for silence. Eventually, peace and calm was restored.

"My future sermons will include God's love of us as well as his wrath. We need to be reminded that he does love us and we should follow his teachings. Go home and remember what you heard today and reflect on how you conduct your own lives."

Four days later, Lilly and I were back at MU attending to our studies. It didn't take long before we were back in our familiar routines, me taking as many courses as the University would allow and Lilly taking just enough to keep her basketball scholarship so that she could have enough time to practice and play games. I continued to help her in courses she had trouble with and I followed her around trying to fit in. It's hard to fit in with people who are all three to six years older than you are, and who have had life experiences that you haven't experienced yet.

However, being with Lilly helped and I quickly became known as her nerd roommate who was helping keep her in college. I even helped some of the other teammates, which made me feel at least a little wanted.

My body was starting to mature and I now had breasts, however small they were. Lilly took me shopping for new underwear to celebrate my new additions. She referred to them as ant hills compared to her mountains. I thought, *she's being a little mean, because hers were not that much larger than mine.*

Boys still hadn't noticed me, except in class when they would ask for help. Both my mother and Aunt Barbara were beautiful and I still held out hope I will be at least half as pretty as them.

A year later my body bloomed into a replica of my mother.

While I didn't get her pretty face, I had her mature body, which has attracted lots of attention from male students. Lilly was running interference for me from the unwanted attentions of the opposite sex.

After three months of this hassle, Lilly and I were studying in our room and I said, "Being pretty is what I wanted, but I had no idea it would bring so many problems. How did you handle it?"

"Do you want your ant hills back?"

I shook my head and she continued. "I didn't think so. Now that you have it you need to learn how to use it. I'll help you get started, but we need somebody who is a master at it. Do you know who I mean?"

"Gloria Masterson!"

"Right the first time. She looks like Marilyn Monroe and has the male population following her around like she's chocolate on a stick that has to be licked."

"I don't want that kind of attention. I just want to be able to smile at somebody without having them climb my frame."

"Didn't your mother tell you anything? She must have had men after her all the time, as beautiful as she is."

"Apparently, she had to study all the time at Harvard to keep her grades up, which didn't allow much time to socialize. Besides, she had a crush on Dad and didn't want anyone else."

"Well, let's talk to Gloria and see if she will help you."

We cornered Gloria in the cafeteria the next day and I asked her for help. She looked at me in surprise. "You're what, seventeen? I bet you're a virgin too."

My face flushed a hot red as I nodded.

She looked at me critically for a moment. "Good, keep it that way as long as you can. You have something that all men want, an untouched beautiful woman. You want me to teach you how to control their responses to you, is that right?"

"Yes. I want to be friendly with men without having them becoming a pest."

"I can help you, but what do I get out of it?"

"What do you want?"

"You're the young nerd whose helping Lilly with her studies. I need help too. I help you and you help me."

"Deal! When can we start?"

"I'll stop by your room tonight, okay?"

A month later I had my routine perfected and Lilly cut my hair. Gloria suggested I change my hair style for a short, more severe business style. Now when I smiled at a man, his eyes widened with appreciation, but usually he didn't come over to strike up a conversation. I learned not to use that smile on a woman, as it had the opposite reaction.

Somehow I must have let something slip in my twice weekly telephone calls that alarmed mom, because she showed up in my room without notice. I said "enter" in response to a knock on the door, and she was there with a smile on her face, which collapsed when she saw my new short hair style. I stood to give her a hug and kiss of welcome, when in surprise, she gasped at my new body shape.

"Angel! You've changed into a woman."

I smiled at her and twirled around, giving her the full benefit of the new me. "I didn't change enough that you didn't recognize me."

"Honey, you've turned into a beautiful young woman. Where's Lilly? She was supposed to call me if anything happened to you."

I laughed. "Come on Mom. I don't think me growing up comes under that situation. I was beating boys off till I learned how to handle them."

"Oh honey. You should have called me. Was it a big problem?"

"Yes. I went from no one paying attention to me to suddenly everyone wanted to date me, even girls!"

Mother looked at me with her big dark eyes as she said, "Noo! I never had that problem."

Suddenly there was a knock and Lilly walked in. When she saw mother she said, "Oh, oh, now the fats in the fire!"

Mother said, "Lilly, thanks for the warning about Angel growing up into a woman overnight!"

"Well, we had our hands full for awhile there until we got some advice from our local Marilyn Monroe. She gave Angel some good advice and it's pretty much under control now. After what Angel went through I'm glad I'm not as beautiful as she is. I have enough trouble keeping the boys at bay as it is."

"Damn it, I wanted to be the one to help you with this part of growing up."

I put my arm around mother's shoulders and kissed her cheek. "You still can. I just learned enough to keep them at bay. Maybe you can teach me how to flirt without getting into trouble."

Mother winked at us. "Okay, how much time do we have before lights out?"

CHAPTER THREE

After mother returned to Kansas City, Lilly and I realized just how much we hadn't known about the world of boys and girls. Lilly asked, "Are you going to practice using any of what your mother told us?"

"I might have been tempted if there was someone I was hot for, but I really don't have time for boys now. How about you?"

"I don't have anyone I'm attracted to either, and I'm not going to tempt fate with a casual relationship. I think there's a special place in Hell for a minister's daughter who does that."

"Okay. If either of us is tempted we will tell the other before we do anything."

Thinking we had all our problems resolved we went back to our studies. It was soothing to our egos that others found us attractive, but for now we had other more pressing needs to fulfill. My junior year at MU I sent out applications to several medical schools, but the one I wanted most was Johns Hopkins University.

The fateful day arrived when I received a packet from Johns Hopkins. I was at my desk with the envelope in hand when Lilly entered. "What's that?"

"It's from Johns Hopkins."

"Aren't you going to open it?"

"I'm scared. What if they don't want me?"

"Oh my gosh! You ninny, just open it."

I looked at her with tears in my eyes. "I just realized that I'm about done here and wherever I go you won't be there with me. It's going to break my heart not having you with me."

I stood up, hugging her tight to me and we both started crying. After we blew our noses and wiped our eyes, Lilly said, "Listen, we're best friends and will stay in contact with each other and let each other know what we are doing. We can still resolve our problems together and share our good times and love interests, if we ever have any."

I nodded my head, then said, "I'm still going to miss you."

"Me too. Now open that letter!"

I punched her shoulder lightly, saying, "Spoil sport. Okay, let's see what I've got here."

After reading everything through twice, I looked at Lilly with a frown on my face. "This is going to be a lot of work. Oh well, I better start jumping through the hoops if I'm going to get it done."

A week later I sent the official application off to Johns Hopkins University School of Medicine with all the attachments asked for. I didn't know if my prior healing history and my present diagnostic talent would help or hurt my applications chances. Time would tell, all I could do was pray I would prevail.

Three months later, a letter arrived telling me an admissions officer from Johns Hopkins would be conducting interviews the following week at MU, and gave me a time and place for my interview. I showed Lilly the letter, who after reading it asked, "Is there any way to prepare yourself for this interview?"

I shook my head. "I have no way of knowing what they might ask. It could be anything, my life goals, hobbies, sexual preferences, anything at all."

"Well, if that's the case don't think about it anymore. Put it out of your mind entirely. Bury yourself in your studies. I know, teach me some more Judo moves. With you leaving I'm going to need to learn how to protect myself."

The next day during our break, Lilly and I went to a local Judo school to practice and purchase a beginning uniform for her. After changing into our uniforms, or gi, we started our training session well away from another class. I wore my black belt, the first time since entering MU. I told Lilly to attack me and not worry about hurting me. We were about the same height, but she outweighed me by at least twenty pounds, which was mostly muscle.

She rushed me, I used the simple move of throwing her over my hip, causing her to land on her back. I quickly knelt beside her and asked if she was alright.

"Oh my body, and I asked to do this. Well, at least it's not as bad as the move you taught me when we defended ourselves against those would be rapists. Okay, help me up."

"Remember, Judo is a defensive routine. You use the others strength against them. Let them come at you. Now I'll show you the move I used on you, so you can throw me."

When I was sure she understood the moves, I rushed her and she responded correctly, causing me to land on my back as she had before. I then proceeded to show her other moves she could counter attacks against her.

We were at it almost an hour when Lilly said, "Enough. I'm beat. This is the hardest workout I've ever done in my life."

I hugged her and was surprised when we received applause from the other students who had apparently been watching us for awhile. I gave them a smile and a low bow, which they reciprocated. Their instructor, a black belt, came over and asked, "Is this your first time here?"

"Yes, my friend wanted some self defense training before we left the University. It was her first time for a full session and right now she is feeling some pain. Lilly, you'll feel better if you take a shower to ease you're sore muscles."

Lilly gratefully left us. The instructor said, "My name is Roger Blevins. Have you held your black belt long?"

"Yes, since I was fifteen, and I'm rusty. I haven't been practicing since starting school. I'm only a first level, but my parents are both mid-level black belts."

"You looked good out there and have a knack for instruction. Even my students were watching you train your friend. What are your plans after college?"

I grinned at him. "Sorry, I'm afraid I'll be heading toward medical school. I plan on being a doctor."

"Wherever you go, keep up your practicing. Who knows, you might need it someday."

Lilly walked with me to the admission officers meeting place with five minutes to spare. I hugged her and she wished me well before departing. I double checked the room number and sat in the chair provided outside the room. At the appointed time the door opened and a tall, thin middle-aged man asked, "Miss Pearson?"

I answered yes and he asked me to step inside. He motioned for me to take a seat before a desk, while he walked around the desk and leaned against the chair back facing me.

"I'm Robert Townsend. Tell me about yourself, something not in your application."

I looked at him in surprise, because I had pretty much told my life story in the application. "I'm not sure what you want from me. I thought I was upfront with you already about my life."

"What has your life been like since you started at Missouri University?"

"It was scary being alone for the first time without my parents and making life decisions mostly without their input. My roommate helped me get settled and broke the ice about meeting new people, and making some new friends. She is now my best friend and we would walk through fire for each other. Is that what you wanted?"

"Yes, that's a start. You began school when you were only fifteen and you're now eighteen. Students at our University usually start when they are twenty-one, so most of your fellow students are going to be older with more life experiences. Do you think you can overcome that?"

"Are you saying that because they are older they can study better than me?"

He smiled and sat down, opened his folder and made a mark, then asked, "You say in your application that you have the ability to diagnose ailments by touch. How do you do that?"

I looked at him in surprise for a moment. "Obviously, you have no idea who I am. I suggest you better look at my application again and this time read it, all of it!"

Townsend's face went white, apparently no one had ever dared confront him before. He visibly composed himself and said, "Humor me. Who are you?"

"Until about three years ago I was that little white-haired girl who healed people by touch. It was a gift given to me by God, who in His wisdom took away this power and instead gave me the power to tell what was causing a person's aliment by touching them. His angel told me I should seek knowledge so that I could better use this power. He also gave me a genus IQ and a eidetic memory so that I could gain the most benefit from my education. My GPA here is almost a five and if you're not smart enough to realize what a benefit I could bring to your University, maybe I would be better off somewhere else."

Townsend looked at me for a moment, then smiled. "That's what I was after. You have to have a strong ego to be a doctor. You have a temper that you should work on, but otherwise everything looks fine. Did you want to be a surgeon or just a general practitioner?"

"I'm leaning toward a surgeon since being in blood doesn't seem to bother me. I'm sorry if I was being discourteous."

"No you aren't, you meant every word."

"True, but I wanted to apologize."

He handed me a sheet of paper. "This is information your parents will need about the cost of tuition and other costs for the first semester next fall. You will also receive a packet in the mail giving you all the other information you will need. Welcome to Johns Hopkins."

I returned to my room and called mother with the news. "Oh honey, that's wonderful news. I know that's the school you really wanted."

I told her about the interview and how I had blown up at the admissions officer. There was dead silence from mother for a few moments before she said, "After that you still got in?"

"Yeah, he suckered me into losing my cool. How many times has that happened mother? I can think of only one other time."

"I can't think of any time you have lost your temper that badly. You say he did it on purpose?"

"He wanted to be sure I had a strong ego. That I would stand up for myself. He said a doctor needed a strong ego."

"So you got in, that's what matters."

"Maybe so, but I'm still pissed at him."

"Honey, let it go. Cool down. Go to the gym and pound on some dummies."

I laughed. "Thanks mom, but it would just hurt my hands. I'm thinking of becoming a surgeon. Tell Dad I love him too. Bye."

Lilly came in and found me sitting at my desk staring at the paper the admissions officer had given me. "How did it go?"

"I got in for next fall's semester. But I'm pissed off at him."

"Wow! I've never seen you this mad at anyone before. What happened?"

I told Lilly the whole story and how Mom had advised me to go punch a bag to get the aggression out of my system. Lilly frowned. "I would have volunteered for another Judo session, but not when you're this angry. I know, let's go get a chocolate sundae."

My senior year passed quickly and it wasn't long before Lilly and I were sitting together waiting to receive our diplomas at our graduation ceremony. Later, after the ceremony we met our parents and talked them into going out together for dinner, before packing up and leaving the University.

We knew of a good steak house far enough out that we could get into if we ate early. We were early enough that we were seated at a table where, at least initially, we were alone in the room. I introduced Lilly's parents to mine and since Lilly was their only child too, they both had a starting point for discussion.

While they were talking, I asked Lilly, "Have you decided on a career?"

"I'm going to try nursing. Who knows, maybe we'll work together eventually."

"Oh Lilly, wouldn't that be great. Is there a school close to Hannibal?"

"Quincy, Illinois has a good school and it's just a few miles north of Hannibal, so I can commute."

"That should work out perfect for you. Do they have a basketball team?"

Lilly's eyes widened in surprise, then she stuck her tongue out at me.

Mom looked at me in surprise, then frowned at Dad. "Jack, our daughter has your sense of humor. She'll probably get herself into trouble over it."

Lilly said, "So that's where she gets it from. I guess I've gotten used to it."

"That's alright Dad, I don't think either one of them has a sense of humor."

"Oh your mother has one, she just doesn't like to be on the receiving end of a joke."

"Well, mother also has messy table manners, because she's dribbled all over her new blouse."

Jenn quickly looked down at her pristine blouse, before saying, "See, she's doing it again."

"I think she just proved my point. If she said I spilled something on my suit, then you would have laughed, not groused about her low brow humor."

"Okay, I get you point. I guess I just don't have the knack for pulling those kinds of jokes. June, do you or your husband make jokes about each other?"

"Heavens no. We are too strait laced for that."

Lilly had to cover her mouth to keep from laughing at that statement. "Mother is the jokester in our family. I take after Dad in that regard."

Reverend Williamson smiled at his daughter before saying, "I wish she had more of my traits, but in all other things she is her mother's daughter."

Jenn grimaced. "I wish Angel could commute to her school too. She has at least another four years of school in Baltimore, and then an internship somewhere. We're not going to be able to see much of her for awhile."

June replied. "I'm afraid that's part of growing up, eventually they leave the nest to start their own lives."

CHAPTER FOUR

That fall, I walked into Mason Hall, which contained the admissions office at Johns Hopkins University. I picked up my first semester class schedule and a map of the campus, marked where the book store and my residence hall were located. My dorm was in Wolman Hall and I had two assigned roommates.

I decided to get my books before checking out the dorm room and my new roommates. Two hours later I parked my rented SUV in the dorm's parking lot and lugged my books to the second floor of Wolman Hall. I knocked on my door, getting no response, I swiped my key card and shoved the door open.

The room was much larger than what I had at MU and had three separate bedrooms, each with a study desk and a small bathroom with a shower. Connecting them was a common area, that included furniture, TV, and a small area for snacks. There was a small refrigerator, microwave, and a coffee maker. A notice was posted that use of a hot plate was not allowed and would be taken when discovered.

Since I was the first to arrive I selected the middle bedroom and dropped my books there. It took me four trips to the car to get all my possessions into my room and I was starting to hang clothes when I heard a knock. I answered the door to find a pretty woman standing beside two large suitcases.

We introduced ourselves and I helped her move her luggage into the common room. Her name was Julie Westerman from Plano, in what she called the great state of Texas. She was elated when she heard I was from Kansas City.

"Great! At least two of us are from the Midwest. Angel Pearson, somehow that name is familiar to me. Don't tell me I'm sure it will come to me. Am I the last to check in?"

"No. I picked the middle room, so you have a choice of either of the other rooms. This is lots larger than my room at MU."

"We may need the extra room with three women living together. I hope you're not a slob, because I'm not picking up after anyone but myself."

There was another knock on the door, which I answered to a petite five foot woman dressed to the nines. She entered without any luggage and we all introduced ourselves. Her name was Robin Lacy from Macon, Georgia, and her southern accent was twice that of Julie's. I grinned and said in jest, "Since we all are from southern states, should we fly the confederate battle flag."

I was surprised that they took me seriously, as Robin asked, "Did you bring one with you? If not, I can have my folks mail us one overnight."

Julie smiled, "Never fear, I've got one in my suitcase. Where can we hang it?"

The two deep southern woman agreed on a spot and we soon had a confederate flag displayed in our common room. *Mother was right, I'm going to have to watch my big mouth.* Robin pulled out her cell and told someone on the other end where to bring her stuff. The two woman then agreed which room they each would take and I went back to hanging clothes.

I was arranging my books according to my class schedule and making sure that they would fit into my book bag with my computer, when I heard Julie yell, "Does anyone want to check out the cafeteria next door?"

Robin's room was overflowing with her stuff and she joined us, saying, "There's no way I'm getting all this into my room. I'm going to have to ship some of it home. I can't even give some of my clothes to you girls because you are both giants compared to me."

I suggested, "When we get back from dinner I can help you

sort what will fit in your room, then we'll stack the rest next to the door for pickup by the moving men. Anything you don't want to keep we can stack downstairs with a free sign."

We found the food passable, but agreed to try other available places to eat before settling on a favorite. The two girls went to the book store, while I returned to our room. I was walking down the hallway, when a handsome man left the room across from mine. When our eyes met I felt a jolt in my gut. We smiled at each other and introduced ourselves.

His name was Jeff, short for Jefferson Blake, from Kansas City. When I told him my name and that I was also from KC, he hesitated before asking, "Are you the girl who heals people?"

I looked up into his gray eyes and said, "I was that girl, but I no longer have that gift."

"Wow! I've met someone really famous. You don't look anything like the pictures I remember, of course you were only about eight then."

"Yes, I've grown up. How do I look now?"

"You look really beautiful. Just how old are you now, because I was at least four years older than you as I remember."

"I'm not quite nineteen, so you're about twenty-three?"

"Almost twenty-four and getting ready to start my second semester. This is your first semester?"

I nodded my head. "I just moved in. Maybe our two rooms can get together, so we can get some pointers on what to look out for."

"Your roommates as pretty as you?"

"I think so. Both of them are southern belles and I think you'll appreciate their accents."

"I'll talk to my guys and get back to you later."

I smiled and left him in the hallway watching me as I closed the door, then leaned against it as I shuddered holding my arms around myself as I took a deep breath and tried to calm myself. I knew I would have made a fool of myself if I had spent another minute with him. No man had ever made me feel like this before.

When my roommates returned, I informed them of a possible date with the men across the hallway. Julie looked at me with a shocked expression. "You really surprise me. I wouldn't have thought you would have the nerve to start a conversation with a man."

"Normally, you would have been right. But, Jeff's cute and from Kansas City and we just seemed to click. He's a second semester freshman, and might give us some pointers."

Robin said, "I'm game, but right now I need help with my stuff. Come on, help me out."

Between the three of us we made two piles, not counting the items Robin decided to keep and had room to store. The pile we were going to discard, we took downstairs and put a free sign on it. The items Robin wanted to send home we stacked next to the entry door.

We were all collapsed on the couch catching our breath when there was a knock on the door. The girls looked at me expectedly, so I hurried to the door and opened it. Jeff and two other young men were smiling at me. I smiled at Jeff and asked, "Are these your roommates?"

"Yes. This here is Bob Peterson and Ralph Masters, both second semester freshmen like me."

"Great. Come inside and meet my roommates, but excuse the mess. Bob and Ralph, these are my roomies, Julie Westerman and Robin Lacy. I'd offer you a soda or a beer, but we haven't shopped yet."

Jeff spoke. "We have. What do you ladies prefer?"

Julie and Robin said, "Beer," while I said, "Pop."

Jeff quickly returned with two six packs of beer and a couple of cans of 7-Up for me. Apparently, I was the only one not drinking beer. We brought out our desk chairs, so everyone had a place to sit and we started to get to know each other.

Bob and Ralph were the same age as Jeff and were both good looking, about the same six foot height, but Bob was a red head, while Ralph was sandy headed. Together, the three might have been taken as brothers, except for their hair color. Jeff was dark haired with a five o'clock shadow of a beard showing on his face. Bob was from Waco, Texas, Ralph hailed from Tallahassee, Florida.

Jeff and I were standing together and watched as the others seemed to couple with people from the same geographical area. I said, "Wow! That didn't take long to make a connection. Jeff, I understand that we get a faculty advisor assigned to us who is supposed to guide us through the next four years. When does this happen?"

"The first week you should receive a letter informing you of your appointment with your advisor. Be sure to check your dorm mail box daily, at least until your e-mail address is on file. Most of your university correspondence will be by e-mail after that. Be sure to study your assigned readings as at least thirty percent of the test questions come from them. A person without a good memory is going to have problems here."

"That shouldn't be a problem for me because I have an eidetic memory."

"I'm glad that they don't grade on the curve here, because you would probably mess it up for the rest of us. Most tests are graded A=95+, B=85-94, C=75-84, less than 75 is unsatisfactory. You should repeat any course that you fail to get at least a B. That's why some students take more than four years to graduate."

Our first meeting with our male neighbors went well, but they warned us that our free time in the future would be severely limited. The first week passed in a blur and we got our appointment to meet our advisor. Mine was at Mason Hall with Dr. Janice Ellsworth.

When I arrived, she introduced herself and said, "I will be your instructor in 'Clinical Skills', a core first-year course. I advise five students from each of the four years and continue this relationship during the four years you are here. Do you have any questions?"

"So you are advising twenty students. Is this strictly course advice or do you advise on personal matters as well?"

"Generally, I limit myself to course advice. If you need personal attention I would send you to our counselor, Georgia Walker. Miss Pearson, looking at your admission application I noticed that you are the Angel Pearson who was documented for having healing powers. Do you not have those powers anymore?"

"No Doctor, not for almost four years now. God in His wisdom took those powers from me and instead gave me the power to diagnose by touch what is causing a person's ailment. I'm attending medical school to make better use of this new power."

"How accurate is this new power?"

"I don't know. Would you like to test it?"

Dr. Ellsworth considered my offer for awhile, then said, "I'll make arrangements and notify you by e-mail when and where to meet me. If there is nothing more, I'll see you at that time."

After dinner that evening I received an e-mail from Dr. Ellsworth to meet her at the Johns Hopkins Hospital, room 618, at seven p.m. I checked my time and saw I had an hour to get there. I knocked on Jeff's door and Bob answered. He called for Jeff, who met me at the door.

"Jeff, I'm supposed to meet my advisor, Dr. Ellsworth, at the hospital at seven tonight. I'm not sure how to get there."

"I can walk you there. It shouldn't take more than fifteen minutes. What's up with you meeting her there, if it's not too personal?"

"She wants to test my diagnostic powers to see how accurate they are. I'm interested too, now that I have some medical knowledge to help me."

"Even if they're weak, in practice it would be a great help in picking what tests to run on the patient. Not so much in school, as you determine what the cause is from the symptoms. Do you want a soda while I finish what I started on the computer?"

Later, we talked about common things we knew of Kansas City until we came in sight of the hospital. "Just go in the front door and take the elevator to the sixth floor. Let me know how it went." He said and then turned back towards Wolman Hall and the studies I had interrupted.

Once on the sixth floor I asked the head nurse where room 618 was, and she pointed where I should go. At the room I knocked and someone said, "Enter."

I opened the door and found Dr. Ellsworth and an older man in a white coat that had his name stitched on it, Dr. Peter Jacobson. He shook my hand told me to take a seat and everyone followed suit. Dr. Jacobson introduced himself and said, "Dr. Ellsworth tells me that you have a unique talent that she wants tested for accuracy. I'm fascinated as well and have arranged three patents for your test. We will take you to three rooms each with a patient, A, B, and C. You do what you do, but don't speak to the patient. When we finish, we will return here and you will give us a recap of your findings. Is that clear?"

Twenty minutes later we were back into room 618. Dr. Jacobson looked at me expectedly, so I began. "Patient A has a thyroid and a pancreas problem; the pancreas appears to be in an early stage of cancer. Patient B has a tumor on the upper right side of the brain. Patient C seems to have cancer of the liver that has spread throughout the body. How did I do?"

Dr. Jacobson looked at me with pride. "You were 100 percent; however, we did not know about the Patient A's pancreas problem. That will be looked at immediately. Maybe if it is early enough we can save his life."

Dr. Ellsworth smiled at me and said, "It's possible we will again call upon your gift in the future. Each time we do we will credit your tuition cost $5,000. Will that be satisfactory?"

"Of course. Although I would have done it at no cost."

"Based upon your past, I would not have expected less of you. However, we want you to feel part of Johns Hopkins and we hope this is just the start of a long relationship. I think we are done here and you may return to whatever you were doing before getting this summons."

"Dr. Ellsworth, before I leave I need to talk to you privately."

"Very well, let's step out into the hallway."

Once the door was closed I walked a few steps away and turned towards her. "When I touched Dr. Jacobson when we shook hands, I discovered that the left pulmonary artery of his heart was over eighty percent clogged. He is in immediate danger of a heart attack."

Dr. Ellsworth's face went white as she realized the danger her friend was in. "Thank you for warning us. I will take immediate action. Wait a minute, what would you recommend that action to be?"

"Aspirin is the only thing that comes to mind."

"Good answer. I'll talk to you later."

CHAPTER FIVE

I knocked on Jeff's door when I got back to the dorm. He answered the door and seeing who it was, grinned at me. "How did the test go?"

Blushing, I said, "100 percent plus. I saw early cancer of the pancreas on a patient that they were not aware of, and I warned Dr. Jacobson that he had a severe blockage of the heart. I guess I had a good day."

Jeff looked at me in awe. "Angel, you have no idea what you have put into motion for yourself. Once the instructors hear what you are capable of I'm sure you'll be placed in some kind of accelerated program and the hospital will want your input on special patients."

"Dr. Jacobson told me that they may call me in to consult on patients and would credit my tuition $5,000 for each consult."

"Wow! It's already begun. You must have really impressed them."

Jeff then gave himself a mental shake. "I've got to get back to my class assignment. Angel, if you want to talk in the future, just knock on my door."

After he closed his door I returned to my room where I found both my mates hard at work on their assignments. I yelled that I was back and took a few minutes to call my parents. Mom put her

phone on speaker, so Dad could hear too when I said I had
something important to say.

"My faculty advisor, Dr. Janice Ellsworth, wanted to test how
accurate my diagnostic powers are. She got together with Dr. Peter
Jacobson, a senior staff member at Johns Hopkins Hospital, and
arranged for me to use my abilities on three test patients. I did
well, I even diagnosed early cancer of the pancreas for one of the
patients, an illness that they were not aware of. I later told Dr.
Ellsworth that Dr. Jacobson had a severe blockage in his heart that
needed immediate attention. The last I heard was that they may use
me to consult on patients and would reduce my tuition $5,000 for
each consult."

I could hear their silence as they were each thinking what this
could mean for me. "Honey, that's great, but what is this going to
mean for your studies?"

"Maybe nothing, maybe everything! I don't know, I just don't
know. Mom, Dad will you send me a copy of Aunt Barbara's
picture. I think I need her here to advice me on my future steps that
I may need to take."

Dad said, "I will get it to you within three days, I promise."

Mom said with a catch in her voice. "Honey, we love you and
let us know of any hard choices you may need to make."

I switched off and laid my head on my desk, crying for a few
minutes into my arms until I felt drained. I blew my nose and
wiped my eyes before starting on my class assignments.

Three days later a large crate with a FedEx sticker was leaning
against my door when I returned from class. I dragged the box into
our common room and opened it, leaning Barbara's picture against
the couch and immediately felt her love. I basked in her love for a
few minutes until I felt stronger, then searched the walls for a good
place to hang her picture.

I was still considering when Robin came in. She immediately
hurried forward when she saw the picture. "That's the self portrait
of Barbara Powers! It is, isn't it?"

I was a little taken aback by Robin's enthusiasm and asked,
"How did you know of her work?"

"It is her picture! How in the world did you get a copy?"

"I got it from my parents. They own the original."

She looked at me as if she was seeing a ghost. "You're Angel

Pearson! How obtuse can I get. I was told the whole history of the painting and of the other water color Barbara when we bought one of her works. I'm so sorry Angel that I didn't connect the dots until now. What in the world are you doing going to a medical school?"

"Long story short, God replaced my healing powers with diagnostic abilities and I was told by Aunt Barbara that I needed medical knowledge to make better use of this ability."

"Aunt Barbara, this Barbara? She talks to you?"

I hugged Robin and because she was so short, her head only came to my shoulder. We then gazed at the picture of Barbara. "Look at her. Take a big breath and let it out slowly and calm yourself. Can you feel the power coming from the picture?"

Barbara upped the flow of love as it washed over us like a tidal wave. Robin inhaled a deep breath as if trying to swallow up more of the love flowing to her. "Oh my gosh, the rumors are true. She is an angel and she talks to you!"

Julie walked into the room just then. She also became enthralled by the picture. I grabbed her hand and pulled her to me and we all stood together with me sandwiched between the two women. After several minutes they seemed to regain awareness of their surroundings and we all collapsed to the floor in a lotus position, still looking at the picture.

I asked, "Where do you think we should hang the picture?"

Robin said, "Honey, I don't care as long as its somewhere in this room."

Julie and I got up, and considered the best place to place it. I said, "Why not move the couch away from the wall and hang it there. We can turn the couch around so that it faces the picture. What do you say?"

The other two agreed and we soon had the task completed. We all sat on the couch and soaked in the power of Barbara's love for a few minutes. I asked, "What did she say to you two?"

Robin said, "She told me to watch after you and to make sure no boy gets too close to you and that I had good taste in art."

Julie said, "She said the same thing to me about boys and that I should now reconsider how I viewed God and angels and how my actions reflect upon my character. Gee Angel, you could have given us some warning of who you are."

"Would you have believed me?"

"Well, no, but subsequent actions wouldn't have been such a surprise."

"I had to bring Barbara to me because of things that are going to change for me. My diagnostic powers were tested at the hospital and the doctors were so impressed that I'm going to be pulled away from time to time as a consultant. There is a good chance that my class schedule is going to change too. I wanted Barbara here to offer advice in case I need it. Besides, she has a calming influence on me."

Robin and Julie echoed that feeling as well. We all left for dinner and dropped off the crates remains as we left the building. Upon our return we were studying for about two hours when I heard a knock on our door.

I looked through the little viewer and saw it was Jeff. I invited him inside where he almost immediately saw the picture of Aunt Barbara, which stopped him in his tracks. "That's the Barbara painting I've heard about!"

"It's a copy. How do you know it?"

"That's one of the most known painting in Kansas City, besides the one of you and your family. She's so beautiful - you two look like you're the same age!"

He moved me to where I stood just to the side of the picture and then laid his ball cap on my head, covering my white hair. "Now stay put, I want to compare you and your aunt."

I could see his eyes moving back and forth between me and the Barbara picture. He walked over and used his fingers to move my jaw slightly before smiling. "You and Barbara could be twins except for your hair color. You really don't have any idea just how beautiful you are, do you?"

We were interrupted by Julie's voice. "What's going on here?"

Jeff turned to find both my roommates standing guard over me. "I was comparing how much Angel looks like her aunt. They could be twins, except for the hair color. Do you all know the history of this painting?"

Robin said, "Yes, Angel introduced us to Barbara today, who told us to watch over her. You know Barbara is an angel, don't you?"

"An angel? Barbara talked to you! So the rumors are true. Did she say anything about being protected by a guardian angel?"

Julie asked, "You mean Barbara is a guardian angel?"

I spoke up. "No, my guardian angel is Olivia. Barbara is a messenger, not a warrior."

Now all three of them were staring at me in awe. "What! You all knew I've led an unusual life. So, I've got two angels looking out for me. Olivia only appears if I'm in mortal danger and hopefully I will never need her again."

Jeff cleared his throat. "But, you have seen her in action?"

"Oh yeah. She's quite fascinating! When she arrives, it's in a flash of white light that is almost blinding, and when she spreads her wings she goes into attack mode and points a silver sword that shoots a lightning bolt of energy at her target. The noise is loud, like a lightning strike and then she disappears."

Jeff said, "I'd like to see that. It would be a sight to behold."

Robin said, "Remember, that bolt of energy killed somebody. I'd just as soon not have Angel put into that kind of danger."

"Dad told me that Olivia first appeared for him when was ten years old and saved him from a car wreck that killed his mother. Sometimes she just keeps me out of harm's way."

Jeff said, "So Olivia is protecting your whole family, not just you."

I nodded, "Am I too weird for you to be my friend?"

Jeff smiled at me and shook his head. "You are a beautiful woman who completely fascinates me." His statement caused my stomach to flutter in a disquieting way.

Robin interrupted. "Back off Jeff. I don't think Barbara wants Angel to get too close with a man at this point."

Jeff said, "It's just as well, because I can't make time for anything more. Love would take too much focus away from our studies."

My stomach flutters stilled as Jeff took another look at the Barbara picture before leaving. Julie shut the door behind him and both women saw the misery on my face. Robin put an arm around me and gave me a hug.

"He likes you or he would have run for the hills when he found out about your guardian angel. So don't despair, you may get together yet."

I mustered up a smile. These girls were friends to stay with me after what they had learned about me. "Okay, that's enough of this.

We need to get back to our studies."

At semester's end I'd earned A's in all classes. I consulted two more times with patients at the hospital, and I heard that Dr. Jacobson had recovered and was back at work. Dr. Ellsworth e-mailed me to meet with her tonight at Mason Hall to discuss my next semester classes.

When I arrived, I found Dr. Ellsworth was not alone. She introduced me to Dr. Mary Kilpatrick, who was in her early thirties, had long auburn hair that appeared to be naturally curly, was about five foot six, slim with an athletic build, and had a cute face with a light sprinkle of freckles across her nose.

Dr. Ellsworth said, "Dr. Kilpatrick is our athletic director and wants you to consider entering one of our sporting programs. We have an excellent women's lacrosse team, soccer, track, and swimming. Are you interested in any of these?"

"Dr. Kilpatrick I have a black belt in Judo and I was wondering if there is somewhere to practice and if others are available to practice with?"

"You say that you're a black belt. Why that's perfect! I've been wanting to start a women's self defense class, but I could never find a qualified instructor. I'll find you a place to practice and we can get together and determine what else you will need to get this started. What do you say? Will you do it?"

"I don't have much time to spare on this project. Are there any students who already have some experience in Judo?"

"Two others, one is a man and they are both upper-class students."

"Okay, I'll need to meet them and judge their skill level."

Dr. Kilpatrick suddenly smiled. "I think you will find a way to make this work for us. Why don't I e-mail them to meet you at the gym tomorrow evening in uniform. Is six okay with you?"

I agreed and she left us. "I feel I've been hijacked into starting this program."

Dr. Ellsworth smiled at me. "She's been trying to get that program started for the last five years, but until now had never had a student or Doctor who could act as an instructor. Now, let's get to the courses you are going to take next semester."

I got to the gym early to check it out and change into my gi. While I was changing I met Jamie Grant, a third degree brown belt and a 2nd year student. We left the change room together and met Mark Andrews, who said he was a fourth degree brown belt and was also a 2nd year student. Jamie was slightly smaller than me, but Mark looked like a football player and I later found out he played ball in college.

I introduced myself and told them I earned a first degree black belt before attending college and hadn't done much training since. "Let's start slow so we don't hurt ourselves. Mark come at me and let's see if I can move all that muscle of yours."

Mark looked like a mountain as he came my way, but muscle memory took over and when I fell backwards he flew over me like he was supposed to. "Okay, Jamie let's see if you can throw him."

She did the same move I had and Mark ended up on his back again. "Okay Mark I'm going to come at you. I know I don't look like I can do much, but I might surprise you, so be on guard."

Mark set himself ready to throw me, but I used one of the sneaky counter moves and he still ended up on the floor. Looking up at me from the floor he said, "Wait a minute, let's do that again in slow motion so I can see what your move was."

We continued for an hour until I could see that even Mark was tired, so I called an end to the session. Before we went to the showers I told them that we were going to start up a self defense class soon and wanted them to be my assistants, and were they interested? Mark asked, "Is it only going to be women, or were there going to be men students too?"

I replied, "That depends on who signs up. If you know of any men or women interested, ask them to sign up when its posted. I hope we don't have more than twenty people, because I don't have free time for more than that, even with your help."

As Jamie and I showered, she grumbled about how much her muscles were complaining. I told her it had been over two years since my last full training session, so I was in the same situation as she was, although I was younger than her and could probably handle it better.

"I know you looked younger. Just how old are you?"

"I started MU when I was fifteen, when I got my black belt, and I already had a year of credits. I just turned nineteen. How old are you?"

"I'm twenty-three and right now I feel every year. What are

you, a prodigy?"

"Not like as you mean. I just have a high IQ and a eidetic memory."

"In that case, they may push you through on an accelerated program. If so, we could have some classes together sometime."

"I'd like that."

"Me too."

.

CHAPTER SIX

A week later I got an e-mail from Dr. Kilpatrick asking me to meet her to plan a self defense course. Eighteen students answered our query, including three men. I called Dr. Kilpatrick and suggested, "We need to e-mail them back and ask for their sizes, so that we can order uniforms. Is this going to be a free course, or was there going to be a fee in addition to the cost of the uniform?"

Dr. Kilpatrick said, "I discussed this with upper management and they agreed to keep everything free, including the uniform. They did this because students were the instructors."

"Did any of the staff express an interest in the course?"

"You know that's a good idea for some of our younger staff members. I'll ask about that for future classes."

Two weeks later we had our first scheduled Judo class. The only students with any experience were the two who were my assistants. I gave everyone the history and purpose of Judo as a self defense practice. When I started the lesson I used Mark as the aggressor and demonstrated how easy it was to use the aggressors strength against them. I then had Mark take the male students aside and start their instruction, while Jamie and divided up the women between us.

After thirty minutes of primary instruction, my assistants and I attacked our students to see how much they learned. None of our students failed to break the attacks. I had them sit in a lotus position around me and had them ask me questions about the holds they were learning. One of the men, Jasper Campbell, asked what would happen if the attacker also knows Judo moves.

I asked Mark to demonstrate a counter move, one that I had already taught him and Jamie. Mark and Jasper stood within the circle of students and begin the demonstration, Mark showing one way to break the Judo move they just learned.

"Remember, the more you learn about Judo, the more dangerous you are to the attacker. There is another form of Judo used for attacking, but we are here to learn self defense. If you find yourself threatened by a gun, run away as fast as you can!"

One of the women held up her hand, and asked, "How old were you when you earned your black belt?"

"Fifteen, about four years ago. It took me five years to earn my belt."

"You started when you were ten?"

I nodded. "My parents gave me a choice of what I wanted to do. They tried to get me to try dance, but they were both black belts, so I went with Judo. I started MU just after earning my belt. If there are no more questions, meet here same time next Wednesday."

This semester I was taking Clinical Skills from my advisor, Dr. Ellsworth. She gave five of her students special attention, so I guessed we were all her first level students. There were three women and two men in the select group and I took note of who they were and asked them all for their e-mail addresses.

I then e-mailed each of them an invitation to meet and form a self preservation plan. The place of the meeting was in my apartment at eight tonight. The four arrived on time and I introduced myself and had them introduce themselves. One of the women was a Hindu from India, whose name was Jara B. Deb-Nath. She spoke English with a British accent and was a slim, short, medium light skinned beautiful woman. The other was Deborah Worth from Dallas, Texas. She was an attractive slim blond who looked like she was raised on a ranch. She wore cowboy boots and was deeply tanned in spite of her blond hair. The two men were dark haired and both were sporting a five o'clock shadow on their faces. They were about my height and appeared to use weights as they had well defined chest and arm muscles.

"I thought that since we were all being advised by Dr. Ellsworth, we should meet and get to know each other. Perhaps we can help one another. Does anyone have any ideas?"

Deborah spoke. "My family is well known in the Dallas area and used some influence getting me into this school. Jara appears to have the same kind of influence. How about you guy's, did you get in here strictly on your merits?"

Jerome and Mack indicated they also had used family influence to get here. Deborah turned to me and said, "Now, with Angel here we have a real celebrity among us. Many people know her as the Healer. What are you doing here if you can heal?"

"About four years ago God replaced my healing powers with diagnostic powers. My Aunt Barbara told me I needed medical knowledge to better use this new ability."

Deborah asked. "Who is Aunt Barbara?"

I pointed to the picture on the wall. "That's my aunt. She's a angel."

The four stared at the picture, which suddenly amped up its energy level so that everyone could feel its effect. After a few minutes Jara blinked and looked at me. "I'm a Hindu and a Catholic, and you talking to God through angels is breathtaking."

Deborah whispered, "Wow! Your aunts a angel. Where's the bathroom? "

The two men appeared about to faint. I quickly got them a soft drink, then Deborah returned. "I haven't done that since that bull chased me under the fence. My point is that we all are special cases that Dr. Ellsworth is handling."

I looked at the two men, who had gotten their color back, and asked, "Jerome, Mack, are you guys okay?"

They both gave me a faint smile and nodded their heads. Mack softy said, "I come from the City of Angels, but I never expected to see one."

Jerome shuddered and then said, "My mother told me I'd better watch my ways or the Lord would visit me. That's as close as I want to get in this life."

I looked at the others for a moment thinking. "Let's have a

meeting with Dr. Ellsworth and clear the air. Do you want to ambush her or let her know we want a group meeting?"

Deborah said, "I think we'll get more information if she doesn't suspect that we know each other."

"Show of hands. Those who vote for an ambush?"

I said, "It's an ambush then. I'll e-mail her and set up a meeting. When I find out the time, I'll e-mail you and we'll go in as a group."

After they left the apartment my roommates came out of their rooms and looked at me questioningly. Robin said, "Are you planning a revolt?"

I smiled ruefully. "Revolt against what? We don't know what's going on and that's what this meeting is going to be about."

Julie grinned. "Both of those men were dreamy looking. They had muscles on their muscles. Come on Angel, introduce me to them."

I smiled at her and shook my head. "After the experience they just had here, do you really think they will want to get together romantically with anyone from this apartment?"

"We might as well be nuns."

Robin said, "Don't be so pessimistic, we can meet boys away from here."

"Yeah, at least until they hear rumors about us. The rumor mill here is as strong as any at your last school."

I said, "Poor babies. Now you know how I feel. Aunt Barbara has even put you two to watch over me."

Two days later our group met outside Dr. Ellsworth's door at the appointed time. I knocked and received Dr. Ellsworth's enter command. Her face went from a smile of greeting to one of uncertainty as all five of us entered.

Dr. Ellsworth frowned, then said, "Angel, what's going on here?"

"Madame, that is our question! We have determined that we all share a common factor, perhaps a uniqueness that has caused you to place us together under your supervision. Perhaps you are not aware that this interest has been working against your other students. They are not receiving as good a tutelage as we have. Is this common factor perhaps because of a deviation in our initial enrollment?"

"Angel, come on now. You can do better than that. You were right, it was because of a common deviation in your enrollment, but we would have approved all your enrollments if you hadn't had this common factor."

I quickly looked at the others and from their expressions I suddenly knew the answer. "We all have eidetic memories!"

The others looked at me in surprise, then with comprehension. Deborah asked, "How did you get that from her clue?"

"People with eidetic memories have a tell on their faces when they access their memory. When Dr. Ellsworth gave us the clue, I watched your faces and my guess was proven."

Dr. Ellsworth smiled at me. "Brilliant! A true mark of a diagnostic genius. It's true I was given the task of monitoring your progress; however, I wasn't aware that I was shortchanging my other students. I'm going to monitor your progress by having you five attend as many classes together as can be arranged. That way the common factors will be the same instructor and the same time of day. Does anyone have a question?"

Deborah asked, "What did you mean when you called Angel an diagnostic genius?"

"She can diagnose an ailment by a single touch, but she also has an analytical mind that she used to discover what your common factor was. By the way, why didn't you two women sign up for the self defense class?"

Jara asked, "Why didn't you include Angel in that question? Did she already sign up?"

"No, she teaches it."

Jara looked at me with new respect. "Angel, is it too late for me to join your class?"

Before I could answer her, Deborah asked to join too. Before I answered I looked at the two men and smiled, asking, "Surely you guys don't need self defense classes with all those muscles."

They smiled back at me and shook their heads. Mack said, "If we need help we know where to come."

I turned to the two women. "Our classes are Wednesday night's at eight. Meet me at the gym at seven fifteen. We ordered extra uniforms that should fit both of you and I'll go over the basic Judo moves that were taught at the first class."

Jara said, "Judo! You're going to teach us Judo."

"Have you had any training?"

"No, but one of my brothers is a black belt. He'll have a cow when he finds out that I've started training."

"You won't get into trouble, will you?"

"Oh no. It's just that such training is not open to women in my country."

"Don't tell anyone, what they don't know can't hurt you."

*   *   *

After her students left, Dr. Ellsworth picked up her phone and called a number. "This is Janice. My first year group showed up wanting to know what factor we used placing them together. Angel was the ringleader and the one to guess it was their common eidetic memory. Yes, she's a strong leader and others are drawn to her despite her young age. She's instructing a self defense class every Wednesday night at eight. I recommend that someone monitor how well she does. Okay, I'll keep you informed."

CHAPTER SEVEN

Wednesday night I met Jara and Deborah at the gym. I had brought several sizes of uniforms with me because Jara was so small. I gave Deborah a uniform my size, but it took two tries to fit Jara. They watched me as I started to put on my uniform, and then followed suit. They were watching to see if I was going to wear underwear, which I didn't. I showed them how the white belt was supposed to be tied, then I placed my black belt on.

Jara asked, "What degree are you?"

"Only a first degree. My parents are both mid-level black belts. Dad taught mother after they met. She told me she was only a mid-level brown then."

Deborah asked, "White belt means a beginner?"

I smiled at her. "Yes, a novice."

When we got to the training floor I demonstrated the basic moves to defend against an attack. When I was sure they understood I told them I was going to attack each of them and they were to use those moves against me. They were both good students and they each threw me according to plan. I then had Deborah attack Jara and after Deborah fell, Jara quickly checked with her to make sure she was alright.

I placed my hand on Jara's shoulder and said, "Don't worry about hurting Deborah, she's a big strong woman. You're the one

I'm worried about because you're so small."

"Angel, don't worry. I may be small, but I'm tough."

"Okay, this time you attack Deborah and get thrown. Are you ready?"

Jana landed on her back and blinked her eyes at me when I bent over her body. "Are you okay?"

"I think so. I think she threw me further than I did her."

She quickly sat up and stood. "What's next?"

I was still going over other defensive moves when the rest of the class arrived. After introducing Jara and Deborah to the other students I assigned them to different assistants, with Jara going to Jamie. I did the circle again with me in the center pulling various students in to demonstrate various moves, before breaking apart into three areas where the students applied these new moves.

Later, after showering and changing back into street clothes, I asked Jara and Deborah what they thought of their first Judo class?"

Jara was ecstatic. "At first it was strange, but as I became more confident in myself, I really enjoyed throwing people around - especially the men."

Deborah grinned at Jara's comment. "Yeah, it felt good. I think all the women enjoyed themselves. Angel, did you get the feeling that we didn't get the full story from Dr. Ellsworth?"

"Yes, I got a tingle from my BS meter. Let's keep our eyes and ears open and hopefully we won't get blindsided."

The next day I got an e-mail from Dr. Ellsworth asking me to consult on a case after my last class. I was to report to Dr. Bill Pullman, Room 412, in the hospital. I arrived at 4:30 and knocked on the door. Not hearing a reply, I tried the door and finding it unlocked, peeked inside.

The room appeared to be a doctor's office with the usual decor. There was no one present, but a tablet was propped on a desk with my name on it. It said, "Be right back, have a seat."

I waited about fifteen minutes before the door opened and a man backed into the room carrying two coffees, being very careful not to spill them. I quickly held the door for him and he thanked me by handing me one of the cups.

As he walked around his desk to sit down I was surprised at how young he looked. My guess was late twenties or early thirties.

He was my height and extremely handsome. He was wearing a lab coat, but he appeared to be fit and slim.

"Hi, I'm Dr. Pullman. I've got a problem trying to find the cause of a patients illness. Dr. Jacobson suggested I consult with you because of your past success."

"Have you got the patient's chart. I don't need it for my consult, but as a medical student I'm interested in the symptoms related to the cause I find."

He gave me the chart, which I quickly read. "Tell me about the patient."

"She's twelve years old and recently returned from a vacation trip with her parents in South Africa. She began having her symptoms within a week after returning home and has now lapsed into a coma."

"Let's look at her. Obviously, she contracted something from a bite, inhalation, or through mouth that is causing the problem. A bite you would have checked for, now what else could cause this reaction? Maybe an allergy?"

He showed me into a ICU unit after we had donned protective wear and masks. My hands were covered in gloves, but it didn't affect my gifts power. To be certain I touched her head, chest, abdomen, and feet, before telling Dr. Pullman I was finished.

We returned to his office and I went to a human body chart on the wall and pointed at the brain. "Her brain is swelling, which is probably the cause of the coma. Her lymph glands have been adversely affected, and her lungs are starting to fill with fluid. There does not appear to be a start point for any of these reactions. What would be a treatment for an unknown allergy?"

"Steroids. In this case a massive dose if we are going to be able to save her. I agree with you that an allergy seems the most likely culprit. If we're wrong, she won't make it."

"Steroids can kill her too, especially a massive dose. Is there a safer alternative?"

"Not that I'm aware of."

"Dr. Pullman you probably know of my past history as a healer. I don't know if it will work, but if you give her a pint of my blood, maybe that will cure her."

"What's your blood type?"

"O"

"Okay, we'll try that and if there's no improvement we'll go with steroids."

Later that night I got an e-mail from Dr. Pullman saying our patient had come out of her coma and was getting better. At the time I was studying and this news lifted a load off my mind. I sat down in front of Aunt Barbara's picture and looked up at her, tears in my eyes.

"Barbara I tried something today that saved a little girl's life. I gave her a pint of my blood which seemed to have healing powers. I didn't know if that was allowed, but I was rushed and needed to do something or the girl would die. Is this something I can do in the future?"

Barbara's love engulfed me and I heard her voice say, "Angel it was your loving nature and care for others that let your blood cure the girl. Use this gift sparingly as your blood was meant for your protection."

I nodded and went to bed, knowing that I would sleep well.

Three days later Dr. Pullman e-mailed me to visit him at my convenience. Later, I knocked on his door and found him in his office.

"Our patient wouldn't take no for an answer and wants to see you personally to thank you for saving her life."

I grimaced, but then agreed. Dr. Pullman led the way to her room where we found her propped up finishing her lunch. He introduced her as Julie Bowman and I took her hand.

"Dr. Pullman, she seems clear of her previous problem. Are there any lingering symptoms?"

"No. She will probably be released tomorrow."

Julie asked, "Are you a doctor? You seem awfully young to be a doctor."

"No, I'm a medical student at Johns Hopkins and was called in to consult because of a gift I have."

"Gift. What kind of a gift?"

"I can tell what is causing an illness by touching a patient."

"Oh, that explains your earlier comment. Dr. Pullman said that you were the reason for my recovery?"

"You received a pint of my blood that led to your recovery."

"Oh! Then you did save my life."

"Yes, my blood has special properties that counteracted the

agent attacking your body. You may find that it will attack other types of infections as well."

Dr. Pullman asked, "Would you answer health questionnaires that Johns Hopkins may send you. I'm sure that they will wish to track your future health."

Julie agreed, while looking at me in awe. She had an inkling of understanding that she had been given a great gift that would follow her throughout her life.

I returned with Dr. Pullman to his office where he asked me to sit. We looked at each other for several minutes, with neither of us giving away our thoughts. He finally said, "You are a quandary for us. You are a wondrous asset, yet you have no official position other than as a medical student. To continue using you as an consultant we need to place you into our official structure somehow. We can't hide you as in the past because today you were uncovered by our patient."

"You could place me under a department, maybe "Experimental Medicine," and have me report to a small cadre of doctors. Give me a title, other than doctor, that will not irritate other physicians until I actually earn the title."

Dr. Pullman looked at me and started to tap a pencil on his desk as he considered the ramifications of my suggestion. He was tapping the pencil so long that I was about to reach across the desk and grab it, when he said, "I like it. I'll get with the powers and see if we can make it work. You better get back to your studies and I'll contact you when a decision is made."

CHAPTER EIGHT

Two weeks later I was officially part of Johns Hopkins new Experimental Medicine under the hospital's umbrella. I even had a title, Intern. When I visited patients with other doctors, I could hide behind a white lab coat with my name stenciled on it.

When my roommates heard about the change in my status, Julie said, "It's started then."

I called Lilly and we caught up on what each other was doing, and at the end of our conversation I told her about my most recent change, being on staff at Johns Hopkins as an intern working under Experimental Medicine.

"What! Girl, this is important. Have you told your folks yet?"

"No, you're the first to hear. I'll call them next. I'm still a medical student and I assume after I get my degree I will continue as a regular intern."

"Girl! Don't guess. Ask them what their plans are for you. You have a vested interest in your career path."

"Okay, don't have a fit. I'll talk to Dr. Ellsworth tomorrow. I better hang up as I need to call home."

I called Mom and when I said I had news, she put me on speaker so Dad could hear. I told them about the hospital's decision to put me on staff as an intern working under Experimental Medicine, a new department.

Mother replied, "Honey, what does this do to your medical training?"

"Good question. I'm going to talk to Dr. Ellsworth tomorrow about it."

After disconnecting the call, I started thinking about the questions I needed answers to. Once they were clear in my mind, I returned to my studies. The next day I arrived at Mason Hall to meet with Dr. Ellsworth.

Once seated before her desk she said, "My, you have been involved in substantial changes at the hospital."

"Yes, that's what I need to discuss with you. Assuming I continue and graduate from medical school, what, if any, changes am I going to have in my medical internship? Is my internship with the Experimental Medicine department going to continue or am I going to have a dual internship?"

Dr. Ellsworth thought a moment before answering. "We are still working on that. Currently, majority opinion is that you will be offered a normal medical internship, with occasional consults as needed. Without you, there is no Experimental Medicine department, and will probably be dropped when you begin your actual internship. We needed that department to explain you working in the hospital. Any other questions?"

"Is there any way to speed up my graduation?"

"What's the hurry?"

"I was hoping to finish school and my internship before my pictures stopped healing people. I really feel a need to use my talents to heal people."

"Angel, all good doctors enter this profession to heal people. You started healing people when you were a child by just touching them. Now you are like us, using hard earned knowledge to cure illness. You still have an advantage we don't have, your gift to tell what's causing the illness by touch. You wanted more. You want to cure the person after determining the cause. This takes time, even with your eidetic memory and genius IQ. To answer your question, we can cut one year by offering you more classes, but this is going to isolate you from the people you want to save. It will be harder for you to relate to fellow humans if all you do is study. Thank about it and get back with me if you continue to want your classes accelerated."

In my heart I knew she was right. I needed human interaction now, because when my internship started my only contacts would be coworkers and patients, working twelve or more hour shifts. My friends would be fellow interns.

"Forget what I said. You're right. Thanks, Dr. Ellsworth for your help."

That evening I told my roommates what I learned from Dr. Ellsworth. Robin came over and hugged me. "Good! I'm glad that you're not going to start an accelerated class schedule. Julie and I need you here and we value your friendship. However, I wish you would change that hairstyle. It just doesn't match the shape of your face."

"Yeah, Robin and I thought we would take you to a styling salon and get that changed. You would be so much more beautiful."

"Hey, I did that on purpose to keep boys at bay."

Julie said, "Well, you're in medical school now and men are better behaved. We need all the bait we have to counteract Barbara's influence. Even if you don't want their attention, your beauty will help attract them for us."

"Is that what they mean by a honey trap?"

Julie laughed. "No! But its close."

The following Saturday my roomies dragged me to the hair salon they went to. They enlisted the help of a stylist and started holding pictures of styles up to my head, trying to determine which would look best, and finally showed me which style they liked best.

"Are you sure? I don't want to change my hair color!"

Robin laughed. "Angel, you wouldn't be you without that white hair. Visualize this picture with your hair color."

"Okay, but if it's a disaster I'll sic Olivia on you."

Julie snorted back a laugh. "Oh please. As if you would or could. Just sit back and let us worry about this."

Later, when the stylist finished and stepped away from me, I watched the expressions on my roomies faces change from interested curiosity to shock.

I thought to myself, *they've ruined my hair!* I quickly stood and turned to the mirror, but instead of a familiar face I saw a beautiful woman with big blue eyes looking back at me. I tried a smile and my face seemed to light up with a glow.

I turned to my friends and asked with a slight smile. "Is this what you were after?"

Robin shook her head. "No! Who's going to look at us if you are in the room. Who would know that this was hiding under that old hair style."

The stylist took my picture and said, "Wow, when this picture goes viral, I'll be famous."

I paid the salon and we left. Standing outside I said, "Let's take this new face out for a spin. I see a Hooters down in the next block, let's see if I can wake the men up."

Julie said, "We've created a monster. Barbara is not going to like this when we get back to the apartment."

When the three of us entered the restaurant all eyes turned our way. Even the busty wait staff gave us a close look. We were seated next to a table of young men who seemed in danger of choking on their food, and suddenly one did until a friend slapped him on his back.

A handsome man quickly came over to our table and introduced himself to us, as Ralph Grimes, a intern at the Johns Hopkins Hospital. He was a tall man, easily three inches taller than me, and had a nice chest and tapered waist.

I smiled at him, which seemed to make his eyes glaze over, and introduced ourselves. Four other men soon joined us, and we were told that they were all interns on a break. "Oh we don't want to disturb your time off. We are first year medical students and know you don't get many of those." I said with another smile that seemed to enthrall them.

Ralph Grimes seemed to shake off its effect and said, "This is the kind of break we were looking for. Three beautiful women who we can talk shop without being boring. Can we buy you ladies lunch?"

I looked at my friends, who nodded their heads. "Sure, but we have questions for you too."

The waitress took our order and we got to know them. This was their first year as interns and had been working long hours with short breaks. Every three days they got a day off, which many used to catch up on their sleep. Ralph looked at me and asked, "Your name is familiar; I know I've heard it recently in regards to a patient."

"Would that patient be Julie Bowman, whose doctor is Pullman?"

"Yes, I believe it is. Angel Pearson, that name sticks in my head. I'm sure I haven't met you before. Your face I would never forget."

"I consulted on Bowman's case at the request of Dr. Pullman."

His eyes got big in surprise as he remembered the connection. "Guy's, meet a fellow intern who's still attending medical school. She somehow saved the life of a twelve year old girl, who no one could determine what was causing her illness."

"Please guys, I'm an intern in name only. The hospital needed to show a reason for my presence with a patient. I can diagnose the cause of an illness by touching the patient."

"But the information I heard was that you saved the patient, not find the cause of the illness."

Julie said, "Angel, you didn't tell us anything about this. You did something you've never done before, didn't you?"

"Guy's, please don't repeat this. I don't want it to get out. I did determine the cause, at least Dr. Pullman and I had it narrowed down to some kind of allergic reaction from when she was in Africa. The treatment for this is..."

Everyone at the table said, "Steroids!"

Dr. Pullman was going to start her on a massive dose of steroids, which we both thought might kill her in her present condition. He couldn't think of any other appropriate treatment, so I suggested he give her a pint of my blood, and if that didn't work he could try the steroids. Luckily, the blood worked as she started to improve almost immediately."

The interns were looking at me in confusion, trying to figure out why my blood would work like that. Robin said, "She's Angel Pearson! You know, the little girl who heals by touch."

Ralph slapped his hand against his forehead. "I'm such a dunce. I didn't make the connection. But why study medicine if you can heal by touch? Oh! I did it again. You can't do that anymore, can you. It appears that your blood still has some power though, that's why you want to keep it a secret."

The other interns looked at me in awe. Ralph touched my hand and squeezed. "I hope I'm still here when you start your internship.

The hospital will be very exciting."

I smiled at the interns. "It's already exciting for me. Maybe we'll all work together in the future."

When we got back to our apartment, we all collapsed on the couch and breathed a sigh of relief. Julie jabbed me in the ribs with her elbow. "Don't keep secrets like that. We're here to help you and that was big. You do know that this will get out, don't you. The guys may keep quiet, but too many people know about it. I bet Dr. Pullman will eventually write a paper on it."

I looked at Barbara's picture and said, "I told them about using my blood."

Julie said, "Well, at least you told her. I bet she told you not to do it again except in an emergency."

"Yes mother, that she did. Thanks girls for taking me out, that was fun and we got to meet new friends."

Robin said, "Enjoy it while you can because we're not taking you with us again when we want to meet boys. They wouldn't even look at us, especially when you turned that smile on."

"That was interesting, wasn't it," I said, grinning wickedly.

Robin said, "Slap her, you're closer!"

"Alright, I'll be good. I need to hit the books again anyway."

CHAPTER NINE

Spring break came and to my surprise, my first year of medical school was finished. I decided to fly home for a week before I returned for the short summer session. I checked with Jeff Blake across the hall, and we both got on the same flight to Kansas City.

We had a direct morning flight from Baltimore and arrived in KC in late morning, where we shared a cab to my parents' apartment. I had talked him into meeting them and promised him a ride home afterwards. Once in the elevator I pushed the penthouse floor, which caused him to raise an eyebrow at me. I gave the camera the safe signal and the elevator started to rise. When the door opened, Jeff was surprised by the security desk facing us with its two armed officers. I signed in for both of us and they took Jeff's picture for their files.

At our apartment I entered the security code, which unlocked the front door with a soft clunk. As we walked inside I yelled "I'm home" in case anyone was there, but getting no response I assumed they were still at work. I used my cell to text mom and let her know I was home.

Jeff was looking around the living room, then he dropped his bags and went to the window overlooking the Plaza. "Wow! You really have a view. What did you say your parents do for a living?"

"They are both partners with Phelps, Phelps, & Woodruff, one of KC's larger law firms. They also are in charge of the Angel Foundation, which distributes my healing pictures."

"I guess that explains how they could afford this penthouse."

"Actually, they got this before they made partner. The Foundation operates out of the other penthouse on this floor. Look at the paintings over the mantel."

Jeff stood in front of the two self portraits and said, "The larger one must be the original of what you have at the dorm. This painting is marvelous, that photo didn't do it justice. She was a very beautiful woman, almost as much as you. The small one is Barbara Messing. I hear her work is selling for big bucks."

"My aunt's work is also selling high and there are not that many pieces out there, which keeps the price up. My parents have this one insured for a million dollars, of course it's not for sale."

My parent's arrived shortly and I introduced them to Jeff, and explained how we met. Jeff smiled at mom and said, "I thought your sister in the painting was beautiful, but seeing you, I believe Angel get's her beauty from you. Except for her hair color you look remarkably alike."

At that comment, mom looked closely at me. "Honey, you've changed your hair style. My, that does look attractive on you. Jack do you think that style will look good on me?"

"Better not, I have a hard enough time telling you apart as it is."

"Oh poo. Angel has white hair." She said before realizing he was joking.

"Jeff, is that short for something?"

"Jefferson. My father is a fan of Thomas Jefferson."

"Jeff, are you a jokester like my husband? I don't think I could abide being the butt of jokes from Jack, Angel, and if you stick around, you."

Jeff looked at me and smiled as my face must of turned scarlet. "Oh, I would never make you the butt of a joke. However, I might conspire with you on a joke."

Mom looked at him and smiled. "I like him. He definitely has possibilities. How much older are you than Angel?"

"Mother! Enough! We're just friends and neither of us has time for romance."

"I know dear, but sometimes it's nice to have shared feelings and comfort from someone conveniently close by."

"Mother!"

"I got you, I finally got you good. Maybe now you will see it's not fun to be on that side of a joke."

"Yes mother. I'll be sure and remember that when I name my first child."

"Now Angel, let's talk about this." She said as she looked at Jeff suspiciously.

* * *

After Angel and her mother disappeared into Angel's bedroom, Jack said, "Don't worry, Angel was just getting a little back at her mother. What do your parents do?"

"Dad has three dry cleaning stores and Mom does the bookkeeping. I'm the youngest of three kids and my sisters work in the business, when they aren't having kids of their own."

"Has Angel made any friends this past year?"

"She has two roommates that seem pretty tight. They take care of her and Barbara has them running interference by keeping boys away from her, and then the four others in her first year shared group, whose advisor is Dr. Ellsworth. Angel did something I don't think had been done before. She got the group together and met with Dr. Ellsworth. I don't know what was discussed, but the rumor mill suggests Angel is a student leader. She teaches Judo once a week, and all her students can be counted as friends."

"She teaches Judo? We didn't know that. What about her consulting work at the hospital, what do you hear about that?"

Jeff smiled at Jack. "Angel has become a student like none other. Most hold her in awe, while some fear her. When it got out that she had saved a twelve year old girl by giving her some of her own blood, even the instructors revere her."

* * *

Angel and her mother came out of the bedroom and approached them. Jenn said, "What's going on?"

Jack answered. "Jeff was telling me that Angel is teaching a Judo class."

Jenn looked at Angel. "Really. How many students do you have?"

"Twenty, including three men. A man and woman had brown belts, so I made them my assistants. Everyone is doing fine and I hope they all come back this fall, but I can't handle any more than twenty, unless my assistants can take on more work."

Jack said, "Angel, you've always been able to do what you set your mind to do. It will work out. Jeff, are you getting hungry? If so, what restaurant do you prefer?"

"I'll go to lunch with you, but then I need to get home and touch base with my folks. I know a great barbeque place that has the best pulled pork and brisket in town."

We took two cars, so I could drive Jeff home after lunch and my parents could return to work. Jeff ordered twice the amount of food I did. I had eaten here before, but it had been at least five years. I felt stuffed as we returned to our cars. My parents hugged Jeff and said they hoped to see him again before we drove away.

Jeff lived in south Kansas City, near the Kansas state line. He directed me to an older two-story house in a established tree-shaded neighborhood. I parked in the driveway and he asked me to come inside and meet his mother.

Following Jeff inside we were met by a pretty, trim woman in her early forties wearing an apron, hands covered with flour and dough. Seeing me she blushed and chided her son.

"Jeff, you should have given me some warning that you were bringing someone home with you. I must look like a witch. Well, come back to the kitchen. I was making bread for dinner tonight."

Jeff grinned at me. "I should explain. Mom plans her evening meals with a different country cuisine every night, and tonight is Italian. Mom, this is Angel Pearson, the woman who has the room across from me in the dorm. She's from Kansas City too. I just had lunch with her and her family and she brought me home."

His mother had gone back to kneading the dough, but was watching me closely as she said, "My son has no manners. I'm Sandra and you're the girl that heals by touch. Since you're attending medical school something must have happened that hasn't hit the news."

"You're right. I've lost that gift, but have been given, as a replacement, the ability to diagnose the cause of an illness by touch."

I thought, *I can see where Jeff gets his intelligence, Sandra you are a very smart and observant woman.*

"You two just friends or something more?"

I quickly looked at Jeff and watched as he went through the same embarrassment as I had with my parents. "We are friends, close friends actually, but not romantically involved. Medical school demands are too much for either one of us to have time for that."

"Poo! When you're ready you will find the time. Do you want to get your hands dirty?"

"May I? I've always wanted to knead dough."

"Wash your hands at the sink and I'll get you started."

* * *

Jeff watched them work together for a few minutes until he was sure they were enjoying the company of each other, then left carrying his bags to his room upstairs. He quickly changed clothes and returned to the kitchen where he found them engrossed in making bread, certain that they had not missed his absence.

He kept company with them, observing how his mother asked Angel about growing up in KC and her early life as a healer. What her parents did for a living and where they had come from originally. Once, Angel looked my way and gave me a wink, letting me know she knew what mother was doing. It was obvious mother wanted to know everything she could about this prospective daughter-in-law, the same grilling he had received from her parents.

* * *

An hour later, Jeff's father arrived home and came into the kitchen, where we all were sitting at the kitchen table drinking coffee. Jeff introduced me to his father, this time using his given name - George. George fixed himself a cup of coffee and sat next to his wife, looking at his son and me sitting next to each other.

Sandra quickly brought him up to date about Jeff's and my history together and how I had helped her make the bread for tonight's meal. "Angel's parents are partners at Phelps, Phelps, & Woodruff. They may give us a discount if we ever need legal help."

George asked, "You're the girl who can heal people?"

Sandra interrupted. "Angel lost that gift and now is attending medical school to heal people in a different way."

"So you want to be a doctor like Jeff? That's a wonderful calling, probably one you were born into."

"Yes, it seems that way. When God took away one gift and replaced it with another, my aunt told me I needed medical education to make the best use of my new talent."

"Your aunt sounds like an intelligent person, what does she do?"

Jeff answered. "Her aunt was Barbara Powers. She died before Angel was born. Her self portrait painting was in the news and part of a TV news magazine broadcast about nine or ten years ago. That painting is in Angel's home and Barbara talks to her through it. Angel thinks Barbara is a messenger angel from God."

George looked at Angel in surprise. "Has anyone else seen or heard Barbara?"

"If anyone becomes close to me they eventually see and/or hear from her. Currently, both my roommates have had contact with her, because I had Dad send me a large copy of her painting. It works just as well as the copies of my picture that heal people."

Jeff said, "I've talked to her as well. She is very protective of Angel, but that's not her purpose. Angel also has a guardian angel, Olivia, who has been tasked to protect her."

I said, "I didn't know that you talked to Barbara!"

"She came to me in a dream. She told me some of your history and that God had plans for you and had assigned Olivia to watch over you."

"Barbara has done that before, sometimes she even takes over somebody's body and talks through their voice. Were you frightened when Barbara came to you in your dreams?"

"Barbara exerts an outpouring of love so great that for me there was no fear, just a desire to please her."

"Did she say anything about the two of us?"

"Yes, but it's too early for you and I to get into at this point."

George and his wife looked at us with curiosity at this

revelation. George said, "Sandra, our son seems to have acquired a higher purpose than just being a doctor."

"I wiped my eyes and asked, "Could I have a tissue to blow my nose?"

Sandra quickly got one for me and her. "Angel, why did you ask that last question?"

"I've had lots of experience with God's guidance in my life. My parents had similar guidance and Olivia's protection. When I first met Jeff I felt a jolt of recognition, I can't say more because I don't understand it. My mother had a similar feeling after Barbara died. Barbara and my father were engaged when she died in a car accident. She had given him that self portrait the day they became engaged. Barbara was my mother's older sister and somehow Barbara's future relationship with Dad was transferred to mother. Mother never saw Dad again until after she graduated from law school and started work at the U.S. Attorney's office here in KC, where Dad worked. Less than two weeks later they were married."

"So you think this may be more of the same guidance?"

"Yes, and Barbara's protectiveness may be because she thinks of me more as a daughter than as a niece."

"You must feel close to her as well, otherwise you would never have asked for the copy of her painting."

"I grew up with her. She's talked to me, advised me, and passed on instructions from God. I love her almost as much as my mother. I missed her advice, so I asked for the copy, hoping it would work."

"Angel, I'm sure that you could have any man that you wanted. What attracted you to Jeff?"

"When you first met George, what did you feel?"

"An attraction that eventually grew into love. But you said you felt a jolt when you met Jeff. What kind of jolt?"

"Like we connected. I never felt that with any other man I've met, so you tell me, what did it mean?"

Sandra asked her son, "What did you feel when you first met?"

"The same. I didn't know what it meant until I heard Angel's story just now."

"So, from what I've heard so far, is that you're connected somehow, but not destined for each other until sometime in the future. Is that right?"

I nodded my head and watched as Jeff nodded his head too. "I'm wondering if this has gone far enough that Jeff is under Olivia's protection too."

Jeff shook his head. "Barbara didn't say anything about that."

"I'll ask her tonight when I get home. She has never told me a lie, but she doesn't mention things that I shouldn't know unless I ask directly."

"Maybe, that's because we might act differently than we would otherwise. You know, change history, like when Barbara died."

CHAPTER TEN

The Blake's convinced me to stay for dinner, so I let my parents know of my change in plans. Sandra asked me to help in the kitchen, where she quickly found I was a neophyte. The men left us alone, so I confessed my mother was not a cook and my father's cooking was what I lived for since they cooked on alternate days.

"Angel, you need to find someone who can teach you how to cook. Surely, Baltimore has a cooking school."

"It would have to be a night school, as that was the only time I had free. My grandmother is a good cook, but she lives too far away to teach me."

I watched, mesmerized as Sandra moved about the kitchen with ease. "What should I learn to cook? Jeff says you cook something different every meal. How am I going to learn all that. Even Dad specialized on one dish."

"Angel, you develop your own special dishes. The list gets longer as you become more accomplished. When I first got married I couldn't cook but one dish. It takes practice and experience. Honey, don't worry about it, you're not going to have time to cook for yourself, let alone others until after you become a resident. I don't know what I was thinking. I guess I was afraid Jeff would starve when he married you."

"So you think that's going to happen?"

"I know it's going to happen eventually."

"What about your daughters, are they good cooks?"

"Better than you, but they're still learning and they get their families fed."

"If we get married I expect to eat out a lot, like my parents. Both being professionals, they don't have much time to cook."

After dinner, I bid everyone goodbye and thanked them for the excellent meal. Jeff walked me to my car and gave me a chaste kiss on the cheek. I winked at him before I left for home.

My parents asked about Jeff's parents and I gave them the highlights of my afternoon. I asked mom to come with me to my room, where I repeated what Jeff had told me about his dream involving Barbara.

"So, you think he's been told not to repeat what she said, and you suspect that involves you and him getting married?"

I nodded. "Mom, I know I have a connection with him because of that jolt when I first looked into his eyes and my physical attraction to him. Was that similar with you and Dad?"

"I felt a compulsion to be with him, so I planned my life to make that happen. When we first met on the job and looked at each other, I thought I was going to faint from the rush of emotion that went through me. He told me it was love at first sight for him. So maybe it's not the same for everyone."

"It must have been strong emotions for both of you, since you got married within two weeks."

"Well, somebody was trying to kill us and Olivia asked us to get married so she could more easily protect both of us. That was the reason we got married so quickly, but we would have done it later on our own. We hadn't even slept together until our honeymoon. I take that back, we never had sex until our honeymoon."

"That sounds like a story I want to hear about sometime. Mom, I'm so confused! I'm going to ask Barbara some direct questions tonight and see if I can get some answers."

"Do you think that's wise? Do you really want to mess with God's plan?"

"Since I'm involved, why not? I wouldn't say no to marrying Jeff, because I already know we have a connection. I just want to know what the plan is."

"Do you mind if Jack and I stand with you?"

"No, it might help."

Mom and I told Dad we were going to talk to Barbara and he was invited to stay. We all stood before the painting and felt a renewed outpouring of love from her.

"Aunt Barbara, I've had a discussion with Jeff and his parents today and he let slip that he had a dream about you where you discussed something that involved the two of us. Is this something that is coming soon or after we're finished with med school?"

Barbara stepped out of the painting and stood before us. She looked at me and laughed. It was the first time I'd seen her laugh and it was a little disconcerting. "Angel, there aren't many people who would challenge an angel like that. Are you afraid that you're not in control, or do you just want to know what's in store for you?"

"A little of both I guess. I feel a strong attraction for him and I think he feels the same about me. I just want to know, when is this going to happen?"

"Things are still in a state of flux, variables could change that could potentially affect when and if you ever become mates. That's why I haven't spoken about this before. Ask Jenn why she married Jack, rather than Jack marrying me. Things change, accidents happen, but remember we have an overall plan for your life that you will enjoy and be happy with. And yes, it could involve Jeff."

Barbara disappeared back into the painting and my parents pulled me into an embrace. I said, "So, she's worrying that something may happen to Jeff like it did to her."

Jenn said, "I think it's obvious that any hookup with Jeff isn't going to happen anytime soon."

"I feel that too. At least now I have a better understanding of what's in store for me. Have you ever heard Barbara laugh before?"

Dad said, "Not since she died, but it was her laugh."

I looked at mom and she agreed, tears running down her face. I gave her a squeeze and kissed her cheek. "It's hard, isn't it, even after all these years."

The week at home passed quickly, but not before the Blake's invited us all over for dinner. I hung out with the men while Sandra and Jenn took measure of each other.

* * *

"How many children do you have besides Jeff?"

"Two married daughters. Jeff is the youngest and my baby."

"Angel has told you about her history?"

"Much of it, but I'm sure there is more. I got on the *Star's* website and made a copy of the articles about Angel saving all those children in that school bus accident, when she was ten. I saw a picture of her covered with blood. She's a remarkable woman."

"Yes she is. I hope it works out that she and Jeff eventually get married. He is such a good man and perfect for her. Together, they could do great things. Angel says that you are a great cook and fix something different every day of the week."

"Well, I hope you like what we're having tonight. We're celebrating Mexico, so it's burrito's, refried beans, and taco's. I also prepared a salad if that's too much grease."

* * *

I walked into the kitchen and asked if I could be of any help. Mom and Sandra laughed.

"Hey, I can set the table."

"I'm sorry dear. I'm pretty useless in the kitchen too, as you well know. Sandra what can we do that doesn't take any skill?"

"How about sitting down and talking to me. Sometimes it gets lonely in here with the kids gone."

By the time dinner was far enough along for me to set the table, mom and Sandra were friends. If things worked out I'm sure they would become close friends. One could only hope.

CHAPTER ELEVEN

The summer session begin and I was back at school. I was only taking two courses; however, both classes were held every day and were supposed to be the most feared by the students. Apparently, the instructors loved to put students on the spot by asking questions of them. That was not the hard part. What was hard was then they had to explain their answer, why was their answer correct, and not just because it said so in the text book.

Dr. Elizabeth Parsons was teaching my first class in anatomy, while Dr. Edger Jackson taught physiology. When I entered Dr. Parsons' classroom, I took my customary seat up front, because unlike many other students I enjoyed being called upon. However, five minutes before class started there were only six other students present. I thought, *it must be because of this being a summer class that there are so few students.*

Dr. Parsons entered the classroom and eyed me as the only one on the first row. She frowned and said, "Everyone come down here and sit behind Ms. Pearson in rows two and three, three students each row. Since we only have seven students this term I'm going to try something different."

I heard a low moan from the students as they took their new seats behind me. After everyone was seated, Dr. Parsons considered us for a moment. "How many have already read all or a portion of the text book?"

We all held up our hands. "Good. Now how many have read all the text book?"

I was the only one who held up my hand. "Well, well. We have our first volunteer. Ms. Pearson please come up here and tell me how much you remember."

I left my seat and climbed the steps up to the podium and faced Dr. Parsons. "Dr. Parsons I remember everything I read. I have an eidetic memory."

"I know my dear. I just wanted to see if you would admit to it. Having a good memory is not sufficient to pass this course. You also need to understand the relationship of the body parts to the whole. Mr. Meyer, please come up here and join us."

While he was making his way towards us I was thinking, *she's going to have us teach ourselves in the relationships of the body*. Meyer came and stood beside me, but as he was approaching I noticed that he was about my height, appeared fit and probably weighed 170 pounds, to my 110, and was quite handsome.

"Alright, Ms. Pearson, please demonstrate by touching Mr. Meyer, the superior position."

I touched the top of his head, then at her prompt, touched each position of his body on command, hitting every point correctly. Dr. Parsons then had Meyer repeat the lesson on me.

"Very good, you may take your seats." She then called two more students up and repeated the same commands until all had their turn.

"Ms. Pearson tell us which side of the body does the right side of the brain control?"

"The left side, Dr. Parsons."

Dr. Parsons continued asking questions of her students until fifteen minutes before the class was to end. "Class, please note this website and download the anatomy of the human male. Tomorrow we will review this information while watching a video of the dissection of a male cadaver. Are there any questions?"

I had an hour before my next class with Dr. Jackson, so I went to the cafeteria and got a cup of coffee. I sat and sipped it reflecting on my previous class for a few minutes, then downloaded the file I was to use for tomorrow's class on my laptop.

Dr. Jackson's class on physiology went as expected and our class size was twenty-five, the size I expected. I suspected Dr. Parsons' class was an experiment of some kind. I liked a good mystery and I was going to see if I could solve it.

The next day I learned as much as I could about the other students before class started. The class progressed as expected, with the video stopped at various stages of the dissection and Dr. Parson asking questions from each of us. The class ended with Dr. Parsons telling us that tomorrow would bring additional questions from the download of the male anatomy.

The next day Dr. Parsons called Meyer and I to the podium again. This time I was asked to identify organs Dr. Parson pointed at on a chart of the human body using a laser. Meyer was asked the same questions, but in a different order. Satisfied with our answers, we returned to our seats and two other students were brought forward for examination, but the questions were different. This continued until all students had their turn.

Dr. Parsons called me forward and handed me the laser pointer and told me to sit back down and use the pointer to identify as many organs as I could in three minutes. I started at the head and worked down until told to stop.

"Congratulations Ms. Pearson you identified thirty-six. Meyer, you are next. Take the pointer and begin when I say."

When we finished my score was highest by three. No one had more than five under my score. Dr. Parsons looked at us for a moment considering. "I am in a quandary. You all have performed higher than the norm, which is why you are in this class. I meant to test your limits as much as your knowledge. I'll think about it some more, but be ready for tomorrow. Dismissed."

I waited outside the classroom and when I gathered all my classmates, I asked them to meet me in the cafeteria. The seven of us gathered off to one side for privacy. I said, "It looks like we all are self starters and high performers, and I'm sure we all are going to get an A from this class. We are obviously a test class for future high performers. Would you mind if we compared IQ scores, because they obviously have this information. I have an IQ of 156."

We all had high IQ's, ranging from 148 to 161. I said, "Wow! I bet we are the highest in the second year class. What do you want to learn from this course? So far it has been too elementary for me, how about you?"

We all agreed to ask Dr. Parsons to step up the course material and see if we could make it more interesting. The next day when Dr. Parsons stepped to the podium I raised my hand.

"Yes, Ms. Pearson. What is your question?"

"Dr. Parsons, our class got together yesterday and decided we wanted more from this class. Is there a more senior version of this class material?"

"You're saying that I'm boring you. You know that this is the first time I've ever had students asking for more work. Ms. Pearson, please stay after class and we will work together to come up with something that will be more interesting for all of us."

I remained sitting as the class ended and the other students left. Dr. Parsons motioned for me to follow her and we were soon at her office. Before I sat in the chair offered I said, "I have another class in an hour."

"I know, Dr. Jackson's physiology class. I think we have time for what I have in mind, so sit down please."

I dropped my backpack beside the chair and gave her my full attention. "I hope I didn't offend you, because that was not my purpose."

"No my dear. You were actually trying to help me as I was floundering in my attempt to make the course interesting to students who were smarter than me."

"I take exception to that Dr. Parsons. We may have a higher IQ, but smarter, I don't think so."

She smiled at me before saying, "You have a kind soul. Everyone you meet in the staff has reported that and has tried to make your life here easier. That and the fact that you are a natural leader and have an instinctive grasp for this kind of work. That's not even considering your diagnostic ability. Would you come back here this afternoon and help me rework this class?"

"How about at one this afternoon. I can give you at least two hours of my time and more if you need it later."

"What seemed to be the biggest problem with the present course?"

"It was geared to students who needed help going from A to B. We are all self starters. We began the class looking for D and you were showing us A."

"Oh my, that won't do. When we meet again I'll have something to show you."

Dr. Parsons came up with a solution; She and Dr. Jackson combined their courses into Anatomy and Physiology for future classes of high performers. We finished the anatomy course early by skipping forward in the text, which satisfied everyone.

My roommates decided to stay with me for the second year, but we had to move out of the freshman dorms. As sophomores we entered the housing lottery and were assigned to McCoy Hall. These apartments were further away from the center of things, but were much nicer. I moved in early and was already settled before my roomies arrived. The room arrangement was similar to our previous apartment, but all the rooms were larger and the furniture was more comfortable.

Julie Westerman was the first to arrive, as she did before. "Hey, help me with this crap. I swear I've got more stuff now than when I moved out. Robin's not here yet?"

"Nope, you're first after me. I hope she doesn't bring a moving van of stuff like last time."

Julie looked around the apartment. "I see you took the middle bedroom again. I guess I'll take the one on the left again as well, so I won't go in the wrong room by mistake." She said with a grin.

I helped move hanging clothes and boxes into the common room, before following her to pick up more from her car. Julie was soon moved into her bedroom and we were sitting on our couch drinking coffee from a espresso machine she brought with her, while looking at Barbara's picture.

I said, "Did you tell your folks about Barbara?"

"You're kidding me. They would think I was bonkers. No, let sleeping dogs lie. They are better off not knowing about her. I did tell them about you though and they were thrilled that I had such a positive example to follow."

I looked at her doubtfully. She smiled and said, "I kid you not. They actually said that."

Our apartment door slammed open, announcing Robin Lacy's presence. "Help me! The moving guys dumped all my stuff out here and took off."

After getting Robin unpacked, the three of us were sitting on the couch catching up on how we'd spent our summer break. This time Robin only had two boxes of stuff that didn't fit into her room and she was going to ship those back home. I told them about my summer classes, but left out my efforts in helping Dr. Parsons with future classes for high performing students.

Tomorrow we would meet with our advisors at Mason Hall for new courses next semester. Tonight we were on our own. I said, "Let's go to the rec room and see if we can find anybody we know."

Julie said, "Does that anyone happen to be named Jeff, that guy you flew to Kansas City with?"

I blushed, which seemed to add fuel to the fire. Robin asked, "Angel, what happened?"

"I went home for the summer session break with Jeff. We shared a taxi from the airport and I suggested he meet my parents before he went home."

Julie and Robin both said, "And!"

"You know what happens when you bring a boy home with you for the first time. They pounced, asking all kind of questions about his background and trying to determine if we were serious. We had lunch together and then I took him home and met his parents."

My roomies said, "Oh, oh! You met his parents too. Angel this is starting to sound serious. Are you sure you want this now?"

"Actually, I haven't told you everything. When Jeff and I first met and we made eye contact, I felt a jolt in my gut, and he told me later that he felt it too. He also had a dream where he had a conversation with Barbara that he says he can't repeat, but it involved us. While I was home I asked Barbara about Jeff and if we would get together sooner or later. She told me to be patient, that we were not ready yet and things could change between now and later. She reminded me of her own death shortly after becoming engaged to Dad, and how her sister - my mother married Dad instead."

Julie said, "Oh my God!" Then covered her mouth in fear looking at Barbara's picture.

Robin hugged me close. "Honey, I feel bad for you. It's probably best if you two wait until you graduate anyway, maybe even after your internship. Okay, let's go see if we can find Jeff."

CHAPTER TWELVE

Dr. Mary Kilpatrick e-mailed me, saying twenty-one students and two staff members were signed up for my self-defense Judo class. I checked on my two assistants who had returned ready to go. Two students from the last class that had reached the brown belt level were also returning. If they agreed to help me I would have four assistants to help run the class, which would work out well.

My first meeting with my new class wasn't as stressful as last year. This time I had many more students with previous training. I had the students separate into two groups, those with training and those without. Six students had no training, including the two female staff members. I had my assistants take charge of the others, breaking them into four groups. My group of six had one man, who appeared to resemble the "before" picture for an exercise commercial. The two staff women were in their early forties, but appeared to be fit.

I demonstrated the first Judo move with the help of John Dye. Once I was sure he knew the move, I rushed him and he used my weight and momentum to throw me over his head as he fell back and used his feet as an assist. I quickly returned and made sure he was alright before asking for another volunteer. We went on until all six students had successfully used the move. I had one of the brown belts monitor my six while I checked on the others.

I then called all the students together in a large circle around me and the four brown belts. I began to demonstrate moves that they hadn't been exposed to before. Using the teach and use method, I soon had all four using these moves and countermoves. I then had my assistants teach these moves to the other students.

At the end of the class I told everyone but the two staff members to hit the showers and be back next Wednesday at the same time. When we were alone I asked, "Ladies, how did this first lesson go for you?"

Dr. Jamison grinned at me and said, "It was exhausting, but I feel wonderful and empowered. Even with the little I learned today I feel I can handle myself if attacked."

"Great, let's hit the showers then, and feel free to tell your friends about your experience."

After leaving the gym I walked over to the rec room to meet Jeff. He was living in a different residence hall than me this term, but we still managed to keep in touch with each other. I sat down at the table he was sharing with two other people, a man and a woman. They were classmates and were comparing notes. The woman said, "So you are the famous Angel Pearson. Did you just finish your Judo class?"

"Yes, I have twenty-three students this term."

"Wow, I don't see how you do it. I have all I can do just keeping up with my studies. Well Jeff, see you later. Bye all."

Soon, it was just Jeff and me at the table. I said, "She's pretty."

"Sherry? I suppose so, but she's not in your league. How did the first lesson go?"

"Good. Better than I anticipated. Even the older members of the staff said they enjoyed themselves. How are you doing with your classes?"

"No problems so far. By the way, I heard that you caused some excitement at your anatomy class this summer. What was that about?"

"Are you familiar with Dr. Parsons' classes?"

"Just that she's a hard ass and everyone tries to avoid her classes."

"She's a good instructor, it's just that she challenges the students more than the other instructors. Anyway, we only had seven students for her class, which I thought was strange. Later, she said we were all high IQ and performing students she was trying a new teaching method on. It wasn't working well for us and I got the other students together and asked them what they wanted out of the course. The next day I told Dr. Parsons what we wanted from her course."

"Wow! How did she take that?"

"She was surprised and said that this was the first time students have ever asked her for more work. She asked me for ideas and she developed a new course with Dr. Jackson, combining anatomy and physiology for future high performing students."

"You mean for high IQ students like you."

"I don't know what their criteria is for that category, but obviously I'm included. You're no dummy. What's your IQ?"

"Lower than you, for sure."

"Come on, tell me. I promise I won't hold it over your head if you're right."

"Okay, please be gentle. Mine is 148, what's yours?"

"See, I told you that you weren't a dummy. I only beat you by eight points. There were others in that class with your IQ, so you will probably take the new class if you haven't already."

"I already did. I lucked out on that."

"You know, my mother had a higher IQ than Dad, with about the same range as us and they got along fine. Each had their individual strengths. They were an unbeatable legal team, and as far as I know they never lost a case."

"Jack seems the dominant personality of your parents."

"Yes, he is usually right in his decisions; but if mom disagrees with him, she guides him into the right direction without bruising his ego."

"So, she's the strong woman behind her man, letting him take the accolades."

"It's still very much a man's world, she likes to say."

"Not for much longer, thanks to women like you and your mom."

I returned to my apartment and put in an hour's worth of study before calling it quits for the night. The next morning I heated up a frozen breakfast sandwich, read the news on my computer, and checked for e-mails before heading out for my first class.

I heard my computer bing at me on the way to class. I was

needed on a consult after my class finished. I met Dr. Peter Jacobson at the hospital as instructed. He asked me to sit down, but was edgy as he fidgeted with a pencil.

"Angel, I have a patient who is dying of cancer. He's heard of your life saving blood. He says he will donate ten million dollars to the hospital if he is cured. Would you consider giving him some of your blood?"

I looked at Dr. Jacobson and thought for a few minutes. "How old is this patient?"

"He's eighty-nine and will die soon unless this procedure is successful."

"If he was in good health, his chances of dying in the next ten years are about ninety percent plus. I've been told not to use my blood in this manner, except in extreme circumstances. I don't believe this qualifies and I won't do it."

"Good! I was hoping you would turn us down, but I was required to try. If you had done this it would have established a bad precedence, where money would qualify who gets life saving treatment. I didn't know how strong-willed you are. In the past you would almost do anything to save a life, but apparently now you have limits."

"God has given my blood something extra that was meant to protect me from disease. I was cautioned not to share with others unless I deemed it appropriate. He didn't share with me His reasons or why I needed to judge who lived and died."

"I don't envy you in that regard, but remember as a doctor we make those decisions all too often. We will not speak of this again and I will pass this on to those who pressed me into asking you."

Returning to my apartment, I collapsed in front of Barbara's picture and cried, feeling sorry for myself for having to make such a decision. I finally told myself, *toughen up, it had to be done and while hard, it was probably going to be easier than others I may need to make in the future.*

Julie and Robin walked in as I wiped my eyes and stood up. They took one look at my reddened eyes and hurried to me, asking what was wrong. I rehashed what had happened in Dr. Jacobson's office.

Julie said, "Cripes, those silly putz. I don't mean Jacobson, but those misinformed people who sent him to ask for your blood.

Jacobson was right too, when he said that sometimes we would have to make this decision as doctors. Honey, are you okay. Can I get you anything?"

Before I could answer, Robin quickly went to fetch us all cups of coffee. When she returned we sat in silence for a few minutes sipping our hot drink which began to sooth my rattled nerves.

Julie said, "You know, I agree with your decision not to sell your blood. Even if he hadn't offered money, in his case it wouldn't have been the right decision."

We all sat a few minutes longer contemplating that statement. I said, "You girls are the best friends I could ever have. You've put up with a lot from me and if there's anything I can do for you, just ask."

Robin said, "Trade rooms with me."

"Besides that."

We all started laughing so hard that we burst out crying in each other's arms. Cried out, we looked at each other's faces and then started laughing again. I said, "I feel much better now. I better get ready for my next class."

Later that day I was returning to my apartment after my last class. I was about two blocks from my destination when a man quickly exited his parked car ahead of me and started running toward me. I dropped my backpack and prepared myself for his apparent attack.

He shouted that I should have given my blood, then was upon me. I used my standard throw back move and he sailed over me as I fell back and used my legs to assist his flight. He landed badly, hitting his head on the concrete sidewalk and lay unconscious. I called 911 on my cell and asked for police and EMT's.

I checked his pulse and finding he had one, I checked for other injuries. I found he had a brain aneurism, but I could do nothing but stand by waiting for help to arrive. Campus police showed up within five minutes, followed soon after by the Baltimore police. I repeated what I told the campus police about his attack on me and his comment as he rushed me. The EMTs arrived and I informed them of his brain injury before they carted him off to the hospital, but not before I warned them that he was dangerous.

I e-mailed Dr. Jacobson about the attack on me and what he said to me and suggested that the patient in question be allowed no visitors or phone calls until the police got involved. The police took my name, address, and cell number and said a detective would contact me later.

I continued to my apartment and found my roomies there. They were shocked when I told them about what happened to me, not two blocks from here. They were pissed when I told them that the attacker was apparently sent by the patient who wanted my blood.

Julie was more vocal than Robin, saying, "Now, I'm really glad you didn't give him any! He certainly doesn't deserve it. Why, he actually paid someone to do you harm. What about the attacker, what's his story?"

"I don't know. He hit his head on the sidewalk and was knocked out, but I detected he had a brain injury. A detective is supposed to contact me later."

Robin asked, "This is Wednesday. Are you still going to have a Judo class?"

"I'm going to try. I'd better contact my assistant, Mark Andrew, and tell him to start without me if I'm late."

I was in my room studying when someone knocked on our door. Robin answered and yelled, "Angel, it's for you."

A man and woman dressed in suits waited for me in the common room. The man displayed a badge and said, "Angel Pearson?"

At my acknowledgement, he continued. I'm Detective Ed Patterson and this is Detective Florence Snyder of the Baltimore PD. "You were attacked a few hours ago by a Victor Kanner?"

"I didn't know his name. Is he alright?"

"No, he died of a brain aneurism within the last hour. We were unable to question him, but your statement said he yelled something at you. Would you repeat that."

"He yelled, you should have given your blood. I assume he was referring to a recent patient I consulted on who offered to give the hospital ten million dollars if I gave him blood and it cured his cancer. I declined the offer."

"So you think this is retaliation for not giving him your blood?"

"Yes. It could mean nothing else. I have no other enemies."

"Who is this patient?"

"I don't know, I've never met the man. However, you can contact Dr. Peter Jacobson at the hospital for that information."

Detective Snyder said, "We were under the impression that you are a medical student. What did you mean when you said you consulted?"

"Detectives, I'm the Angel Pearson of the persona - The Healing Angel. I used to be able to heal by touch. I'm now attending medical school hoping to continue to heal people the old fashioned way."

Snyder's face blanched as she realized who she was talking to. "I didn't connect your name. You've grown up into a young woman. I'm so glad I got to meet you."

Detective Patterson cleared his throat, bringing Snyder back to her job. "Consulting?"

"I have been given the gift of a diagnostic ability in place of my healing powers. I've been called in to diagnose difficult cases; however, in this case it was the patient wanting my blood."

"Have you used your blood in the past?"

"Yes, one time. A young girl was dying and as a last resort we used some of my blood to try and save her. It worked and she was released from the hospital soon after, fully recovered."

Patterson said, "Somehow word got out and this rich patient wanted your blood to cure him. Do you mind telling me why you turned him down?"

"Primarily because he was eighty-nine and didn't have long to live anyway. Secondary, I was told by God not to use my blood in this manner unless it met my test of last resort."

Snyder said, "The little girl met that test for you?"

"Yes, but that was before I was given the limit by God."

"You speak directly to God?"

I smiled at her and shook my head. "No, an angel speaks to me."

We were interrupted by Julie. "She's not crazy. We have talked to her aunt too."

"Her aunt?"

I pointed to the picture on the wall. "Barbara Powers, my aunt. She was about my age when she died and that's a copy of her self portrait."

"That's Barbara Powers! Her art is selling for big bucks. You say she's now an angel?" Patterson said doubtfully.

Snyder looked between the picture and me and said, "I can see the resemblance. We'll contact Dr. Jacobson and get back with you later."

CHAPTER THIRTEEN

I arrived at the gym on time for my Judo class and we had just started dividing up the students between my assistants, when the doors burst open with a loud bang, and four men started running towards me. I yelled, "Brown belts with me! All white's get behind us!"

As the four men approached us I yelled, "Disable them if possible!"

There were four women and a man facing the charge of the four large men. We spread out to meet their charge, causing them to do likewise instead of concentrating on me. I wasn't watching my assistants, trusting in their training, while I concentrated on the largest of the group heading for me.

They were silent as they slowed to take our measure, but they only saw one large man they needed to worry about. They rushed us, my opponent smiling as he reached for me. I broke his reaching arm as he flew over my head, and then turned to see where I was needed. All four men were on the floor, all but one with a broken arm. He stood and pulled a knife, slashing out at any who approached him. I swiftly approached him from the rear and gave him a rabbit punch behind his ear, knocking him out.

I turned to one of the students, and asked her to call 911 and ask for police and EMTs. I motioned for the other students to approach and watch the downed attackers. They silently looked at me and my assistants in awe.

Again the campus police were first on hand, followed soon after by the Baltimore PD. A sergeant from the BPD ruefully said as he took in the downed men. "Pretty stupid to attack a class of Judo students. They look like they went through a meat grinder. Which one had the knife?"

Mark Andrews said, "He's the one without a broken arm. Angel popped him from behind while he was trying to cut me."

"Well, that's assault with a deadly weapon. He'll get special treatment. Which one is Angel?"

"The one over there with the black belt, our instructor."

The BPD sergeant approached me and asked, "Are you in charge of this class?"

I smiled. "They did pretty good for their first actual attack, didn't they?"

"I'm Sergeant Burke and if I remember correctly, this is your second attack today. The other guy died from his injuries. What's going on that would warrant this?"

"You better call in Detectives Patterson and Snyder and get them in on this. Apparently, someone set a bounty on my head and these detectives know who it is."

He used his cell to call in for those detectives and turned back to me. "Tell me what happened here?"

The police were just finishing up interviewing all the class members, when Patterson and Snyder arrived. They came over to where I was sitting on the floor in a lotus position and helped me stand. Patterson said, "This has got to stop. I talked to Dr. Jacobson and he put Jacob Roberts in isolation about three hours ago. Somebody else is hiring these guys, maybe one of them will give us a name. Did anyone get away?"

"No, it was just these four. One of them used a knife. Maybe you can use that for leverage in getting what you want."

"Which one was he?"

"The others are getting loaded up by the EMTs. The one you want is over there in cuffs, I only knocked him out."

"Jeez! What did you do to them?"

"All but that one had broken arms. He was trying to slash everyone with that knife, so I rabbit punched him behind the ear.

When we were attacked I told my Brown Belts to try and disable them. They did good work."

Soon everyone was gone but my class. I called them all into a circle around me. Once settled, I told them what I thought was going on and why. "I'm sorry that you got involved in my mess, but sometimes things happen. Did you White Belts learn anything from this show?"

One of the new students held up her hand. "I hope future classes aren't this exciting, but you did show me that if properly trained I will be able to defend myself."

"That's the purpose of this class. Now Brown Belts, please stand up and everyone give them a big hand for their performance tonight."

Thunderous applause followed. Mark and Jamie, my first two assistants, pointed at me and Mark saying, "Angel saved the day by getting us set and aimed at our attackers. Without her, this could have turned out badly for us. I found out recently that this is the second attack she's endured today. I hope this is the last one."

My whole class gave me a hug before they headed for the showers. I trailed along behind them a little misty eyed, but feeling good that I was appreciated. When I got back to the apartment my roomies were waiting up for me.

Julie said, "President Smithson e-mailed us to tell you that he wants you to come to Mason Hall as soon as you got back to the apartment. What happened? Are you in trouble?"

"My class was attacked by four men tonight. No students were hurt, but three of the attackers ended up with broken arms, and we were held late answering police questions. I guess I had better head over to his office. Any advice for me?"

Robin said, "Yeah, don't lose your temper, and say yes sir a lot."

I entered Mason Hall and started looking around for a clue where to find the president. I then went with the obvious and headed for Dr. Ellsworth's office. I noticed that a light was on, so I knocked on the door. Dr. Ellsworth's voice said, "Enter."

I entered the room to find it packed with staff and I said to myself, *oh my!* President Smithson was present and he pointed at a chair and said, "Please take a seat Ms. Pearson."

I sat down and scanned the crowd, looking for any friendly

faces. Everyone was solemn faced, so I set my eyes on the president, who was watching me closely.

President Smithson began pacing in the limited area of the office. He turned to me and said, "Dr. Georgia Wilson, one of your Judo students, gave us a description of what happened tonight. Apparently, you and your assistants handled yourselves well when you were attacked. In fact, this was the second time you were attacked today and the first attacker died from his injuries. Tell me how this all started?"

I hesitated a few moments before responding and he prompted me by saying, "Well, what is the problem?"

"I'm sorry President Smithson, but I'm trying to maintain control of my temper. This started by an ill-conceived attempt by someone on your staff trying to grab a ten million dollar donation by asking me to donate some of my blood to a patient, which I refused. Apparently, the patient took exception and set a bounty on my head."

"What! Dr. Jacobson is this true?"

"Yes sir. I agree with Ms. Pearson's statement that it was ill conceived and never should have been considered."

"Have we done anything like this in the past?"

"No sir. However, Ms. Pearson is unique to our hospital and perhaps the world. Her blood apparently has properties that can cure many or all illnesses. But accepting money as a qualifier to receiving such treatment is abhorrent."

"Ms. Pearson you have used your blood to cure an illness before?"

"Yes sir. A young patient, Julie Bowman, was dying and the only treatment available for her was a massive dose of steroids. The attending and I agreed that her survival was unlikely. I suggested that we should try a pint of my blood, because of my past history as a healer. If it didn't work, then we could try steroids. The blood worked and the patient was released about a week later cured."

"Yet you turned down another patient's request. May I ask why?"

"An angel told me I should use my blood in this manner sparingly. It was meant for my protection and should be used as a gift only in rare instances. I was given the responsibility for making those decisions."

President Smithson looked at the staff and said, "I'm going to draft a letter to all doctors tomorrow that no one is to try in any manner to try to influence Ms. Pearson in donating her blood. Ms. Pearson do you want me to place an addition to this order?"

"Yes sir. If a young patient is dying and there is no conventional method of treatment, please let me know and I'll make a decision regarding the use of my blood. It's possible that a smaller amount of blood will achieve a satisfactory result, but that's for another time."

President Smithson looked solemnly at me and said, "Please forgive us for the treatment you received and I hope you continue to stay with us as long as possible. I have a feeling that you are going to make this institution more famous than it already is. Dr. Jacobson, please have the person responsible for this in my office tomorrow. This meeting is over."

Dr. Ellsworth said, "Angel, please stay for a few minutes. I need to talk to you."

After the room emptied except for the two of us, Dr. Ellsworth asked, "How did your Judo students fare? Any express a desire to drop the course?"

I shook my head. "No, in fact most thought it was exciting, after the fact. Many are excited that now they have a means to defend themselves and are anxious to attend the next class."

"When you gave the students their instructions, both Brown and White Belts, were you surprised that they followed your orders without hesitation?"

"I never thought they wouldn't. In Judo, the instructor quickly gains a rapport with his student, so that the student follows the instructor's commands without thought. The Whites didn't have enough experience to do battle, so I put them behind us. The Browns and I were sufficient to handle those four men, even if armed with knives, which one was."

"What would you have done if they were armed with guns?"

"I would have told them to scatter and run away, with me leading the way."

"Somehow, I doubt that. I'm sure you would have told them to run, but not you."

"Dr. Ellsworth, are you aware that I'm protected by a guardian angel? I was safe, but my students could have been hurt by stray gunfire if they had stayed."

"You're not pulling my leg? A guardian angel?"

"My family is protected by Olivia, a guardian angel who first appeared to protect my Dad when he was in a car wreck that killed his mother. My mother and me were eventually included in her protection over the years since. Olivia has great power and has killed several people who have mortally threatened our family."

"You've seen her in action? It's not just stories dreamed up by your parents?"

"I was little and with my parents when we were threatened. She appeared in a flash of light and carried a bright sword with her wings spread, and was a sight to behold. In this case her presence was enough to cause the men to run away, so I didn't see her use her sword. Dad and Mother told me she points it at the threat and fire consumes them, leaving nothing but a husk."

Dr. Ellsworth shuddered. "I can see why you felt safe. Why Judo then?"

"Olivia protects me only from a mortal threat. Anything else is up to me."

"Is this the angel you referred to when talking about the use of your blood?"

"No, I'm blessed in knowing two angels. Barbara told me about my blood. She's my aunt, my mother's sister, who died years before I was born. That's another story and I'm bushed. It's been a very busy day for me."

"I'm sorry. Go ahead and get some rest. I do want to hear that story sometime when we have the time."

My roomies were still up when I got back to the apartment. Julie and Robin quickly came into the common area when they heard me enter, and looked at me expectantly. Sitting together on the couch, I said, "I met the president in Dr. Ellsworth's office and she and about six others were there. It was a little scary at first, then I got a little pissed. After all, none of this was my fault."

"We told you not to lose your temper!"

"I know, and I tried real hard. When Dr. Smithson asked how this started I was a little mad, so I gave him the story and my thoughts about how stupid I thought it was."

Robin gasped, "You didn't!"

I nodded. "Dr. Jacobson backed up my story and agreed with my conclusion. I thought President Smithson was going to pop his cork he was so mad. He said he was going to write a letter to all hospital staff to not bug me about giving blood. He even asked me if I wanted to add anything to the letter, which I did. President Smithson apologized to me and hoped Johns Hopkins and I had a long future ahead of us."

Julie said, "Wow! You've had some day. Come on, let's go to bed I'm pooped."

CHAPTER FOURTEEN

The next day I didn't have any classes until late morning. I was still in my pajamas sipping a cup of hot coffee when someone knocked on the door. I looked through the peep hole and saw it was Jeff, so I quickly opened the door and let him inside.

He held me by the shoulders, looking at me closely, then said, "I just heard about your adventures yesterday. Are you hurt, you look okay."

I smiled at him. "Jeff, I'm fine. The other guys aren't though."

Jeff's relief was evident as he sighed, letting his breath out slowly. "I vaguely remember reading about your parents having problems with people attacking them, but I thought we were safe here. Is this going to be part of your life too? If so, I want you to teach me Judo so I can help protect you when we are together, like your mother and father protected each other."

I hugged him tightly and looked into his eyes. "Okay, but I'll have to give you special lessons until you catch up with the rest of the class. Can you meet me at eight tonight in the gym?"

At his nod, I said, "I'll arrange to get you a uniform and meet you there."

We stood holding each other and were about to kiss when Julie said, "Ah, ah, ah! No more of that. One kiss and you two will want to bed each other. Jeff, go off and take a cold shower, study, do something else, leave. She's presently off limits, so scram."

Jeff looked surprised. "I see you have a Rottweiler to watch over you, so I'll see you tonight at the gym. Bye."

After he left Julie and I looked at the door and sighed. Julie said, "So you're going to teach him Judo. You want one of us there to keep you honest?"

"Please. I don't think I can trust myself around him anymore. Maybe you and Robin can take turns."

"I don't blame you. He's hot."

That evening we met in the gym and I told him where to go to change into his uniform and meet me here without shoes. I was going through my warming up exercises when he returned. I told him to watch me and then do his own exercises. Fifteen minutes later I judged he was ready and I started showing him the basic moves.

An hour later he was flat on his back begging for mercy. I started to move towards him to cuddle, when Julie said, "Ah, ah, ah! None of that. I think he's done. Better flip him over and scoop him up and send him to the showers."

Jeff frowned at Julie, but slowly got off the floor and headed to the showers. Julie said to me, "I better go with you to the showers, to keep you honest."

The following evening Robin was our chaperone. Later, when the lesson was finished she asked, "Angel, that looks like fun. I think I'm going to join up next term."

Jeff looked at me and grinned, saying, "Are you sure you want to go flying?"

"There is that, but I'd like to see if I can do that to one of you big guys."

After Jeff and I showered and changed we all headed back towards our dorms walking together. Jeff and I were talking about various Judo moves we had used tonight, when suddenly three men rushed us from the darkness. We were almost blinded by a bright light as Olivia arrived between us and our attackers. She spread her wings and raised her sword as she prepared to smite them. Whatever their original intentions, they all dropped their weapons and turned to run.

Olivia shouted, "STOP!"

They stopped so suddenly, that two slid to the ground. The

remaining man standing slowly turned to face Olivia. She slowly approached them and loudly demanded, "WHY ARE YOU SEEKING TO HARM ANGEL?"

The two on the ground appeared to have fainted, while the man facing Olivia was trembling, a wet stain spreading over his pants. Olivia shouted, "TELL ME!"

"We were paid a thousand dollars each to kill her. Dr. Peter Hedrick told us to make it look like a mugging."

"WAS HE ALONE, OR ARE THERE OTHERS WHO ARE INVOLVED?"

"I don't know of any others. He was alone when he paid us half and said we would get the rest when we did the job."

"WHEN THE POLICE ARRIVE YOU WILL REPEAT WHAT YOU TOLD ME OR I WILL RETURN AND END YOUR DAYS ON THIS EARTH. DO YOU UNDERSTAND?"

"Yes, please don't kill me. I'll tell them everything!"

Olivia turned to me and winked, then disappeared in another flash of light. Robin said, "I already called 911. Jeepers creepers, so that's Olivia. I don't blame those guys, I would have fainted too if I had to face her.

I called Dr. Ellsworth and told her what happened to us and how Dr. Hedrick was involved.

She said, "Holy Crap. President Smithson will stomp all over that SOB!"

This time the BPD beat the campus police to us. We told our stories and I advised them to check the money in their pockets for Dr. Hedrick's fingerprints. After they hauled away the three attackers, I told them we would be at my apartment waiting on the detectives to arrive.

My roomies, me, and Jeff were having coffee while waiting, still trying to calm our nerves when Detectives Ed Patterson and Florence Snyder arrived. I let them in and asked, "Do you want anything to drink?"

Patterson said with a frown, "Got something stronger than coffee?"

I shook my head and looked questioningly at Snyder, who shook her head while trying not to smile at her partner's discomfort. He said, "We barely got to Dr. Hedrick before President Smithson and four of his campus police arrived. He was fit to be tied that a member of his staff would be involved in trying to kill one of his medical students. Hedrick confessed that he paid to recruit those muggers in an attempt to change your mind about giving your blood. Later, he wanted revenge for setting President Smithson against him. Those three attackers couldn't talk fast enough fingering Dr. Hedrick as the one who paid them."

Detective Snyder said, "What's got Patterson so worked up is that everyone says that an angel protected you and got them to finger Dr. Hedrick."

I said with a slight smile, "Why Detective Patterson, don't you believe in angels?"

"I don't believe in anything I can't see!" Patterson said with a smirk.

Julie said, "Angel, don't do it!"

However it was out of my hands. Barbara decided to put her two cents in and stepped out of the picture and stood before Patterson, saying, "Why Ed, that's a little short sighted of you considering all the evidence to the contrary."

Patterson's eyes got big as he looked at the beautiful woman standing before him. "Where's your wings?"

"Ed, I don't need wings, but if you insist…" She spread her wings, which made her look entirely different.

"Okay, okay. I'm convinced. Where's your sword?"

I said, "She's a messenger, not a warrior like Olivia."

"Oh! Angel, you really keep strange company."

"It's who I am. I wouldn't be me without my angels to protect and guide me."

Jeff put his arm around my shoulders and said, "We like the package, just as she is."

Detective Snyder smiled before saying, "So you have a boyfriend now. Congratulations Angel."

I blushed, but winked at her. "Is there anything you need from us. It's getting late and we have classes tomorrow."

"Write your statements out and sign them, and we will be on our way."

We all used our laptops and quickly printed out our statements, signed and dated them, and handed them to the detectives. They checked them over and then said they would get back with us later.

Jeff hugged me and then gave me more than a sisterly kiss on the lips. I held my fingers to my lips as he left the apartment, a single tear sliding down my cheek.

Julie looked at me with comprehension and said, "Ah! Angel, I know it's tough. Come here and I'll give you a hug."

Robin joined in the hug. I sighed, "Thanks guys, but I'd rather it was Jeff hugging me."

We broke up and went to our rooms to get some sleep. I thought to myself, *maybe I'll dream about him making love to me*.

The next day, I received a text message from President Smithson. He wanted to meet with me ASAP. I texted back, thirty minutes in Dr. Ellsworth's office at Mason Hall.

It was a beautiful fall day, with trees showing their colors and only cool enough for a light sweater. I took my time enjoying the day and noticed many others along the way doing the same. I still had fifteen minutes before the meet time, so I sat on a bench near Mason Hall and watched students and staff walk by.

I wasn't paying close attention to people as they approached me, so I was surprised when someone stopped in front of me. I looked up and saw President Smithson standing there.

He said, "You're enjoying the day too I see. This is my favorite season and it's too bad it doesn't last longer. Mind if I sit with you?"

"Please, go ahead."

We sat there in silence for several minutes before he sighed and spoke. "It's been a trial for you, hasn't it?"

"How do you mean?"

"Having to explain why you came here, and knowing that many people thank you are delusional when you tell them the truth."

I smiled at him and asked, "How about you. Did you immediately believe me?"

"I noticed that you used the word 'immediately', it seems that you make your point pretty quickly. No, I originally thought there must be another reason for your healing powers, but the evidence kept piling up and I was forced to believe what you say is fact."

"What's going to happen to Dr. Hedrick?"

"Whatever his legal problems, he's not coming back here. I've never before had a staff member conduct himself in such a manner that it would bring such dishonor to this institution. If you elect to remain as a student, your tuition and lodging will be free for the reminder of your education here."

"Wow! You don't have to do that. How about when I graduate, I'm not sure how an internship here works?"

"If you want an internship at this hospital, you will have it. Even if I'm no longer the president, and I'll throw in free lodging as well."

"You make it sound very attractive. Maybe I shouldn't tell you this, but ever since I was told I needed medical education, this place stuck in my mind. It's as if there was a plan for me to come here."

"I feel even worse now. That you had to go through this at my school, I feel ashamed."

"Perhaps I was sent here so that you could clean house. Sometimes old establishments need a shake so that new ideas can flourish. I don't blame you or the school for what has happened, only those evil doers get that blame."

"Shall we go inside. I'll want to tell the others inside what we have agreed to out here on this beautiful day."

I was a little surprised that only Dr. Ellsworth and Dr. Jacobson were present when we entered the office. President Smithson preceded me into the room and sat behind the desk.

"I met with Ms. Pearson outside and we have come to an agreement. Her past and future tuition and lodging is going to be paid by Johns Hopkins and upon graduation, if she so desires, we will offer her an internship at the hospital. Her lodging will be paid during this period as well. I didn't discuss this with Ms. Pearson, but I would like to reimburse her for past and future consultations at $10,000 per occurrence, instead of the $5,000 per our original agreement."

Dr. Ellsworth asked, "Should I order a check be made for all past tuitions and lodging to be paid to her parents?"

President Smithson asked, "Ms. Pearson is this correct?"

"Yes please. They paid these fees for me."

Dr. Ellsworth added, "Ms. Pearson will also receive a check for her past consultations. Angel do you remember how many you've done? I'll check to be sure."

"I believe it's been ten, not counting the one where I was asked to donate blood."

"If that's the correct number, then you'll be getting a check for $50,000 that you can apply against other expenses here. Do you have an account in the campus bank? If so, I can make a direct deposit for you."

I gave her my account number and the meeting came to an end.

CHAPTER FIFTEEN

Five days later I got a telephone call from Mom. "Angel, I've got this on speaker for Jack. What's happening with you at school? We just got a huge check in the mail from them that says it's for reimbursement of tuition and lodging. You haven't dropped out of school have you?"

I stifled a giggle. "Mom, you know me better than that. I've put it all in a letter to you and Dad, but the short story is that a patient wanted to use my blood to cure his cancer and when I refused he sent people after me to try and change my mind. That didn't go well and he tried again, which failed. Then a hospital staff member tried to have me killed, but Olivia interfered and made them confess who hired them. The President of Johns Hopkins got involved and apologized, offering me free education and lodging, and after graduation an internship at the hospital if I want it."

There was silence at their end for almost a minute, before I prompted, "Mom, Dad, you still there?"

Mom answered. "Honey, you should have called us. We still want to be a part of your life. I don't care how far away you are, when our little girl has people trying to hurt her we want to know about it. You know we have talents too, so use them in the future. We're looking forward to reading that letter and if we have questions we'll call you back."

"Yes, Mom and Dad, I'm sorry and I'll do that next time, but remember I have two angels looking out for me too. Jeff even insisted I teach him Judo. He told me that if I'm going to be in danger, he wanted to help protect me."

"It looks like you have matters well in hand, but Angel please remember that your parents worry about you all the time and no matter how old you get, you will always be our little girl."

Okay, Mom, I'll try to do better. School work is fine and it won't be long before I'll be home for Christmas break. It will be nice to see everyone again and send them my love if they ask. Bye."

*   *   *

Jack and Jenn looked at each other in wonder at what their little girl had accomplished. Jenn buried her face in Jack's chest and sobbed. Finally, looking into his face she said, "Angel is all grown up and making decisions without us. Our little girl has left the nest and spread her wings, leaving us behind."

"It is a little lonely here without her. Do you want to raise another child?"

Jenn looked at him in sudden interest and thought for a moment. "I'm too old for pregnancy and child birth, but we could always adopt another child. Do you want to look into it?"

*   *   *

Jeff and I flew home together for Christmas break. My parents picked us up at the airport and took us to my home, and I was going to take Jeff to his home later in the day.

Angel Foundation was still in operation, sending my healing photo's worldwide. I have begun to suspect that the pictures healing powers would continue until I became a doctor. As soon as I got home, I stood before Barbara's painting, telling her I was home again. The love coming from the painting to me was all I needed to know that she welcomed me back.

Jeff stood beside me as we both gazed at Barbara. He said, "I can't get over how talented she was. You look about her age and close enough alike to be sisters. You are both beautiful women."

Dad walked up behind us as Jeff made his comment. "Jenn makes it three beautiful women. If she was fifteen years younger you would think they all were triplets. By the way, you and a date are invited to the firms Christmas party at the Crowne Plaza tonight."

I quickly looked at Jeff and asked, "How about it. Do you want to mix with the rich and famous with me?"

He gave me a quick kiss on the cheek, then frowned. "What's the dress code?"

Dad said, "You need a tux. If you don't have one, come with me and we'll see if one of mine will work."

Jeff followed Dad out of the room and I asked, "Mom, do you have something for me to wear?"

She motioned for me to follow her and we joined Dad and Jeff in the master bedroom closet. Dad and Jeff were the same height and build, so I didn't expect Dad would have a problem finding him a tux. Me, I wasn't so sure of. Mom and I were about the same height, but I was slimmer around the waist.

My parents' had a huge his and hers closet; however, Mom used up almost half of Dad's side too. I was astounded by all the gowns Mom accumulated over the years. Luckily, they were hanging by date of purchase and she pulled the three oldest for me to try on.

I went into her dressing room and with Mom's help, put the oldest one on. The gown was simple form-fitting from my breasts to just below my waist, where it flared out slightly, with a slit to mid thigh. The blue material appeared metallic. I stood before her full length mirror and caught my breath in surprise. It was beautiful on me and fit like a glove. I felt like a princess.

"Mom, this gown is absolutely out of this world."

"Don't tell your father, but I splurged on that. It's a Vera Wang original. No one else at the party will be wearing anything that pretty."

I checked how the bodice covered my breasts and found it had a built in brassiere and I wouldn't have to wear one. I had Mom unzip me and I removed my bra and resettled my breasts into the cups before zipping the gown back up. We looked at the mirror image of me and I had to admit, I looked hot, partly because the built-in bra made my breasts look bigger than they were, showing lots of cleavage.

"Honey, you look better in that than I ever did. Don't let Jeff see you in that until tonight. The other women are going to have a fit of envy when they see you. Don't move, I'm getting my phone to take your picture. "

After I had changed back into my street clothes we joined Dad and Jeff. Dad said, "We lucked out. One of my older tuxes fit like it was made for him and I gave him a white shirt to wear with it."

I said, "Great, we found an old gown of moms that fit me too."

Dad looked at Mom and said, "Was it the blue one that I liked so well?"

Mom smiled, which prompted Dad to say, "Jeff, prepare to have your socks knocked off when you see it."

Jeff called home and told them he was here and Sandra asked to speak to my mother. Mom laughed shortly after she began talking, and then said, "Fine. We'll be there shortly."

Mom looked at Jeff and said, "Your mother invited us over for lunch, so get your tux and stuff and we'll head over there."

My dad and Jeff disappeared into the master bedroom, and I quickly asked, "Mom, you and Sandra seemed awful chummy. What's going on?"

"We talk almost every week and we've gotten together for lunch a few times too. They've been over for dinner, you know, friend stuff."

"Mom, please! You would have had to cater the one held here."

"What's wrong with that. They know I can't cook and I never ordered anything too fancy. They seemed to enjoy it, so no harm, no foul."

Once we arrived at the Blake house, I helped Jeff carry his tux and shirt in. Dad brought two bottles of wine, a red and white, depending on what was being served. Jeff led the way into the house, yelling that company had arrived, which brought both of his parents. They welcomed their son home with much hugging and kissing, then it was my turn.

Sandra took the tux from me and asked, "What's this for?"

Jeff replied, "I'm taking Angel to her parents' firm Christmas party tonight at the Crowne Plaza."

Sandra held up the tux and said, "I assume it's going to be a fancy one. My, our boy is coming up in the world. If everyone is hungry, lunch is ready."

Jeff grabbed the tux and some luggage and took them to his room, while we took seats at the dining room table. Sandra and George served us barbeque short ribs, fried sliced potatoes, and a tossed salad. Jeff soon joined us and fixed his own plate, sitting down next to me. Sandra mentioned that she used her own special sauce on the ribs and hoped we liked it.

No one said anything, aside from asking for more ketchup or sauce for over twenty minutes. Sandra brought us each a wet cloth for our sticky fingers after we had finished eating.

Dad said, "Those were the best ribs I've ever eaten. That was the best meal I've eaten here and Sandra serves great food."

Jeff used his wet cloth to wipe some sauce off my nose, then asked, "How about me. Do you see any on my face?"

I had him turn his head, then said, "No, you weren't as messy as me. Sandra please don't feed me this very often or I'll get fat."

"Angel dear. You are a little too skinny. Are you exercising too much? Jeff, you look like you've lost some weight too."

I said, "I'm teaching him Judo at school. That's probably the reason. He's trading fat for muscle."

Jeff looked at me for permission to explain and I said, "Go ahead. They should know."

"Angel had some problems at school, but we think it's all been resolved. She was attacked three times. The first was a man who died when she used a judo move throwing him over her head where he landed head first on the sidewalk. The second time was at a judo class she was teaching, when four men attacked. They were all disabled, three with broken arms. The third time I was present with one of her roommates walking back to the dorm, when she was attacked by three men. Olivia, her guardian angel, appeared that time and persuaded them to surrender and tell the police who was behind the attacks. The perpetrator was arrested and for the last two months we've had no trouble."

Sandra said, "You mentioned your guardian angel before when you were here, but I didn't pay close enough attention. Her name is Olivia and she's supposed to protect you?"

"The last I heard she protects our whole family."

"Why didn't she appear earlier with the first two attacks?"

"She protects me from mortal attacks. Muggers I take care of myself. That's why I have a black belt in Judo."

Sandra looked at her son. "That's why you're taking Judo lessons. You want to help protect Angel."

George said, "It sounds like she can take care of herself pretty well."

"George, if somebody was trying to hurt me, wouldn't you try to protect me?"

"Yes, and if I knew Judo I could do a better job of it."

Dad said, "Jenn and I both have black belts in Judo and we have had several instances where we had to use it. Olivia has stepped in and saved our bacon a few times too."

I said, "The point we're trying to make is that we live interesting lives that at times are not safe. When Jeff joins our family he will also be at risk."

Jeff said, "You're too late with that warning. Maybe if you had given that warning when we first met it might have meant something, but I'm hooked now."

"Oh Jeff, me too." I said and put my arms around him.

After we broke apart both mothers had tears in their eyes as they looked at the young couple.

Sandra got a box of tissue, pulled one for herself and offered it to Jenn, who took one for herself to wipe her wet eyes. Angel also had tears, but Jeff used his finger to wipe them away.

Sandra said, "Now that we have that behind us, what plans do the two of you have while on break?"

I said, "Why, to see our family, relax, and catch up on what's happening."

"Jeff, what time does this shindig start tonight?" Sandra asked.

Dad said, "We'll pick him up here at 6:30 and bring him home when it's over."

"Well, we have a little time then. Tell us what you two have been up to besides having people trying to hurt you?"

Later, after returning home, I moved my bags into my room. Mom helped me hang and put away clothes from the bags, all the time asking personal questions. I finally sat on my bed and patted the space beside me. She rolled her eyes at me and sat.

"Mom, to answer your unasked question, no I've not made

love with Jeff. The most we've shared is a few kisses, which burned my lips. I've got lots of friends, including some staff members and I'm happy with that. I think even President Smithson likes me after we had a long talk together."

"Oh honey, I just want you to be happy. I remember how I felt about your father and how I planned my life so that we could be close again. I was really lonely during that period."

"Oh Mom!" I said and gave her a hug.

Pulling back, I looked at her in astonishment. "Mom, you're pregnant!"

"I know."

"Does Dad know?"

"Not yet. I was going to wait a while longer to make sure it's going to take before telling him."

"Mom! It feel like it's almost two months along. Tell him!"

Dad showed up at my doorway in response to my raised voice. "What's going on?"

Mom stood and faced him. "Jack, you know what we discussed earlier about our empty nest. Well, I'm pregnant!"

"What! I thought you gave up on that idea because of your age." He said as he hurried to her side and hugged her tightly. He gave me a questioning look over Mom's shoulder.

"Mom, have you seen a doctor yet?"

"About three weeks ago. He said it looks alright for now, but he wants me in every month for a checkup."

"Well, I'm going with you on the next one. How come you told Angel first?"

"I didn't, she knew when she hugged me. I was going to wait until after the next checkup to tell you."

CHAPTER SIXTEEN

Later that evening we stopped to pick up Jeff, who asked for Dad's help in tying his bow tie. The evening was a little cool and Mom and I were wearing a wrap over our gowns. We parked in the underground garage of the Crowne Plaza and took the elevator to the main floor of the hotel, where Dad checked where the party was being held. It was one floor up and since Mom and I were wearing gowns, we took the elevator.

Leaving the elevator, we first checked our wraps and then went to the ladies room to freshen up, leaving the men behind. Later, as we approached them I noticed how large Jeff's eyes got as he looked at me.

He took my hand and said, "Wow! Your Dad wasn't kidding when he said that gown would knock my socks off."

I leaned close and gave him a kiss on the cheek. "Thank you for the compliment. You look quite handsome yourself."

We entered the large room as a group, with Mom and Dad leading the way. Christmas music was playing and two open bars were at each side of the room. George Phelps and his wife, Marilyn, were talking with another couple, but quickly excused themselves and headed our way. George was the Managing Partner of Phelps, Phelps, & Woodruff, where Mom and Dad were partners.

Marilyn came right to me bypassing Mom and Dad. "Angel! That gown looks familiar and my, you look gorgeous in it. Who is this handsome man with you?"

"Marilyn, this is Jefferson Blake, but goes by Jeff. He is a fellow medical student at Johns Hopkins. He is also a resident of KC, and yes he is very handsome. I don't know yet if he dances, but I'm going try him out."

Not to be outdone, Jeff bowed to Marilyn and took her hand. "Are you the famous Marilyn Phelps who set up the Angel Foundations mail operation?"

Her eyes widened as Jeff took her hand. She was momentarily speechless until she looked at me and I winked. "Angel, you put him up to do that, didn't you?"

"Nope. I found he has a wicked sense of humor to match mine."

"Oh Lord. Poor Jenn. With you and Jack, he makes three she has to watch out for. Wait a minute and I'll introduce Jeff to George."

Marilyn got her husband's attention and brought us forward. George's eyes brightened as he recognized me. "Angel! My, you've grown into a beautiful woman."

Marilyn said, "George, this handsome man escorting Angel is Jeff Blake, also a medical student at Johns Hopkins. It just happens that he is from KC too."

George asked, "Jeff, what does your father do?"

"He owns several dry cleaning stores on both sides of the state line."

"Blake, you say? I was trying to recall if we ever had any dealings with each other."

"I doubt it, unless you do tax work."

Dad spoke up. "I checked already and we haven't, but I left my card with George, his father."

"Well, he must be a great guy if we share the same first name. Why don't you young people mingle and dance, enjoy yourselves."

I thought this might be a good time to see if Jeff could dance. I learned while at MU, but hadn't had much opportunity to dance. Some slow music started and I pulled Jeff onto the dance floor. Surprisingly, he was a very good dancer and I followed his lead as we glided across the floor. There were only two other couples with us on the floor and we made them look bad.

We danced twice more before going to the bar. Neither one of us were drinkers, so we ordered soft drinks and found the table where my parents were sitting. Clarence Woodruff, another partner, came by and said hello.

I asked, "Clarence, how are the two Barbara paintings selling?"

"Great! I only have two of your Aunt's left to sell, which I may keep for myself. Messing's work keeps going up in value. That watercolor painting used in healing is still my favorite." He said before leaving.

Jeff said, "I know what painting he is referring to, but I can't recall what it looks like."

Dad pulled a copy out of his wallet and gave it to Jeff. "I remember now. It's the family portrait."

Jeff held it up to my face for a moment. "You still look like her a little bit, but the grown up version is much prettier," he said before handing the picture back to Dad.

I suggested to Jeff that we see what was on the buffet, so we joined others in line. When I sat back down with my plate of goodies, Mom handed me a handful of napkins, saying, "Honey, if you spill anything on that gown it will be ruined, so be careful."

I looked at the food on my plate and then at my lap and shuddered. I carefully tucked two napkins into the top of my gown covering my breasts, and several more in my lap. I looked at Mom and she nodded. Jeff looked at me and just smiled, then before I could do anything he snatched a sticky bun off my plate, saying, "You shouldn't be eating this anyway and if it dropped in your lap you would never forgive yourself."

I glared at him, but then reconsidered. He was right after all. Dad said to Jenn, "Does that bring back memories?"

"Yes, but I would have given him a jab in the ribs whether he was right or not."

"Jenn, you were always a little physical with me. I eventually learned to stay out of your reach when I did something like that."

Jeff quickly looked at me and I responded with a wink, and took something off his plate that wouldn't make a mess if it fell into my lap. Marilyn followed our playfulness with interest and asked Mom if she would go to the ladies room with her.

* * *

Once there, Marilyn checked to be certain they were alone. "Jenn, those two appear to be closer than just classmates. They appear to be serious about each other."

"Yes, you're right. Barbara told Jeff and Angel to back off for awhile as the time was not right for them yet. They both think they were meant to wait until after med school or maybe even their internship. It's been difficult for them as its obvious that they were meant for each other."

"So, the intrigue in your family continues, now it's Angel's time."

"I'm afraid Jack and I aren't out of the woods yet. Marilyn, I'm pregnant again."

Marilyn looked at me as if I was a crazy woman. "What! Are you sure?"

I raised my eyebrow at her.

"Of course you are. How far along are you?"

"About two months. Angel hugged me today and sensed it with her diagnostic abilities, so I was outed. I hadn't even told Jack yet."

"How did he take that?"

"He wanted to know why I told Angel before him. When I said she hugged me and sensed I was pregnant, he was all concerned about my health. We discussed adopting earlier, but this was a surprise even to me."

Marilyn gave me a lopsided smile. "Be careful what you wish for, you of all people should have realized that. Are you going to keep it a secret for awhile?"

"Yes, I want to be sure this baby is going to stay with me before making it public."

"Jenn, keep calm. You were meant to have this child, so don't be concerned about losing it, even if you are a bit older to be having another baby. How does Angel feel about having a sibling?"

"I don't think she's even thought about it. I was the middle child in our family and I always had either a sister or brother while growing up. Both of my children will grow up alone. I wish now

I'd had another baby while Angel was still at home."

* * *

When Mom and Marilyn returned to our table, I could see from their faces that some serious discussion had taken place. I pulled Jeff toward the dance floor so we could talk while dancing.

"Jeff, Mom is pregnant again and I have a feeling that their lives are going to change, much like when I was born. She's trying to keep it a secret because she's afraid she might lose it. That's not going to happen, this is according to plan. Would you tell your mother what's happening and maybe she can offer Mom some advice when she's ready?"

"I will, she's had three kids and was your mother's age when I was born. They've become close friends and I'm sure they'll get together."

We danced in silence, with my head on Jeff's chest, each lost in our own thoughts until the music stopped and we returned to our table. I noticed that Marilyn gave me a sad smile, as if she knew about my romantic problems.

Later, after the party was over and we took Jeff home and before getting out of the car, he gave me a long kiss that made me forget everything else as my emotions peaked. Mother turned and watched me as I touched my still burning lips.

"Are your lips still burning?"

"Yes, but not as bad now. Do yours do that when Dad kisses you?"

"No. It's not supposed to do that. I think that's a warning to you not to go any further. When it stops burning, then it will probably mean it's finally time for you."

When we got home, Mom helped me out of the gown, and hung it back in the closet. Mother looked at the gown wistfully. "This was my first gown and I can't get into it anymore, not since I gave birth to you. It fits you like a glove, so this is going to be my Christmas gift to you."

I hugged her tightly. "Thanks Mom. I don't know when I'll have occasion to wear it, but if I do I'll be the best dressed woman there."

"Is Jeff going to church with us tomorrow?"

"No. He's going with his parents. We're going to try to get together Monday, weather permitting, for a jog. Remind me to call Lilly tomorrow after church."

Christmas break flew by and Jeff and I were back at Johns Hopkins getting ready for our next term before we knew it. I met with my advisor, Dr. Ellsworth, who arranged my schedule of classes for the semester.

I asked, "Is it possible for me and my roommates to apply for an apartment in Charles Commons for the fall semester."

"What kind of rooms do you want?"

I smiled at Dr. Ellsworth. "What can I get for three women?"

"You're now in McCoy Hall. You can get rooms like that, only at Charles Commons they are slightly bigger; or we can put you into a suite. Suites are nice because they come with a kitchen."

"Put us down for a suite then and if that can't be arranged, we'll settle for the smaller apartment."

"Angel, you don't realize what status you have here. If you want the suite, that's what you get."

"I plan on staying for another summer session, can I go ahead and move in then?"

"You can if there's any available, and I'm sure there will be."

"Okay. That sounds wonderful. I'll tell my roomies where they will be staying this fall."

After picking up my books and supplies I returned to the apartment. I did a little house cleaning and sat down on the couch facing Barbara's picture. I basked in the feeling of love coming from her picture for awhile, then decided to bring Barbara up to date on Mom's pregnancy.

I started to tell her, when her voice came to me. "Angel, don't be concerned about Jenn's pregnancy. It will be easy for her with little or no morning sickness and delivery will come as expected. You will have a sister and she will progress much as you did. She will be given healing powers at the age of ten and the Angel Foundation will continue as before, at least in the beginning. There may be a name change to reflect the new healer, but that is minor. There are other changes coming that involve you, but that's not until after you've become a doctor. Don't be discouraged about you and Jeff being married. It will happen and you've already guessed when."

I sat stunned on the couch trying to fathom all that had been revealed to me. Then I sat in silence wondering whether to reveal any or all of what was to come to my parents.

"Barbara, am I free to share all this with my parents?"

"Yes, I think it will calm their nerves."

I smiled at her in relief, then thought, *I'm going to have a sister!*

I called Mom, "Where are you and do you have time to take this call?"

"It's okay. We're in our office alone. I'll put you on speaker for Jack."

"Barbara just told me I'm going to have a sister. She said your pregnancy is going to be easy and when my sister is ten she will be given healing powers. Apparently, I'm going to be involved with the foundation after I become a doctor. There's more, but those are the highlights."

There was no response at first from mother's end, then I could hear her crying in relief. Dad said, "Angel, this is astounding news. I'll call you back after we absorb what you told us. How amazing - another daughter who will be a healer."

I heard a sound behind me and found both my roomies standing with their hands over their mouths, trying not to cry. I said, "I didn't hear you come in. Did you hear all of it?"

Julie said, "You're going to have a sister that will have healing powers like you did. That means you don't have to worry about the healing stopping!"

They both sat down on the couch on either side of me and hugged me tightly. Robin asked, "Did you know that your mother was pregnant?"

"I found out during break when I hugged her and my gift kicked in. Mom said she hadn't known very long and hadn't told Dad yet."

Julie said, "Wow! I bet that was a surprise."

I smiled ruefully. "To put it mildly. Listen, I have some news. I arranged for us to move into a suite at the Charles Commons this fall."

Robin said, "What! How did you arrange that. Everyone wants into that dormitory. It's got a fitness center and Nolan's, the best dining hall on campus."

Julie said, "Angel has a lock with President Smithson. I bet he'll get her anything she asks for."

"Maybe, but I'm not going to push my luck. How did you two fare on your classes this term?"

CHAPTER SEVENTEEN

About two months later I received an e-mail summons from Dr. Ellsworth. She and President Smithson asked to speak with me immediately. I was a little nervous because I had no idea what their concern might be.

Dr. Ellsworth said, "Ms. Pearson when you first enrolled in Johns Hopkins University you were placed in the Vivien Thomas College, which is one of four colleges in the school of medicine. Last year you failed to enter the Olympics for your college. Why was that?"

Her tone was serious, so I responded in a like manner. "It wasn't required and I didn't see how it could benefit me in graduating."

President Smithson responded, "Ms. Pearson, the Olympics challenge our students to better themselves and if the best students don't compete, then that defeats the purpose. Students are ranked according to how they perform in the Olympics and so far you are a no show. I'm sure that you don't want to be considered a no show when it comes time for your internship."

"No sir, I don't. Where can I sign up."

"You will meet with Dr. Abel tomorrow. Please contact her and arrange a time. I'm happy that we've had this talk and I'm looking forward to Vivien Thomas College being one of the top performers in this year's Olympics."

Dr. Grace Abel was a older woman in her late fifties, gray hair in a pony tail, and wore colorful loose clothing that she unsuccessfully used to hide a trim body. I knocked on her door and she bid me to enter. Once inside I told her my name and that I wished to enter the Olympics for the Vivien Thomas College.

"You didn't enter last year, why was that?"

"I didn't see any advantage to me at the time. President Smithson changed my mind."

"Did he? That's unusual for him to send me someone. I'll have to look into this. I'll e-mail you later for a meeting of all contestants, which describes what needs to be done. For now fill out this questionnaire and be on your way."

The next day Dr. Abel e-mailed me, asking me to meet her at my convenience. I e-mailed her back with a time later today.

When I arrived I took a seat at her request. Her attitude was different this time and she stared at me as if I was the goose that laid the golden egg. "Ms. Pearson, please forgive me if I was abrupt with you yesterday. Normally, when a student doesn't enter the Olympics it's because they're not a good student. You have straight A's in all your classes and Dr. Parsons has given you a great recommendation. That's never happened before. President Smithson tells me that you are a natural leader and that the students are drawn to your charisma. Last year our college came in last. I want your help in putting together a winning team this year."

She passed me a list of students in my college with their GPA's, then a list of those who were signed up. I quickly scanned the lists and said, "Whoa, this can't be right. Less than half are signed up."

"It's sad isn't it. I'm going to give you a week to get more signed up and then we'll talk again."

I looked at her doubtfully, but put the lists away and left, *what have I gotten myself into.*

I had two free hours, so I went back to my room and started working on the assignment. The lists had e-mail addresses, so I composed a plea with my name on it and sent it to everyone in the Vivien Thomas College who hadn't entered the Olympics.

That evening I asked my roomies which college they belonged to. Neither were with mine, Julie's was Florence Sabin and Robin's was Helen Taussig. Sabin College won last year. I told them the task I had been given and they shook their heads sympathetically.

Robin said, "Thomas really stunk last year. Nobody wants to be part of a losing team."

I composed a pamphlet asking Thomas College members to enter the Olympics, telling them they needed to participate or risk losing their internship chances later. I plastered the posters everywhere on campus.

A week later I received an e-mail from Dr. Abel asking me to meet her that evening. After I was seated, she smiled at me. "I've never seen a pamphlet touting the Olympics before. It's created a large increase in entries for all the colleges, especially ours. We are up to eighty percent now and I think we will make a good showing this year. I'm going to send e-mails out to all our entries for a meeting Thursday evening. I want you there to help me hand out the rules and generally make your presence known."

"Why me?"

"Because you are responsible for most of these people entering and they need your moral support."

At the meeting I was surprised at the number of students who knew me by sight and came over to introduce themselves. Apparently, my consulting work and the personal attacks on me were well known.

Dr. Abel brought the meeting to order. "The rules that were passed out, basically say all entries from the four colleges take the same test to qualify for the actual contest to be held in one month. The top four scorers from each college will compete against each other. A question will be asked and the first team that hits the buzzer gets to answer. If the answer is incorrect, that team is penalized ten points, if correct they receive twenty points. The incorrect question is open to any team that hits their buzzer after it is declared incorrect. If no team buzzes, then a new question is asked. Winner is 100 or more points. Teams will have three minutes to consult on their answer. The qualifying test will be given here to all college entries in two days beginning at one p.m."

I stood and explained further. "It's just a test on what you have learned, and the seniors should do better than the rest of us, but that's to be expected. Hopefully, we'll be a senior someday and our time to shine. Be a team player and do the best that you can, who knows you might make the team. If not, we will cheer for our team. Good luck and I will see you Saturday."

Dr. Abel joined me as we watched everyone leave. "My, President Smithson was right when he said you were a born leader. Were you always this way in high school and undergraduate school?"

"No, I was home schooled from when I was ten until I was fifteen when I started Missouri University. I had other battles to fight there because of my age."

"What do your parents do, are they doctors?"

"No, they are both partners in a law firm."

"So it's in the blood. Angel, I want you to do as well as you can and make that team. Even as a sophomore you will add greatly to the team."

I took the qualifying test for the Vivien Thomas team for the College Olympics and my score was the fourth best, which meant I made the team. Not bad for only two years of classes. My roomies couldn't believe I actually made the team. President Smithson e-mailed me his congratulations and wished me luck.

I looked at who my teammates were and they were all seniors; however, I had the best GPA. There were no sophomores on any of the other teams, and all but two were seniors. I counted myself lucky that I had made the team, no matter how it turned out. Dr. Abel e-mailed me and the other team members to meet with her next week for a strategy session.

When we met I expected to be told not to use the buzzer even if I thought I knew the answer, and I was right. Their reasoning was the seniors had exposure to more classes than me and I might earn them a penalty if I buzzed in. I didn't point out that my score was only three points below third place and ten below first. I'm naturally a competitive person and it rankled me, but this was a team effort and I went with the flow.

The day of the Olympics I was stressed, probably more than for any test I've taken in the past. The questions initially were easy for me as they covered classes I had taken, but our team never beat the others on the buzzer. After five questions they called a break and we were zero, Sabin had ten, Nathans had twenty, and Taussig had forty.

Our team huddled and I pointed out, "We need to beat the

others on the buzzer whether we knew the answer or not. It's our only chance of getting points and I didn't want Thomas to come in last again."

Dr. Abel smiled at my confidence and asked, "Who's got the fastest reflexes?"

I said, "Me, because of my Judo classes."

"Alright, beat the others and let's hope we can answer the questions."

Our team beat the others three times in a row and we knew the answers, giving us sixty points and the lead. The next question we missed, knocking us back to fifty points, but no one else attempted to answer it either. The next two we answered correctly, giving us ninety points. But my buzzer malfunctioned on the next question and Taussig got the answer, bringing them to sixty points. They fixed my buzzer and we got the next question. The others on my team didn't know the answer, but I had an inspiration and said I thought I knew the answer. The team said go for it and we won! I answered the winning question.

Later, as our team was celebrating our win. Dr. Abel asked, "How did you came up with the answer?"

"I was stuck too at first, then it struck me. The question was asked backwards from what was in the textbook. When I turned it around it made sense."

"Well, you earned your spot on the team and I want you back next year."

When I carried my individual trophy into the apartment my two roomies gave me another celebration. Julie said, "I never thought your team had a chance until you started hitting the buzzer. Wow, that was exciting."

The remaining days of the semester passed quickly and I flew back home with Jeff. Like last year I was only taking a week off before returning for summer school. Jeff was taking the full summer break.

Jeff and I entered my home and found both my parents there waiting on us. Mom was definitely showing her baby bump now, but appeared happy and excited as she rushed to hug both of us. After the welcome home greetings, I asked, "What's up?"

"It's our turn to host your return home party. Jeff's parents will be here in about two hours, so let's sit down and catch up on what's been happening before the caterers get here."

I asked Mom, "How are you feeling with the pregnancy?"

"A lot better than when I was carrying you. It's just like what Barbara told you, it's much easier this time. Jack has been very attentive and loving, which has helped too. Now tell me about you two?"

I grinned. "I've had no more people trying to do me harm. I'm doing well in school and I promoted three more of my Judo students to Brown Belts, including Jeff."

Jeff said, "I've got the bruises to show for it. Did you know that your daughter is much stronger than she looks?"

Her father said, "Angel, be careful and don't take out your frustrations out on Jeff. It's not his fault that you are both in a holding pattern. I'm sure he's as frustrated as you."

Jeff's face was flushed. I hugged him and looked into his eyes saying, "I'm sorry. Maybe I could kiss the bruises and make them better."

He responded, "Angel, don't do that! I can hardly keep my hands off you as it is."

Mom and Dad looked at each other and sadly shook their heads. Dad said, "When your mother and I first met on the job, it was like being hit on the head with a club. She teased me the way you just did with Jeff, only much worse. We didn't have to wait like you two, but the sexual tension was so heavy you could cut it until we married less than two weeks later. You two may have years to wait, so go easy on each other and be kind, don't tease."

"Mom, what did you do to Dad?"

"Never you mind, I'm sure you're wise enough to guess the ways a woman can tease a man."

Dad and Jeff both rolled their eyes at that comment, while I tried to figure out what she actually did. *I'm going to find out what they did together during that period before they got married.*

I rubbed Mom's belly and asked, "Have you thought of a name for my sister?"

"Well, it's not going to be Angel. Do you have any thoughts?"

"How about Elizabeth or Alice Jennifer Angel Pearson?"

Mom and Dad looked at one another. Dad said, "We'll think about it some more, but you came up with good ideas."

CHAPTER EIGHTEEN

Jeff's parents arrived shortly after the caterers left. Sandra and George were given a tour of the apartment, but the Barbara's were the highlight after so much had been told about them. Sandra and George stood before the mantel gazing at them, basking in the glow of love emanating from the elder Barbara painting.

Sandra looked over at Jenn and said, "I wish I had something like this at home that I could go to and receive a dose of love. This painting is so real. I can feel her presence, and all of you look alike."

George agreed, "Angel, I can see where you favor both Barbara and Jenn. If it wasn't for the age difference people would think you were triplets."

Mom said, "Food's ready if you're ready to eat. We're having Italy tonight. Pasta with three kinds of meat and chicken. Sandra, I'm sure the bread is not as good as yours, but whose is?"

My week at home passed quickly, but my feelings about leaving Jeff behind were mixed. I loved him, yet being so close to each other without consummating our love was torture.

After my return to medical school I checked with admissions and found I was assigned to Charles Commons dormitory as promised. I moved my things into my new apartment before obtaining needed materials for my summer classes. It didn't make it any easier to be without Jeff, but at least I had something else to think about.

Compared to my old dormitory, this suite of rooms was like staying at a fancy hotel. The common room included a gas fireplace with a mantel, where I placed Barbara's picture. The common room was easily twice the size of our old place, and included a small kitchen and dining area. Each bedroom had a larger study desk and storage area for clothing and other items.

Dr. Mary Kilpatrick sent me an e-mail asking if I would teach a small Judo class this summer. She had requests from three students who wished to attend. I replied, "Yes. The first class to start Wednesday at seven p.m., and we need to place an order for thirty new uniforms in assorted sizes for the fall term."

The two courses I was taking this term didn't require much time for me outside the classroom, and I needed the distraction the Judo class would give me. I was waiting for my students when they arrived on time. The three were all new sophomore women having just completed their freshman year. Jessie Graham was a brunette of about my 5 foot, 10 inch size and shape from Tulsa, Oklahoma. Betty Cassidy was a petite 5 foot, 3 inch blond from Tupelo, Mississippi. Helen McCoy was a tall willowy 6 foot red head from Boston, Massachusetts.

I had not yet changed into my uniform, so I introduced myself and we got to know each other's backgrounds. I found that these three had heard about my previous experience with attackers, one that had happened during a Judo class, and they wanted to be able to defend themselves.

I led them to the locker room and gave them each a uniform. They watched how I donned my uniform, then they followed suit. After we returned to the gym floor I had them help me in placing the practice mat. I adjusted their white novice belts, then used Helen as a form to demonstrate the various basic holds they would learn to use. Eventually, after I was sure they were ready, I had Helen charge me as an attacker. I grabbed her arms and fell backwards using my feet to help gently throw her over me where she landed on her back.

I checked to make sure she was not hurt, then helped her up and asked the others if they had seen me use the moves I had previously demonstrated. They all agreed, and I told Helen that she now was going to use those moves against me, which she did with little effort. We took turns until they all had defended themselves successfully.

Jessie said, "When attacked, you and the brown belts broke their arms when you defended yourselves. How did you do that?"

"That comes later in your training, when you are brown belts. Now you learn the basic moves to defend yourselves. If you continue your training through the next term, maybe, if you do well, you will earn your brown belt."

Later, after the session ended and we showered and dressed, I asked if any wanted to continue discussions at the rec room. The four of us found a empty table and we got to know a little more about each other. Helen told us that she'd run in the Boston Marathon a few times, but usually finished far back in the pack. Betty, the smallest of us, said she was raised to be a lady, but wanted to be able to defend herself. Her brothers were always there to defend her at home, but they weren't here. Jessie was a tomboy and tried to do almost everything physically her brothers had done. As an adult, she realized a woman needs an edge in defending herself.

Betty said, "Angel, I've heard rumors that you are something special in the medical world, but no one knows the whole story."

"What have you heard?"

"Some say that you are a healer, that you can touch somebody and they are cured. But that doesn't make any sense, if you could heal why would you be here. There is a rumor that you are called in to consult on special cases, what's that about?"

"Please don't spread this around, but I used to be able to heal by touch. Now I have the ability to diagnose illness by touch, but I was told by an angel that I needed medical knowledge to make better use of this ability. So, the rumors were partially true."

My three students looked at me in awe. Betty said, "An angel talked to you?"

Jesse snickered. "What! That she talked to an angel is the most fantastic thing you got from her revelations. What about she used to heal and now can diagnose illness by touch. How would you like to have that ability?"

I smiled at the women. "So you believe me?"

Helen snorted trying not to laugh. "Even without the rumors, you are famous on the campus. You starting medical school when you were only eighteen, then these rumors, the attacks against you that were defended so spectacularly, and the way you made your college team for the Olympics when you were only a sophomore and lead the way to victory. By the time you graduate they'll probably put up a statue to honor you."

Betty repeated, "But she spoke to an angel. That's big where I come from."

"Actually, I know two angels. Olivia, my guardian angel, and Barbara, my messenger angel."

Betty's mouth hung open at this revelation. "You have a guardian angel too!"

Jessie asked, "Why take Judo if you have a guardian angel?"

"Olivia only protects me from a mortal danger. I need Judo for all other attacks."

Helen asked. "Has Olivia helped you since you've been here?"

"Yes. Rather than kill my attackers, she made them tell the police who hired them to kill me. President Smithson has been very protective of me since that last attack."

The three looked at me in speculation, but before they asked I said, "If it hasn't already happened, I'm sure it will come out soon. I don't want to comment until it does."

The summer session passed and I was looking over the study materials for my fall classes, when my roommates, Julie Westerman and Robin Lacy, arrived. I helped them move their belongings inside, then showed them what the new apartment offered. Robin had a big smile on her face as she said to me, "Thank you, thank you! We finally have an apartment that I have enough storage room. Angel, have you tried out Nolan's yet? I heard that it's the best on campus and it's on the first floor of this building."

"You guys know I can't cook, so I've eaten there a lot. Be sure and try the veal cutlet. I've got us some frozen breakfast sandwiches that we can nuke in the microwave in the mornings, and popcorn for snacks."

Julie exclaimed. "Hey, we have a machine for one cup of coffee or tea. Awesome!"

I said, "Pick your rooms, I'm still the one in the middle."

I helped my friends move their things into their rooms, then went back to reviewing my class materials. Later, Julie and Robin appeared at my door.

Julie asked, "How did your week at home go with you and Jeff?"

"Frustrating for both of us. It was worse than having an itch that you couldn't scratch. I didn't get any relief until I returned here. On the bright side, Mom seems to be having a much easier pregnancy with my sister than she did with me. I even suggested a name for her."

Robin said, "I assume it's not Angel II."

"Ha. I suggested the first names of the women in our family. She will have a long name if they follow through with the idea."

Julie nodded. "It's not fashionable now, but at one time it was common practice to name children after close relatives or people in power. What classes have you signed up for this semester? Maybe we can take some of the same ones you did."

I showed them the courses I was taking, which they wrote down and left for Mason Hall to get their classes lined up. I thought, *it's strange how empty the apartment seems after they leave.*

I called Lilly, my old roommate from MU, to see how she was getting along. She was in her last year attending nursing school in Quincy, Illinois, not far from her home in Hannibal, Missouri.

When Lilly answered, she just gushed with happiness on hearing my voice. "Angel! I finally found him. The man of my dreams and he feels the same way about me. I'm engaged! Can you believe that, I'm engaged to be married. He's in training here too, and we're going to wait until after graduation to get married."

"Congratulations! Lilly, please set the date so that I can come. I would really like to see you get married. Is he religious and has he met your father yet?"

"Yes and no. His mother is very religious, but not like my father. I just got engaged and we plan on telling father this weekend. Oh Angel! I so want you to be my brides maid, but I know you can't. Tell me your next break and we'll try to work the wedding into your time off. Oh Angel, I'm so happy!"

After I disconnected, I sat with tears of happiness running down my face. Lilly was getting married! I then thought of my own frustrated love life and laid my head down on the desk and cried real tears of despair.

I felt someone touch my shoulder and turned to find Barbara standing next to me. As she embraced me, I suddenly felt much better. She used a finger to wipe away my tears, saying, "Angel, try to be more patient. Your time will come, I promise you. You will attend Lilly's wedding and you will meet the young man she has chosen. Tell her to try to get a position in or near Kansas City after graduating and you may eventually meet again."

I searched Barbara's face looking for a clue of what would happen in the future if fate didn't interfere. I hugged her and nodded before she disappeared. I centered myself, inhaling deeply, then went into the common room and stood in front of Barbara's picture.

"Aunt Barbara, thank you for your support. I really needed it and I'm better now."

I received a call from Jeff, which I answered with a sigh. He wanted to meet and I suggested the rec room as a neutral place. When I arrived he was already seated at a table, where I joined him. He pointed at the cup of coffee he had gotten for me, which I sipped gratefully.

We were now at about the same grade level because of my two summer sessions, and he asked what courses I was taking. When I told him, he smiled. "I've got two of your classes. Are you still teaching Judo?"

"Yes. You better sign up before it fills, I seem to have become a minor celebrity according to my summer class students."

"Not so minor, according to what I've been hearing. Dr. Peter Hedrick was fired by Johns Hopkins and is facing criminal charges for the attacks against you. You are the top topic of the rumor mill and it keeps building with each thing you do."

I said with a slight smile, "You mean I've become well known for my many exploits."

Jeff placed his hand over mine. "Angel, you will always be at the center of whatever you do. It's just who you are. I've known that since I first met you and am resolved to follow in your shadow."

"I might be a bright star, but that doesn't mean that you can't shine too. I need you to be as bright as possible to help me later in what's to come. I've just got a clue that I'm going to eventually be in Kansas City."

I then told him about my conversation with Lilly about her upcoming marriage and Barbara's message to Lilly. Jeff pondered that news for a moment. "Apparently, this is going to happen after we become doctors, so that is at least four plus years in the future."

"Hopefully, we would be married by that time. Do you want to go to Lilly's wedding with me? I'm sure it will be on a weekend, if it's not during Christmas break."

Jeff squeezed my hand and gave me a smile. "You just want to show Lilly that you have a man too."

"That, and it's lonely attending a wedding by yourself. I suppose I could get my parents to go with me."

"No. I was just kidding you. Of course I'll go with you. I'll be beside you supporting you as she gets married."

My two roommates chose that moment to arrive at our table and sit down. I stuck my tongue out at them and said, "We were just talking about Lilly's wedding. You remember, the girl I told you about that I roomed with at MU."

Julie said, "The preacher's daughter who's going to nursing school."

"Yes, they plan on getting married as soon as they graduate. Her fiancé, Robert Cox, is attending the same school."

Julie said, "So, you're not just making moon eyes at each other."

"Right. Although, that sounds like fun. What do you say Romeo, want to make moon eyes at me?"

Ignoring the comment, Julie asked Jeff, "Did Angel tell you about our new digs at Charles Commons?"

"You're in Charles Commons! How did you work that?"

Robin replied, "Angel has pull with President Smithson. She asks for something and she generally gets it."

"Wow! Angel, is that true?"

"It seems that way, but I don't want to push it too far. I don't want to use up all my good will, because I may really want something some day. Do you want to see our palatial apartment?"

We soon arrived at our eleventh floor south tower apartment where Jeff entered our domain slightly intimidated, but impressed. "Hey, this is a suite. Boy, you girls are really lucky to get a suite.

Besides being expensive, there's at least a year wait getting one, and Nolan's is in this building too. Now I'm jealous."

Julie said, "I told you so. She's got pull. Jeff, you still got the same roomies?"

"Yeah, but if you want dates they already have girlfriends."

"Poop! Do you know anyone else that's not scum that might like to come to our house warming?"

Jeff grinned at Julie. "What's wrong? You two should have guys hounding you."

Julie pointed at Angel. "That's why. When guys find out we are roomies with her they get intimidated. What are the rumors about her? Do they think her guardian angel will zap them, or what?"

"It's intimidation by association."

"Oh please. As if we have any special powers. Maybe if they see all of us in a social situation, they won't be scared of us."

Jeff said, "I guess you can advertise like Angel did for the Olympics. Some will come just to check you out."

Julie said, "Okay. Angel, help us out with a flyer for our housewarming party."

CHAPTER NINETEEN

The following Saturday evening my apartment was packed with friends and students, some just curious about the famous Angel and her roommates. An hour into the party, several staff members arrived including Dr. Ellsworth. They were apparently curious about the party and how the students were behaving. Dr. Ellsworth asked me to come outside into the hallway.

"Angel, beginning this semester we are going to start our junior and senior students into a modified internship on Saturdays at the hospital. For one Saturday each student will work with a doctor from a different department, so that they may be exposed to different kinds of medicine. You might even find the department that you will want to specialize in later after you graduate. Of course, your first year of internship does this too. However, this tease may whet your appetite for what is to come. After each student has worked in three departments the program will stop until a review is made of its usefulness. I'm particularly interested in what your take on this project will be, so put some thought into how you benefited from it as a junior."

"When is this going to start and may we pick the departments we work in?"

Dr. Ellsworth looked at me in surprise at first, then said, "Right off the starting line you came up with a good idea. The answer is Saturday after next, and you may pick the department if there's an opening. Anything else?"

I smiled as I said, "No, but I think it's a good idea. It doesn't even have to be done every year, every other year will work just as well."

Later, after everyone had left I told my roomies about the coming internships. Julie and Robin stared at me in surprise, then Robin said, "When did you hear that?"

"Dr. Ellsworth came by the party and told me. I think it's a great idea."

Julie said, "I bet you have already picked your three departments."

"Yep. Emergency, family practice, and pediatrics."

Robin and Julie quickly headed to their rooms to make their own selections, while I sighed and looked at Barbara's picture. "You would have thought that by now they would have selected the departments that interested them. Did you see any boys from the party that would be a good match for Julie and Robin?"

Barbara answered me non-vocally. *Several were good matches, but time will tell if a connection is ever made. It is up to them.*

Monday, every junior and senior received an e-mail outlining the new test internship and asking for our three department choices, which will be honored if possible. At my first class everyone was excited and talking about the new program.

The following Monday we each received a letter of the dates and departments they would be working in. I found out later that the start date for some students was a month away. However, I started the next Saturday at emergency medicine, followed by my picks at the following Saturdays. Dr. Julia Song was famous for how her department was run under her tight leadership. She was a small slender Asian woman who took no prisoners when her policies were violated.

When the ten of us reported to her in a small conference room, Dr. Song gave us a strict set of rules. "Don't talk unless a doctor is asking a question, observe and take notes which you can ask questions about later. If a staff member tells you to move out of their way, move up against a wall. If you faint, another student will place you out of the way of staff. If you fail to follow these rules you will be dismissed from further consideration by this department."

Dr. Song left and our leader was Dr. Brad Lowry. He told us to follow him and observe what is happening and follow Dr. Song's rules or we were toast. Before entering the main emergency room we all donned gowns to protect us from blood splatter. Upon entering we found only one patient, a middle aged man with an apparent broken arm.

As if on cue, the doors opened with attendants pushing a gurney that held a blood stained woman, screaming in pain. I watched as a male student fainted, striking his head on a piece of equipment as he fell. I quickly approached him, grabbing a wad of gauze as I knelt and applied it to his head wound. Looking up I motioned for Dr. Lowry to approach me, which he did.

I quietly said, "He's got a depressed fracture of the skull and needs immediate attention."

He looked at the wound and grimaced in agreement. "Nurse, get another team in here and page Dr. Holmes to come to the emergency room for a head wound. Students, move back and make way for the trauma team. Not you Ms. Pearson, stay with me."

I stood near Dr. Lowry, out of his way, but close enough to observe everything he did as the trauma team arrived and placed the student on the gurney where he was wheeled to a work station. A doctor hurried inside and conferred with Dr. Lowry, who I assumed was Dr. Holmes. They both looked at me and then Dr. Holmes hurried to the injured student, where he began his examination.

Dr. Lowry said, "Follow me and observe."

I stood as close as I could get and watched Dr. Holmes work on the student.

Holmes asked, "How did you know he had a depressed fracture, because it's not immediately apparent from the wound?"

"I've consulted here before because of my ability to diagnose by touch. He was bleeding internally as well."

"You must be Ms. Pearson. We can use you here, so hurry up and graduate."

Dr. Lowry took my elbow and we joined the rest of our group. "Students, please follow me back to the conference room. I'll show you where to discard your gowns on the way. Ms. Pearson please use the scrub station over there before joining us."

I returned to the room where all the students were waiting. I thought at first it was for me, but then Dr. Lowry came in closely followed by Dr. Song. Dr. Song looked at us for a moment, then gave a crooked smile. "I understand you all had a bit of excitement while you were in the ER. Ms. Pearson please come up here. I've heard about you and I want to shake your hand."

I blushed a little at the accolade, but quickly made my way to her and shook her hand. Dr. Song then turned to the students. "It was lucky that Ms. Pearson attended your classmate, Ralph Jennings, because he was quickly diagnosed with a depressed fracture of the skull, which may have kept him from having brain damage. In case you didn't know, Ms. Pearson has the ability to diagnose ailments by touch. She has helped the hospital before while attending JH medical school."

One of the students held up her hand and was recognized by Dr. Song. "This question is for Angel. You didn't know that he was going to faint, did you? You didn't hesitate a bit. I saw you grab some gauze and go right to him and then motioned for Dr. Lowry."

"I'm trained in Judo, which gives me quick reactions. I knew he was hurt when I saw his head hit the equipment, and when I touched him I knew what his injury was and got him help. If you're asking how I got this gift, it came from God."

Dr. Song asked, "Any other questions? If not, I have a lesson for you. Don't work in ER if you faint at the sight of blood. Everyone take off except for Ms. Pearson."

When it was just the two doctors and me, Dr. Song said, "I would be proud to have you work towards a residency in emergency medicine. Your talent is sorely needed and I know you will save many lives here. Even without your ability, you have shown quick clear thinking. That ability is also hard to find. When you graduate, please consider us first."

I thanked her for her interest in me and told her I was strongly considering her department, before leaving for the rec room to unwind. When I arrived there I immediately headed toward the counter and got a cup of coffee. Looking around for a table my eyes were drawn to Shelly Beaman, who was waving her arm at me to get my attention. I headed toward her table where most of the interns I was with earlier were sitting.

I didn't know everyone, so we introduced ourselves. I sighed after taking a sip of my hot coffee and closed my eyes, settling myself. George Bushman was watching me and when I opened my eyes, he asked, "Does that help?"

I gave him a weak smile. "Usually, but it's been a stressful morning."

I looked around the table and they all were intently looking at me. "How about the rest of you, what's up?"

Shelly said, "What did Dr. Song want?"

"She was trying to recruit me for her department when I select my residency."

"Wow! You are only a mid-junior and you have a department head trying to recruit you already. I'm jealous." Shelly said.

George frowned at Shelly, saying, "Are you forgetting we were all standing around while Angel took charge and tried to help Ralph. Even without her gift she did more than the rest of us."

I looked at the others considering, before saying, "I have an eidetic memory and can repeat word for word what Dr. Holmes said during his examination of Ralph. Are you interested?"

They all straightened up in their chairs and leaned towards me, while Shelly said, "Please help us. We didn't hear anything and saw very little."

I then repeated what I saw and heard from Dr. Holmes. When I finished they looked at me in awe."

George shook his head in frustration. "You are a rising star at the University and will be the same at the hospital when you start your internship. To compete we are going to have to choose a slightly different track than you do."

"Poo! There's room for several more just like me. I might not even stay at JH after my residency. Make your decisions based upon your own interests and abilities, not on me."

George asked, "By chance, do you have a boyfriend?"

"Actually I do. His name is Jeff Blake."

"Crap! He's another rising star. I bet you both try for the same department when it's time. Thanks for the information on Ralph. Not everyone would have done it after Shelly's performance."

They all left the table, while I sat and allowed the tension leave my body until I felt in balance again. I looked around the room and watched another group of students enter, one of which was Jeff. I raised my hand to get his attention and he waved. A few minutes later he was sitting with me with a cup of coffee in front of him.

Jeff sighed and then grinned. "You must have been released early, how did it go?"

"There was an accident in the ER when Ralph Jennings fainted and struck his head. I attended him and found that he had a depressed fracture of the skull. Long story short, Dr. Song wants me for an residency in emergency medicine. How did your tour go?"

"Damn! Angel, you really lead an interesting life. I was in pediatrics and nothing strange happened, but it was still interesting. You were going there next, aren't you?"

"Yes. When you do ER, I'd be interested if they mention me. Dr. Lowry knew me by name, so apparently I've already got a reputation."

My phone chimed, telling me I had an e-mail. I looked at it and frowned. "Jeff, Dr. Ellsworth wants to see me in her office. Do you have dinner plans?"

"Do you want to meet at Nolan's at six?"

"Okay, I'll see you then."

I knocked on Dr. Ellsworth's door and she invited me inside. "Sorry, but President Smithson hasn't arrived yet. I hear you had a little excitement at the ER this morning."

I nodded. "It was interesting. Have you heard how Ralph Jennings is doing?"

"He's in intensive care, but is expected to fully recover thanks to your quick action and diagnoses'. Dr. Holmes doesn't think he has any brain damage, but tests still have to be run."

We continued to talk about the intern project until President Smithson arrived. He smiled and congratulated me while shaking my hand, then said, "I have a problem with the department heads. Word quickly got around about Dr. Song's offer to bring you into her residency program. They all want equal access to you so that they can expose you to their departments' merits. So, in the future you will be given a personal tour of each department by senior staff members. Each department will have two hours of your time beginning this afternoon at one with the anesthesia, and then dermatology departments. Next Saturday you begin with family practice and continue with three other departments. I know this is outrageous, but I couldn't think of any other way to keep the department heads happy."

"How many Saturdays is this going to take?"

"Four, unless something comes up. Will you do it?"

"Yes, but the other interns may take a dim view. I'm already getting flack for preferential treatment from my group today. This may hurt your intern program. I would suggest a conference with all department heads touting the high points of their departments to the interns. Instead of just me visiting each department, maybe it should be the top five performers and we could answer questions from the interns at the conference."

Dr. Ellsworth smiled at President Smithson. "Didn't I tell you. She's a problem solver and a natural leader."

President Smithson's face relaxed and he took a seat next to me. "Okay, this sounds much better and it takes the pressure off Ms. Pearson. Is there enough grade spread for a clear top five?"

"I'll check, but I think so. Ms. Pearson is currently number one, but I'll need to check on the others."

"Very well. Compile a list and e-mail those five to meet here Monday at six p.m.. We'll see how they respond. Ms. Pearson, we seem to place a lot of responsibility on your shoulders, but that comes with being a doctor. I'll talk to you later."

CHAPTER TWENTY

I returned to my apartment and made myself a sandwich, which I was eating when my roomies entered. They both looked at me in contemplation before taking seats with me. Julie said, "We just heard about Ralph Jennings fainting and hitting his head. Is it true that you may have saved his life?"

"I told Dr. Lowry that he had a depressed skull fracture and needed immediate help. Dr. Lowry seems to thank my quick reaction may have saved him."

"I guess! There's also a rumor that Dr. Song wants you in her residency program. Is that true?"

I shrugged my shoulders in frustration. "It's gotten out of hand. President Smithson talked to me a few minutes ago saying that all the department heads want equal access to me, so I suggested a procedure that might keep everyone happy, including the interns. Instead of just me, the top five performers are going to visit all the departments. Later, after all the interns have visited three departments, a conference of interns and department heads will meet. The department heads will tout their strong points and then the interns may ask questions of them and the top five performers."

Robin said, "Angel! You're one of the top five? You never told us, but I guess we should have known. Who are the other four?"

"I don't know. We meet Monday evening. I wonder if Jeff is

one of them? I guess I could ask him, we're having dinner tonight."

Julie said, "You two have the patience of Job. But, I guess your faith gives you the strength you need."

My roomies fixed themselves something to eat and we sat in silence, each with their own thoughts. A knock on the door brought us back to reality, and Julie went to see who was there. We could hear her laugh, then she returned with a handsome man.

Julie said, "This is Peter Cook, who I met at our housewarming. We're going out, so keep him company while I clean up."

Peter looked around, then said, "Your apartment looks different without so many people in it. I don't think we were introduced. It's Angel isn't it?"

I stood and shook his hand. "I'm sorry, I don't remember meeting you at the party. I must of stepped out or you were lost in the crowd of people. What year are you?"

"Oh, I'm not a student. I'm a freelance writer for the *Baltimore Sun.* Are you by any chance the Angel Pearson who is famous for having healing powers?"

I yelled, "Julie! Please come out here."

Julie quickly came out of her room wearing a wrap. "What's wrong?"

"Did you know that this guy wants to write a story on me?"

Julie's face turned red in anger. "Peter, is that true?"

"Hey, I've got to make a living."

Julie went to the door and opened it, saying, "Please leave."

Peter grimaced, then left. Julie shut the door and leaned her body against it, with bright tears in her eyes. "Damn it, and he was good looking too. Using me to get to Angel, how low can you get."

I said, "Don't worry about it. He was scum. I'll help you find someone who deserves you, but first I better call Dr. Ellsworth and alert her to the reporter."

Later, I got on my computer and looked up George Bushman's phone number and called him. When he answered I said, "George, this is Angel. One of my roommates would really like to meet you. Her name is Julie Westerman and I think you'd really like her. Are you up to a challenge, because she's my roommate and you better treat her right."

"Julie Westerman, I know her from one of my classes. Can

you put her on and I'll talk to her."

"Sure, hold on."

"Julie, George Bushman wants to talk to you." I handed the phone to Julie and winked at Robin.

Julie started talking and made her way to her room, where she shut the door. Robin said, "Okay, now it's my turn. Who do you have in mind for me."

"I just met George and he seemed perfect for Julie. What kind of man appeals to you?"

"I want someone like your Jeff. Tall, handsome, muscles, and smart."

"My, you don't want much, do you. How about if I can find one with only two of those traits?"

"Oh Angel, all he needs to be is male and have a good personality."

"Well, that makes it easier. I'll keep my eyes open."

Julie came out of room, smiling, and handed my phone back to me. "Thanks Angel, George asked me out for dinner tonight. I've seen him in class, but I've never talked to him. He seems real nice, how do you know him?"

"He was one of the interns with me in the ER today. He stood up for me when one of the female interns gave me a hard time and later asked me if I had a boyfriend, so I knew he was available."

Robin said, "Angel, you're not a bit shy are you. You set yourself on a goal and full speed ahead. I'm not going to wait on some man asking me out. If he looks good, I'm going for him."

Julie laughed. "Yeah sure, the little Georgia girl chasing after a man. This I've got to see."

"Well, I can flirt can't I?"

"Yeah, yeah, "I said, "I'd better keep looking. Julie, maybe George has a friend who's available."

Six weeks later, all the interns had audited three JH hospital departments and the five top performing students had completed their tour of the departments. The conference was underway and the department heads had just completed their individual pitches trying to get the interns to pick them for their residency.

Now it was time for the interns to ask questions from the department heads and the five top performing interns. President Smithson was the moderator and took the first question, which was addressed to me by George Bushman.

"Angel, of all the departments you visited, which appealed to you best and why?"

"First of all, you asked which appealed to me. Everyone has different backgrounds which influences the choices they make in life. My number one choice was emergency medicine, mainly because of my gift. However, in two or three years it may be family practice or some other department I don't even consider now. Does that answer your question?"

The questions continued for two hours, eighty percent were to one of the five top performing interns. President Smithson finally brought the conference to an end due to time constraints, not because of lack of questions. He dismissed everyone except the five top interns.

He told us to keep our seats and then said, "I want to congratulate you for the way you conducted yourselves and the excellent answers you gave to the others' questions. The department heads will follow you closely for the remainder of your time at the University. When you start your internship you will be given special treatment in an attempt to attract you to their department. Choose wisely according to your own interests. The choices you make will influence your entire career. At this time we plan on doing this each year, so you seniors will be full time interns next year. Feel free to advise your former classmates if they ask for it. Good luck to all of you. You're all dismissed except Ms. Pearson."

When everyone else had departed, President Smithson took one of the chairs and placed it facing me and sat down. He sighed in relief. "I'm going to place a stool at the podium next time. My feet are killing me. How did you think the program went?"

"It seemed the other interns were more interested in what the top five said, than what the department heads had to offer. Maybe in the future their participation could be limited to informational booths set up before and after the meeting."

"If we did that it means the heads will try harder to impress you five when you visit their departments. I was really impressed on how much you each took away from your visits. Your classmates seemed impressed with you, as you received more questions than any of the others."

"Maybe it's because of all the attention I've received since I've been here. Especially, the College Olympics."

"There is that, but you seem to draw people to you and your causes. Take me for instance. I've never taken this close of interest in a student before, and when you continue into the hospital as an intern I'm sure it will continue. Do you have any questions?"

"No. But I do appreciate your interest and help during my sometimes difficult times."

Six weeks later on a Friday night, Jeff and I were driving from the St. Louis airport to Hannibal, Missouri. It was the weekend of Lilly's wedding and we were invited to stay with Lilly's parents and attend her wedding the next afternoon. We arrived at eight p.m. and it was already dark as I guided Jeff to their home with little help from the streetlights obscured by trees.

Lilly met us as we pulled into the driveway. I had no sooner gotten out of the car when Lilly grabbed and hugged me. "Oh Angel, you don't know how much I've missed you. But enough about me, I want to see this man you brought with you."

I introduced Jeff and Lilly to each other and then started carrying our luggage inside. Lilly's mother, June Williamson, met us in the kitchen and after giving her a hug and kiss, I introduced Jeff to her. June looked at us intently for a moment, then said, "I've got you in two separate rooms upstairs. I don't know what your relationship is, but here you sleep separate."

"Mother! You know how God has taken her under his wing. That comment was insulting."

I said, "June, I would have asked for separate rooms. We love each other very much and it would be too tempting to sleep in the same room."

Lilly grabbed a bag and said, "Follow me and I'll show you your rooms, then come with me so I can see if your bridesmaid dress will fit."

Alone with me in her room, Lilly broke down in sobs, her head on my shoulder. "Lilly, what's wrong? Did you and Robert have a fight?"

She raised her head from my shoulder and looked intently at me, wiping a tear away. "No, Bob is a saint. It's just me. I guess it's pre-wedding nerves. Everything is ready, Father is going to marry us in our church, and you're here. You've got a man too, but very frustrated by the looks you give each other. What's the story on that?"

"Barbara tells me it's not time for us yet, but wouldn't or couldn't tell me when we could be married. When we kiss I get a burning sensation. Barbara tells me that is God's warning that's it's not yet our time. I think our time is either after med school or our internship. I think it's after our internship, which means another three years."

"Oh Angel, no wonder you're frustrated. What did you mean when you asked me to try getting a job near Kansas City?"

"Barbara mentioned Kansas City in my future. But based upon my future medical training, that's at least five years in the future. Also, Mom is pregnant with another daughter who is supposed to be a healer when she is ten, like I was."

"Oh my, another healer in the family. Yes, it sounds like Kansas City is in your future. In ten years, Bob and I will be well situated. Which field are you going into?"

"I'm strongly considering a position in ER, because of my diagnostic gift. The Emergency Medicine Department Head at Johns Hopkins Hospital wants me very badly, but I'm not certain yet."

"I anticipate having enough pull in the future to dictate what staff I work with. I have an idea developing, that if it goes as planned, will put Kansas City at the center of medical development."

Lilly said, "Bob and I both have jobs in KC at different hospitals and I'll get him to try for an ER job as soon as possible. Let's try that dress on now and see if it fits."

Later, we all met in the kitchen for a sandwich and light conversation about the wedding. Reverend Williamson came into the kitchen and I introduced him to Jeff and told of his background.

"So you met in medical school and now have a personal relationship, that even a man of God can see is frustrating for both of you. Apparently, God is not ready for you to be married yet."

Lilly said, "Yes father, Angel has been told to wait until her medical school training is complete, she thinks until after their internship. When they kiss, Angel has a lingering burning sensation, which Barbara says is God's warning that they aren't ready yet."

Reverend Williamson said, "You indeed have been touched by the Lord to receive such guidance. Daughter, have you made all your preparations for your marriage tomorrow?"

"Yes Father. Bob will be here at about ten in the morning to change clothes. His parents will be at the church for the one p.m. ceremony. We will all return here for the reception and change our clothing, then later Bob and I will leave on our honeymoon to Florida."

Jeff said, "Do you want us to hide your car so it won't get covered with junk?"

"It's Bob's car, so ask him tomorrow. I hope he says yes."

Bob showed up shortly after nine the following morning. Of course no one would let him see the bride. He agreed to Jeff hiding his car, while I followed in the rental and brought him back to the house. Bob was nervous, but seemed a perfect fit for Lilly. They had common interests and each had played basketball in school.

Bob took me aside and asked me about Lilly's and my time at MU. "She's told me some wild stories about you and her. She said that you used to be able to heal by touch when you were younger, but now you diagnose illness by touch."

I smiled at him. "Bob, it's all true. When we first met and she realized who I was, she panicked, thinking God was playing a trick on her for leaving home to get away from her dad. We made a deal where she would help me, a fifteen year old home-schooled girl, fit in at MU and I wouldn't preach at her. She's still my best friend, so take good care of her. I've got friends in high places that would make you very sorry."

Bob stared at me with his mouth open in shock until Jeff walked up and said, "Don't worry, her guardian angel only protects her and doesn't act as an assassin."

"I didn't scare you did I? Well, maybe you should worry a little. Lilly knows some Judo I taught her, so don't piss her off."

Bob suddenly smiled. "Lilly said you liked to joke around, and for your information she can clean my clock without using Judo. How much Judo does she know?"

"Not much. Just enough to get out of trouble and run away. Me, I'm a black belt and can do a lot of damage in just defensive mode. Jeff here is a high rank brown belt, but it won't be long before he's a black belt."

"I looked you up on Google after Lilly told me about you. She was lucky you were her roommate at MU. She's a self-assured woman who's not afraid to go after what she wants. We still have a little black bias here, but she either ignores it or if she thinks it's warranted, she'd come right back at them until they back off. She told me that you didn't have any bias toward her. It was like she had a great tan as far as you were concerned."

"Look at me, pale as a ghost and white hair. She did have a great tan and I was envious. Besides she had breasts and I didn't then. She was a woman and I wasn't yet. She taught me a lot of things, and being the subject of racial prejudice was one of them. I had no tolerance for it when I was with her. The first time it happened I got right up into the man's face and told him to back off. He did too, even as small as I was then. Lilly told me she fought her own battles, but I responded that if she didn't in the future, I would. I guess I forced her to defend herself and it wasn't long before the bigots left us alone."

"Wow! You were her best friend in every way. She's never found anyone to replace you since MU, except maybe me. She needs to be near you again."

I told Bob about my tentative plans to return to KC after my internship, but it was going to take time. I said, "Try to get into ER, since I'm interested in that field of medicine. I visit Kansas City often because Jeff's and my family are there, and I can visit you two as well. Things are going to start happening soon. My mother is going to have a baby girl, who in ten years is going to be a healer, like I was. Can you imagine the upheaval in the medical world with two of us in Kansas City."

CHAPTER TWENTY-ONE

After the wedding and reception, Jeff and I flew back to Baltimore, arriving on campus in time to have dinner at Nolan's. Waiting on our food I said, "Lilly was a beautiful bride, wasn't she?"

Jeff smiled slightly. "You will too, and I bet she'll break a leg getting there for the wedding. I liked Bob. They're a good match and he loves her deeply."

"Yes, she picked well with him, and he's smart too. She sometimes needs a little direction. Her father seemed more laid back this time, not nearly as uptight as my last visit and Lilly's relationship with him was much more relaxed."

Jeff said, "I had a hard time not laughing at the expression on Lilly's face when her mother inferred she wasn't going to allow any hanky-panky between the two of us."

"June could tell we were a close couple, she just didn't know our situation. Oh, I wish this waiting period would end, I'm ready to be a blushing bride."

Christmas break arrived and once again we were back in Kansas City. Mom was due any day. She hadn't worked in a month and was happy to see us. We phoned from the airport, so she knew we were on our way. I called to her after we dropped our luggage by the doorway, and could hear her answer from the bedroom.

I hurried into the master bedroom and found her propped up in bed, a novel lying by her side. She smiled at us as we entered and held her arms up for a hug and kiss. I sat on the bed, while Jeff took a nearby chair.

"Mom, how do you feel? Can I get you anything? I thought someone would be staying with you in case you had any problems."

"Oh, Jackie left just before you arrived. You can take care of me now, since you both are almost doctors."

I laughed. "Hardly. Maybe in a few more years. But let me know if anything happens, so we can call your doctor. Where's his information?"

Mother pointed at the night stand. "Over there. When you touched me what did you feel?"

"You are very close to delivery and my sister is ready to meet us. You are both in good health, so you shouldn't have any problems."

"See, you are almost a doctor. Probably better than the one I have. He couldn't tell me what you just did."

Jeff said, "She's got you there. Has my mother been by to see you?"

"Sandra's been here almost every day for the past month. Where does she get her strength?"

"Mom has always been there for her family, and I guess you are included even though Angel and me aren't married yet."

"Yes, she includes Angel as family, and me by association. Did you call Jack that you're here?"

"No, I'll do that now."

After I disconnected I said, "Dad says he'll be home shortly. He had to pick up something for you."

"Oh, he's been doing that about every week. He's such a good husband and father. Jeff, be sure you do the little things for Angel that remind her how much you love her. Angel, you do the same for Jeff. Sometimes we need reminders that our loved ones need us."

After Dad came home, Jeff headed home to his parents. I called Lilly to let her know that I was in town and invited her and Bob to visit me at the apartment tonight. They lived in Raytown, not far from the Plaza area by interstate.

I had just cleaned up our dinner mess of Chinese delivery, when the Cox's arrived. Mom hadn't gone back to bed yet, so I introduced Bob to both my parents. Lilly immediately asked Mom how she felt.

Leaning back into the couch, Mom said, "I understand that you both are registered nurses here in Kansas City."

Lilly answered, "Nearby. I'm in Independence and Bob's in Lee's Summit. We live in Raytown, which is about half way between them. I'm working in the ER and Bob is trying for the same thing."

Mother looked at me with a raised eyebrow. "I have a feeling that my daughter has a hand in this somehow."

Lilly looked at her husband and smiled. "I told you where Angel got her smarts from. Angel wanted to position us so that we would be helpful in a few years when she comes back to KC."

"Angel dear, please explain?"

"Well, in about ten years, my sister is supposed to become a healer, probably much like I was when I turned eight. By then I expect to be well established at Johns Hopkins Hospital in some capacity, probably emergency medicine."

"So that explains why you two want to get into the ER. You want to be well trained by the time Angel returns. What about Jeff?"

"That's not clear yet. I'm sure he's going to play a bigger part than just being my husband. Obviously, my main talent is my diagnostic ability; however, I'm going to be able to do more than that. Jeff may become a surgeon, but until we receive more guidance that is all we know."

Barbara suddenly stood before us. Everyone was startled, but Bob would have jumped out of his chair, but for Lilly's restraining hand. "I told you we might see Barbara, so pay close attention."

Barbara looked at Lilly and smiled. "I see you have a husband now and you're both trained nurses. Angel will need you later."

Barbara turned to me and shook her head. "Angel, you are always in such a hurry to know what's next. I know you need information so that you can make plans for what is needed. I believe in your case you need to be a general practitioner and Jeff your surgeon when its needed. He already has the required talent, even though he doesn't know it yet. You will find that your talent has greater depth than you now realize. When you next use your talent, probe with your mind the problem you find and see if you can make adjustments. When you are interns you will be much too busy for marriage, that must wait until your second year of residency. Jenn your baby is ready, call for an ambulance and your baby girl will be delivered within an hour of your arrival."

Barbara disappeared, and Dad was calling for an ambulance. Lilly and Bob hurried to check on Mom, who said, "My water broke."

I hurried for towels. Lilly and I started shoving the towels underneath Mom, when she started having contractions I checked the time. Ten minutes later, the EMTs arrived to wheel Mom out of the apartment, and we rushed to our cars to follow her to the hospital.

CHAPTER TWENTY-TWO

A mere two hours later I was gazing at my new sister, Elizabeth April Alice Jennifer Barbara Angel Pearson through the glass at the neo-natal unit. She was shrouded in pink, sucking one finger peacefully. Her presence awed me. I finally broke eye contact to call Grandmother Pearson and report the birth of my new sister and her name.

"Why that poor thing. You shouldn't have burdened her with so many names, but tell Jack and Jenn I'm happy for them and hope to see my new granddaughter before I'm gone."

"Oh Grandmother, you have to stick around for at least another ten years so that you can see another miracle."

"Oh dear. Okay, but I need a little help now and then by a visit from Jack's first child, you hear me?"

"Yes Grandmother, I haven't been a very good granddaughter. I'll try to do better in the future."

Two days later, Jeff and I pulled into the long lane leading up to Grandmother's house. Grandmother was in the yard feeding her chickens. She watched me get out of the car and started smiling. I ran to her and gave her a hug and kiss on the cheek.

"Angel darling, you gave me a start. You don't want to do that to an old person. My guilt trip seemed to work though. I'm going to have to try that on your father too. Whose that handsome man coming our way?"

"That's Jeff Blake, my future husband. He is handsome, isn't he."

When Jeff reached us, I introduced them to each other. Jeff, the charmer, said, "May I call you Grandmother too. I don't have any living grandparents and Angel and I are going to be married in a few years, as soon as the angels let us."

"Oh you poor man, you've been caught up in this family's odyssey too. Yes, I'm grandmother to several people now, blood relationship or no. I guess that is my contribution. Come on inside and I'll make us something to drink."

Once inside and fresh made lemonade in our glasses, Grandmother asked, "I assume you met each other at that medical school back east?"

Jeff held my hand and nodded. "Yes, we met in the dorm soon after we arrived. We both believe we're meant to be together. But our angels want us to wait until the second year of our residency at Johns Hopkins Hospital. That's about four years from now."

"Angel, you've already spent most of your life in school, is it finally coming to a end?"

"Formal school is ending, but on-the-job training hasn't started yet. I'm going to have a year of internship leading to residency training in my specialty. Once my training is completed, the angels say I will eventually return to Kansas City and my sister will be a healer when she is ten, much like me."

"Another healer in the family. How do you feel about that?"

"I wondered for years why God took away my healing powers and gave me another gift, now I know why."

Grandmother was eager to see pictures of her new granddaughter, so I used my smart phone to scroll through the dozen or so pictures saved on it. I said, "It's strange, but she has a birthmark on her back shaped like a small cross. It's just like my birthmark and in the same place. Do you think it means anything?"

"It must mean something. It happening once is one thing, but twice, that must have some meaning. Angel, do you have a picture of you and Jeff I can have. It would be nice to look at it when I think about you."

I pulled one out of my purse and gave it to her, which she gazed at for a few moments before putting it away.

"I'll have Dad send you one of your namesake too. I believe she will resemble me when she is older. All the women in our family resemble each other."

"I know. When Barbara died, I thought Jack would die too. I was in bad shape as well. Olivia appeared several days after the funeral and told us that she intervened in our mourning by blunting our emotions so we could function again. Years later, when Jack brought your mother here I thought she was Barbara at first. But then, I realized who she was."

Jeff spoke. "I've heard the story, but until now I didn't realize how her death caused the upheaval in so many people's lives."

Angel took Jeff into her arms. "Honey, you now stand in the same position as Barbara did when she died. Please stay close to me as much as you can, so that Olivia can protect you too."

"Do you think Olivia will take me under her wing someday?"

"Probably. Mother and I were. Olivia, if you're listening, see if you can get this done sooner rather than later."

We stayed the night. At bedtime Grandmother didn't say anything, she simply pointed at Dad's room for me and fixed the couch for Jeff. She made us a big country breakfast before we left the next morning for Coffeyville to visit mother's family.

I was the navigator as I guided Jeff to my other Grandmother's house. Jeff honked the horn as he parked in front of the garage. Alice came outside, closely followed by Jamison. Seeing me get out of the car, they rushed over to give me a happy welcome. After many hugs and kisses and a little tears, they realized I'd brought someone with me.

I introduced them to Jeff and my grandparents gave him a long measuring look. Alice said, "Elizabeth called me and told me about Jeff. He's your future husband and I don't see a ring on your finger."

I looked at Jeff. "Yeah, what about that."

Jeff looked at us in a panic. "Honey, you should have said something. We've known for years that we were going to be married, I guess I was waiting for the angels' go ahead before getting the ring."

I pointed at a ring on his pinky. "Give me that until I get a real one."

He smiled as he removed the gold ring and placed it on my

finger. It was a little loose, so Alice used tape to make it fit. She pointed at Jeff. "Don't you think you should give him a kiss to go with the ring?"

I winked and turned to Jeff, and placed my arms around his neck before kissing him passionately. He was a little slow at the start, but soon had my passion for him accelerating to a point he broke us apart before I lost control. Jamison placed his arm around Jeff's shoulder and steered him to a chair, sitting down next to him.

"Jeff, I understand you're from Kansas City too. What does your family do?"

While Grandfather kept Jeff busy, Grandmother was grilling me about our relationship. I was still touching my burning lips when I told her about my problem. She frowned, then muttered. "That's just not right. But I guess it's a good reminder when you get passionate with each other."

"He is a good man and we're very much in love with each other. I just wish this waiting period was over."

I then shared pictures of their new granddaughter and my parents' reasoning for her long name. Grandmother laughed, "So the women of the family each have a claim on her with our names. April was Jack's mother?"

I nodded. "We need to tell my sister who each of these women were, so that she can honor them."

Grandmother said, "I wonder which name or names she will claim as hers."

Before we left that afternoon, Uncle Ben and Aunt Judy arrived with two children in tow. Our family keeps getting bigger. Chuck and Gloria were three and two respectively, but Gloria was the stinker as far as misbehaving. Judy finally picked her up and took her outside for a few minutes. When they returned, Gloria was rubbing her butt. I looked at Grandmother and smiled, who after looking at Gloria, smiled back at me in satisfaction.

Jeff dropped me off at my parents apartment building before heading home. He took my hand and kissed the ring he gave me, saying, "I'm getting you a real one. I'll pick you up tomorrow and we'll go shopping."

I was carrying my bag into the apartment, when Dad came from his bedroom. He said softly, "I brought Jenn and the baby home this afternoon and they're both asleep."

I smiled. "What's the matter Dad, was it easier with me?"

"I was younger then, that's the difference."

"Well, let's take turns on the feedings. Go ahead and try to get some sleep. Where's the baby?"

"Come with me and I'll show you where everything is. Be sure the formula isn't too hot when you give it to her."

Elizabeth started crying then and Dad got to supervise me in the proper way to feed and change a baby. When Elizabeth was asleep in her crib, Dad went to bed. I took a shower and got an hour's sleep before Elizabeth woke me for another tour of duty. Later, after returning to bed I vaguely recall crying, which quickly ended. When I heard her crying again, I knew it was my turn. Checking the time I figured I had gotten a little over four hours sleep this time.

It was almost six a.m., so I decided to stay up after I had Elizabeth changed and fed. I took another shower and got dressed. I was reading the newspaper and drinking coffee when Dad came into the kitchen.

"You want anything to eat?"

"No. I ate cereal and toast earlier. Can I fix you something?"

He looked at me with a raised eyebrow. "You've learned to cook?"

"Simple stuff I can do. I've got to learn how to cook some things for when I'm married. By the way, look." I said as I wiggled the finger with the ring on it.

"How did you get that?"

"Grandmother Powers and I guilted Jeff into giving me this until he gets me a proper ring. He said we'd go ring shopping today. By the way you need to send Grandmothers Pearson and Powers a picture of Elizabeth. I showed them the ones on my cell."

"Angel, would you check on your mother and see if she's ready for a shower. Let me know and we'll take one together."

I checked on Elizabeth on the way and she was still asleep. Mother had her head up and looking around when I walked into the bedroom. "Hey sleepyhead, Dad wants to know if you're ready for a shower."

Mother rubbed her face and smiled at me. "I slept good and didn't hear the baby once."

"That's because Dad and me took care of her. You want

something to eat after your shower? Don't give me that look, Dad did the same thing. I know how to prepare some things, mainly things Jeff likes. I'll never be as good as his mother and he knows it, so he doesn't expect much from me."

"Okay, tell Jack I'm ready for a shower, but to keep his hands to himself."

"Mom! You play shower games. Is that how I was conceived?"

"Move… Go get your father."

I passed the word to Dad, "She's ready for the shower, but you're to keep your hands to yourself."

He gave me a slight smile as he said, "I wonder what she meant by that?"

"Dad, dad, dad. That's so lame."

Dad muttered as he left, "Kids grow up too fast."

Jeff arrived and after checking if my parents needed anything, we went ring shopping. Three hours later I was wearing an engagement ring and showing it off to Mom and Dad. Mother took my hand and brought it closer so she could see the ring. "Honey, it's small and pretty, but I'm surprised Jeff could afford this. Expenses at that school are terrible, over $60,000 a year."

"I know. I just wanted the ring to show our commitment to each other. Don't tell anyone, but I paid for it over Jeff's objections. I told him he could pay me back later when he starts making the big bucks."

"Angel, where did you get the money? You haven't asked us for any in over a year."

"The university pays for my tuition and housing, and a nice consulting fee whenever they need my help. I've got over $50,000 saved up for trips home, food, and whatever else I need."

"Well, if you or Jeff need money let us know. We consider you an investment in the future. Where is Jeff and what are your plans before going back to school?"

"Jeff and I want to host an engagement/Christmas party here before Christmas, and your parents are coming here soon to see Elizabeth. I think they plan on bringing Grandmother Elizabeth too. They will probably stay in an hotel, since you're getting crowded with me home. Don't worry about planning anything, Jeff and I and his mother will take care of that. Sandra can hardly wait to see Elizabeth. By the way, what are you going to call Elizabeth?"

"You mean besides Elizabeth? None of the others names seem to sound good together. I have a feeling that she will make that decision when she gets older."

I laughed. "I bet it gets shortened to Liz or Lizzie."

Mother looked at me and shook her finger. "Don't you start saying it. If it happens, let someone else do it. Angel come over here and feel my stomach. Does it feel right to you?"

"Nothing feels wrong. What's your concern?"

"When I had you, it felt different somehow. Now, I feel stronger and my fat is leaving faster than before."

"I wouldn't complain about that. Let me use my gift in a different way."

I probed with my mind, slowly feeling my way around the abdominal cavity and her uterus. Withdrawing, I placed my hand on her cool forehead, then checked her lymph glands before moving down to her breasts.

"Mother, your breasts are full of milk, why not try and breast feed Elizabeth. I didn't find anything wrong elsewhere."

"Well, she's due for a feeding. Would you get her while I get ready."

Dad followed me back into the bedroom, where I helped Mother position Elizabeth for her first breast feeding. We watched for awhile and everything seemed to be working.

Mother said, "She seems to like it better than the bottle. How do you tell if she's had enough?"

Dad said, "The book says if you have a good supply, about fifteen or twenty minutes. Really, it's just trial and error. She'll finish when she's ready."

Twenty minutes later Mother pulled Elizabeth away from her breast and tried to get her to burp. She performed as expected with a little leakage and I took her to check on her diaper. Fed and changed I placed her in her crib and watched for a reaction. She appeared to be happy and went to sleep.

I told my parents that Elizabeth was asleep and I was going to take a nap.

*   *   *

After Angel left the room Jenn said, "I think Angel will make a good mother when it's her time. She already has the confidence of a doctor, and she tried something different with me in addition to checking my health status. You remember what Barbara said about the depth of her gift. I wonder just what she can do now."

CHAPTER TWENTY-THREE

Our engagement/Christmas party was in full swing. It was mostly a family affair and included my grandparents, Lilly and Bob Cox, and Jeff's and my parents. Elizabeth, my baby sister was cared for by all. Sandra brought food, and Dad furnished the alcohol and other drinks. When the guests first arrived many immediately went to view the Plaza Christmas lights in full view from our penthouse windows.

I approached Grandmother Pearson and put my arm around her shoulder, giving her a hug. "This sight never gets old no matter how often I see it. Grandmother, what do you think of my sister and your namesake?"

"She's a beautiful baby, just like you were. This family is going to be even more famous when she gains her power and you join her. I hope I'm still here when that happens."

"You're not that old. I'm sure another ten years is not impossible, you'd be less than ninety. I'll ask Barbara to put in a word for you."

Grandmother looked at me tearfully. "Barbara was taken from us so early. I still get sad when I think about it."

Mom joined us as we both turned and gazed at Barbara's picture over the mantel. Mom said, "She's a constant reminder of her love for our family. Her love flows to us as we open our hearts to her. I bring Elizabeth in here when she gets upset and she immediately calms down."

I asked, "Have you made any plans for a nanny yet?"

"I've made inquiries, but haven't decided on one yet. I'm not as eager to go back to work as I was with you. I'm getting older and I'm breast feeding this time. I'm thinking of taking six months off."

Lilly and Bob joined us in front of Barbara's painting. Lilly said, "I've told Bob of my experience with Barbara, which I admit sounded a little farfetched."

I said, "Bob, look into her eyes and mentally ask her a question. Don't be surprised if you get an answer."

Bob's eyes seemed to glaze over for a few minutes. Lilly touched his arm and got a zap of power, causing Bob to become aware of us again. "Wow! That was awesome. I asked her what plans she had for us, and she answered. She said we were to train ourselves to be outstanding ER nurses because Angel and Elizabeth would need us in eight to ten years."

"Lilly, I'm sorry I ever doubted you. This is awesome. It looks like we're going to be part of something big in the future."

Jeff and I were at the end of our mid-senior year. We both had entered the College Olympics on competing colleges, me on Vivien Thomas and he on Daniel Nathans. We made our teams after taking the qualifying tests and were now in a friendly competition with the five colleges facing each other.

My college won last year's Olympics, due in part to the strategy I recommended. The others were sure to try to beat us by using it too. The student body's interest in the competition revived after our college moved from last place to first last year.

The Captains of each team called their members together for a strategy session. Our five member team consisted of two juniors and three seniors based upon the top scores of the qualifying test. The top score of the team was the Captain, in this case me. Our strategy was to buzz first without worrying about whether we knew the answer or not. Each right answer received twenty points and each wrong answer got a minus ten points. If a wrong answer was given, then it was open to the others. If no college team buzzed, then a new question was put forth. First college to reach 100 points would win.

When the contest started our team quickly got three questions correct. Jeff shook his finger at me and I responded with both hands raised in a victory sign. His team got the buzzer and answered the question correctly. Three more questions and we were ahead, eighty for Thomas, forty for Nathans, and twenty for Taussig. We needed one more right answer.

We buzzed in first, and then pooled the team for the answer. Two of us thought we knew the answer, which we recited to the other team members, who then decided which answer we would offer. Luckily, they picked my answer and we won the Olympics twice in a row.

President Smithson gave each of our team a small trophy, while a larger one would be placed on display with other past winners. Our pictures were taken with him, which would appear in *The Johns Hopkins News-Letter.* Later that evening we had a small party at my apartment, with my team and members from several others, including Jeff. During the party, both President Smithson and Dr. Ellsworth arrived.

The President held up his arms for quiet. "Students, I want to congratulate those of you who participated in the Olympics. This year it was a fight just to be able to get a question, and there were no wrong answers. That's a first. Either you're getting smarter or we gave you easy questions."

A few laughs and half hearted booing ensued before he continued. "Next year will be the last Olympics for you juniors, so put some effort into the next one. Before Dr. Ellsworth and I leave, I'd like to see Ms. Pearson and Mr. Blake."

I motioned them to follow me into my room and then shut the door. "What's up?"

President Smithson said, "I want to congratulate you both on your engagement. Have you set a tentative date for your wedding?"

I looked at Jeff and smiled. "Right now it's the second year of our residency, but that's subject to change. Jeff's surgery residency is going to take longer, which may affect our plans. I should tell you that I recently learned that my gift has a greater effect on my abilities. I seem to be able to manipulate body tissue, at least in a small way. I'm still learning what my limits are. I would like a patient to be attached to a 4D Ultrasound Machine so that I can visually observe what I am doing. Of course, it would have to be a patient already scheduled for surgery."

Dr. Ellsworth said, "You think you can perform an operation without surgery."

"In some cases I think I can. This is still early for me in my research of my abilities. I would like to start small, like a appendectomy. If I can't do it, the surgery staff can perform it the normal way. I would like to view such an operation first, to make sure I know what I have to remove and then cauterize bleeders."

President Smithson said, "Just to make it clear to me, you want a patient hooked to a 4D Ultrasound Machine so that you can visually see the organ you want to remove in real time. What are you going to do with the organ after it's detached?"

"May I demonstrate."

At their nod, I went into the kitchen and returned with a raw hot dog, which I cut a small piece off and placed on a Kleenex. Using my mind I caused it to quickly disappear into dust.

President Smithson said, "That's why you need to see what you're doing. Dr. Ellsworth, this needs to be looked into further. It's nothing we can train others to do, but as long as she is here we might as well use her the best way we can. Now, the reason we asked about your marriage plans. We hoped you would put it off until residency, which you already have done. Internship is a poor time to get married with all the pressures associated with it. Dr. Ellsworth will get back to you on this other matter."

After they left, Jeff picked up the hot dog and took a bite from it. "They didn't seem too surprised by your performance. It was like, oh, that's nice. What else can you do?"

I laughed at his humor. "I only told them a fraction of what I think I can do now. I'm still learning what I'm capable of."

I wasn't planning on taking summer courses this year because Jeff and I were now at the same grade level and would graduate together. Besides, I needed to bond with Elizabeth this summer. This break will also give me time to consider what my eventual move to Kansas City will mean if I can't get Johns Hopkins to back me.

I got an e-mail from Dr. Ellsworth to meet her at Dr. Jacobson's office in the hospital. I knocked on his door at the appointed time and was asked to enter. Dr. Jacobson stood and shook my hand and introduced me to Dr. Jacob Holmes, one of the hospital's top surgeons. Also present was Dr. Ellsworth.

Dr. Jacobson said, "Please tell Dr. Holmes what you would like to try."

"I think I can remove an appendix without surgery. Since I've never done it before it would be prudent to schedule a surgery in case I fail in my attempt."

Dr. Holmes said, "You have the power to diagnose illness or injury by touch. Now you believe you have more to offer us. How confident are you that you can do this?"

"Almost 100 percent. But, I've never done it before, so there is some uncertainty."

"You want to observe an actual surgery to see the appendix and how it is attached. I saw you in action, so you're not afraid of a little blood. Do you intend to be a surgeon?"

I smiled at him. "I'm not trying to put you out of business. I couldn't if I wanted to, no I'm just testing my abilities. My fiancé, Jeff Blake, is going to be a surgeon and I would really appreciate any help you give him. I've been assured that he has a natural talent for it."

"He's in your class?"

At my nod, he said, "Dr. Ellsworth please note that for when his residency comes up. I can use a great surgeon. Okay, are you free tomorrow at 3 p.m.?"

I said yes and he responded, "Great. Dr. Paul Givens has one scheduled for that time. Be there at 2:30 and scrubbed in. Dr. Givens will be expecting you."

When I entered the ER everyone was ready. Dr. Givens asked, "You Pearson?"

"Yes, Dr. Givens. May I stand at your elbow so that I can better observe?"

"Not so close that you touch me. I'll kick you out if you nudge my elbow."

"Yes doctor, I understand."

Dr. Givens quickly made his incision and used his fingers to open the cut wide enough for me to see the appendix. He then explained how he was going to cut it from the body and seal the incision. I watched as he completed the surgery, then I carefully backed away and left the OR. I was joined by Dr. Givens as I was scrubbing my hands.

"Ms. Pearson did you get the information you needed?"

"Yes doctor, I have an eidetic memory and I'm grateful that you allowed me to observe. Did Dr. Holmes tell you what my purpose was?"

"No. He was really closed mouthed about it. Will you tell me, I've heard rumors about what you do, but this procedure doesn't fit that."

"I'm sorry, if he didn't tell you he must have a good reason. Maybe later, it will all come out."

After returning to my apartment I e-mailed Dr. Ellsworth, telling her I finished my observation of the operation and thanked her for her help and I wished to wait until this fall to do the second part of my test.

My mid-senior term came to a close and Jeff and I returned to Kansas City for the summer break. We walked into my apartment to find Elizabeth crawling on the floor. I yelled that I was home, while Elizabeth looked up at me in surprise and delight, holding her hands up to me. I stooped and picked her up, her hands immediately reaching for my white hair.

Mom hurried into the room and stopped, smiling as she watched me with Elizabeth. Jeff moved my luggage out of the way and hugged Mom. Holding Elizabeth in front of Barbara's painting, I smiled. "Barbara, how do we look. Both of your nieces standing before you with so much talent waiting to be unleashed on the world."

Suddenly Barbara stood in front of us and held her hands out for Elizabeth, who willingly climbed into Barbara's arms. Barbara gazed serenely at Elizabeth and then turned to me. "Angel, you have done well and Elizabeth is now under Olivia's protection. When you and Jeff marry, he will receive her protection as well. Elizabeth will be a healer as you were, but her power will be limited to her touch only. Your power is expanding in ways you have not even considered. Eventually, when Elizabeth receives her power, the pictures of you will no longer work as a healing source."

Barbara kissed Elizabeth on the forehead and handed her back to me, before vanishing into the painting. Mom took Elizabeth into her arms, who was chortling happily from all the attention she was getting.

I said, "Well, we got a little more information. But why so

much in riddles. Was Barbara that way when she was alive?"

Mom said, "You mean her saying your powers expanding in ways you have not considered? Yes, that's pure Barbara. She used to drive me crazy when she did that. Well, it did make me think about what she might mean. If she had said you could read other people's minds, you might stop at considering other things you could do."

"Well, I can't read your thoughts, so put that out of your mind."

I looked at Jeff and smiled. "I can read yours though, it's down the hall."

Mom interrupted. "I can read body language too and Elizabeth needs changing."

"Yes, I can smell her too."

We were in the nursery changing Elizabeth when Jeff joined us. "You didn't really read my mind did you?"

I winked at mom. "You better operate as if I did and you'll never get into trouble."

"That's what I thought. It was body language wasn't it?"

CHAPTER TWENTY-FOUR

The summer break was over and Jeff and I were back in school. We only had one semester to complete before graduation and the beginning of our internships at Johns Hopkins Hospital.

Dr. Ellsworth was making sure my scheduled courses for the coming semester would result in sufficient credits to graduate. "Ms. Pearson you appear to be set with these courses. Do you still intend to do the appendectomy we discussed previously?"

"Yes. Can we have another meeting with Dr. Holmes so that we can make arrangements?"

"I'll e-mail you a time and place that won't conflict with your class schedule. Anything else?"

"Yes, I won't be able to continue my Judo class due to my other interests. Please tell Dr. Kilpatrick that I'm sorry I didn't give her more warning. Ask her to try Jamie Grant and/or Mark Andrews. They are my most experienced brown belts and should be able to teach a beginning class."

A week later I was scrubbing in with Dr. Holmes for the scheduled appendectomy. I was going to do my thing and then Dr. Holmes would do a regular operation to see how well I had done. A technician used the 4D Ultrasound to give me a real time view of the appendix. I placed my hand on the patients abdominal region above his appendix and mentally felt my way to the target, a swollen appendix. I mentally moved the organ and watched the screen of the machine as the appendix moved.

Now feeling sure of my myself, I mentally felt the appendix, as if I was using my fingers, until I was at the connection to the body. I cut the connection, sealed the cut, and then started the destruction of the disconnected appendix. I watched the Ultrasound screen until nothing was left.

I turned to Dr. Holmes and said, "I've finished and I believe I was successful. Now it's your turn to verify."

Dr. Holmes had the technician remove the machine, then proceeded with the surgery. After the cut was made he opened it sufficiently so that I could see that the appendix was no longer there. Dr. Holmes checked the surrounding tissue for additional damage before looking at me.

"You did it and the cut is properly sealed. I'd say it was a first class surgery. All I have to do is sew him up."

"Dr. Holmes may I attempt a seamless repair of the incision?"

Without comment, he moved out of way and I placed my hands on the incision and slowly closed the cut until it was sealed. Using a wipe I removed the blood from the area and revealed a pink line where the incision had been.

Dr. Holmes looked at it and then me, eyes wide, in surprise. He then instructed his team to move the patient to the recovery area and motioned me to follow him to the scrub room. We removed our masks and gloves and started our cleanup.

Dr. Holmes asked, "Was that seal up something new as well?"

"Yes, after completing the surgery I thought it would be the next logical step. There was no risk to the patient and why leave a scar if I could fix that too."

"Damn it! Why don't you want to be a surgeon. You could be the greatest one in history with your talent."

"I may be one on a part time basis, but I have other talents that I'm just now learning about. Besides, I've been told to concentrate on being a GP, while Jeff should be the surgeon."

"Who told you this?"

"An angel, who's also my aunt."

"Well, I can't argue with that. This Jeff, he's your fiancé, the one you told me about before."

At my nod, he said, "I'm going to pull him in to watch me

operate. Maybe I can fast track him when he starts his residency."

The following day I got an e-mail from Dr. Ellsworth asking for a meeting to discuss my future with Johns Hopkins. I called Jeff and told him of the e-mail. "Jeff, since we are joined at the hip, I think you should attend this meeting with me."

"How much are you going to tell them about your plans?"

"Well, since my future is somewhat dependent upon what they are willing to do, I better give them enough to want to back me."

"Have them schedule the meeting around both our schedules. Also, President Smithson should be present."

Six days later I got an e-mail that scheduled the meeting to be held in President Smithson's office that evening at six. I called Jeff and asked, "Where should we meet so we can arrive together."

"Let's meet at Nolan's at four-thirty, eat light and plan on what we want to say."

This was our first time to meet President Smithson in his office. I thought, *he must want to put this on an official level.*

President Smithson secretary announced us and we took a seat together on a comfortable couch, while the others present all sat in chairs facing us. President Smithson, introduced Dr. Ellsworth, Dr. Jacobson, and Dr. Holmes to Jeff.

President Smithson said, "Ms. Pearson it seems likely from your recent activities that you have an agenda planned that probably involves Johns Hopkins. Would you care to enlighten us?"

I looked at Jeff and squeezed his hand. "Yes, you are right. I have a tentative plan that won't bear fruit for about ten years. My sister, who is now five months old, will become a healer when she reaches her tenth birthday. I'm not sure what powers I will have by then, but I'm trying to be prepared, hence the test last week. I was told by an angel that Jeff has a natural talent as a surgeon, and he was to help me in that capacity when I needed him. For this plan to work I need the backing of a well known, respected medical facility. I was hoping that Johns Hopkins would open a satellite facility in Kansas City."

President Smithson looked at me unblinking for several minutes as he thought. Finally, he seemed to shake himself and said, "My, you don't dream small. I assume you need a operating hospital. With a healer on staff, that's going to be quite a draw.

That's not even considering what kind of a draw you and Jeff will have."

"Dr. Holmes, what kind of draw do you think Ms. Pearson will have?"

"Surgery without cutting people open, that's unheard of. But, her other talents may be even greater. If Mr. Blake is even half as good a surgeon as Ms. Pearson claims, he'll be another big draw."

Dr. Jacobson said, "Research will need to be done to estimate the size of the facility needed. We might be able to purchase an existing facility and rehab it, and forgo a needs investigation. I recommend we do what we can to get this done. We have a little less than ten years, let's not sit on our hands."

President Smithson polled the others in the room and they all agreed to proceed. He then looked at me and shook his head. "I never dreamed that this was what you were considering. Okay, I'll get the ball rolling for Board Approval for this project and we'll see what happens. Ms. Pearson what do you envision this hospital being after it's open to the public?"

"The healing portion would have to be restricted to terminal or otherwise patients who couldn't be helped by conventional medicine. I believe my talent will be between conventional medicine and my sisters healing powers. The reason for the restricted use of my sister's powers is that she'll be young and the sheer numbers of ill patients. I think I was given these extra powers to fill the void between conventional medicine and her healing powers."

Dr. Holmes said, "That means a triage protocol would have to be established that separates the patients into three groups. Those for conventional treatment, those that Ms. Pearson can treat, and the hopeless. Depending upon the draw I would expect an eventual need for at least a 1,000 bed facility. There would be a large transient population, especially for those patients healed. I anticipate longer stays for Angel Pearson's patients, but shorter than the conventional patients."

President Smithson asked, "Anything else?"

I said, "Forgive me if I appear to be self serving, but my parents are partners in one of the largest legal firms in Kansas City, Phelps, Phelps & Woodruff, LLC, and they have experience with legal matters relating to the period when I was a healer. I'm sure they could help you find an existing facility or a location for a new hospital without it making the news."

President Smithson shook his head and smiled. "No, not self serving, but well prepared. Dr. Ellsworth get that information from Ms. Pearson and we'll include it in our presentation to the Board."

After we left President's Smithson office, we went to the Rec Room to discuss what just happened. We got coffee and found a table far enough away from other people to avoid anyone hearing what we were saying.

I took a sip of my coffee and sighed. "Ahh. That went well. I've been dreading that conversation for awhile and then they initiated it. How fortuitous can it get."

"Angel, remember who is pushing this. It's starting to come together and we needed the lead time to get the hospital in Kansas City."

I placed my hand over his. "Jeff, it won't be long before we graduate and start our internships. Dr. Holmes is going to fast track you through surgery, and I'll bet he'll shave years off your residency."

"I think that's wishful thinking, but next year you can start looking for a wedding dress."

"I want to be married in Kansas City, near our families. My roomies can come there as my bridesmaids. Have you someone in mind for best man?"

"I'm in the same spot as you for your maid of honor. Who should it be?"

CHAPTER TWENTY-FIVE

Jeff and I finished medical school and it was graduation time. Grandmother Powers was babysitting Elizabeth, now nine months old and trying to walk. The apartment was now child-proofed to keep everything out of her busy hands.

The winter graduation class held 546 students. My roomies wouldn't graduate until next summer. I showed my parents the fancy dorm where I spent the last two years, while Jeff showed his parents around campus. We met in the Rec Room and explained how the ceremony was supposed to happen tonight. My roomies had already departed for the Christmas break, so my parents were staying with me tonight. Jeff's parents were going to stay in his dorm room too. We would all depart tomorrow for Kansas City, and Jeff and I would return to the hospital after the first of the year to start our internship.

Jeff and I watched our parents gush over the campus while we sat back and basked in completing the first hurdle in getting our doctorate. Neither of us was dreading the hard work of the internship. It would be another hurdle before becoming a medical doctor.

Mom asked, "Are you staying in the same dorms when you return next year?"

"No, interns can't stay here. These units are for students. We'll have to find something nearby that will not be too expensive. I'm not sure yet if that's going to be free for me, but I have enough saved for at least a year and I'm still paid a consulting fee."

Sandra said, "Jeff, it sounds to me like you and Angel will be in good shape as soon as you get married."

"Maybe another year mom. That's what we are planning anyway. I was promised a fast track in my surgery residency, which may not take as long as normal. In the meantime we've got reservations at Nolan's for dinner, then on for our graduation. In the morning we'll meet at the airport for our flight back to Kansas City."

Mom placed her hand on my arm and asked, "Angel, who is the Valedictorian for your class?"

Jeff said, "You don't know? Angel why didn't you tell your parents that you are our Valedictorian. She's been working on her speech for a week now."

"I don't know. I guess I was embarrassed to be singled out as the top of my class. I was going to let it be a surprise when I did my speech."

Dad and Mom hugged me and she said, "This from the one who said she was never shy. Well, we are happy that you are receiving this honor, but would be just as happy if you came in last."

She then laughed. "As if that would have ever happened."

Sandra and George asked, "Jeff, what was your rank?"

"I made the top ten."

I said, "Now who's shy. He came in third and we both made the honors list. Your son is no slouch and I'm counting on him becoming a great surgeon."

Sandra said, "Jeff! You should have told us, we're so proud of you and Angel. Getting such an honor from so prestigious a medical school as Johns Hopkins is really a great accomplishment."

After my speech, President Smithson gave one of his own, praising my contributions to the school while attending classes the past three and half years. "No student before has ever made Valedictorian in less than four years. Another startling thing she brought to the school was her diagnostic ability that the hospital used in over a dozen instances during her studies here. She started self defense Judo classes shortly after beginning school and in one instance she and her more advanced Judo students foiled an attack against them, resulting in injuries only to the attackers. In short, Angel Pearson is more than a top student, she is probably the most outstanding student this University has ever graduated. She is going on to intern here at Johns Hopkins and we expect to hear more of the same from her in the future."

After thunderous applause, the top ten students received their diplomas from President Smithson, me leading the way. Jeff and I sat next to each other until everyone received their diplomas and then pandemonium ensued. We eventually met our parents outside where Jeff talked his parents into coming to my apartment for awhile.

The Blake's marveled at how much nicer my apartment was than Jeff's. Jeff started to say something, but I jabbed him in side with my elbow and when he looked at me I placed a finger over my mouth. There was no need to let them know my room and board was no charge to me.

Mom sidled up to me and softly said, "Sandra knows about your arrangement with the University on free room and board."

"Is she alright with it when they have to pay Jeff's way?"

"She figures you are a special case and doesn't begrudge you for it."

Jeff and I stood in front of the picture of Barbara with his arm around my shoulders. "Angel, when we come back we're really going to be kept busy. We'll have to meet when we can and try to stay in contact by phone. If you have a really lousy day, talk to me and I'll do the same."

He looked at Barbara's picture and said, "Watch out for her and let me know if she needs my help."

Instantly, Barbara stepped out of the picture and smiled at us. "Jeff, you and Angel are both emotionally strong and should have no problems you can't overcome. Angel, watch your temper because you will be tested. Just remember who you are and what is yet to complete."

Barbara disappeared back into the picture and the senior Blake's gasped in surprise. Sandra said, "So that's your Aunt Barbara. Seeing is believing, you have an actual angel in your family."

Sandra asked, "Angel, what did she mean when she said watch your temper?"

I smiled at her and looked innocent. "Me? I don't have a temper."

My parents and Jeff started laughing together. "Well, not much of one anyway." I said as I stuck my tongue out at them.

Mom said, "Angel, take what she said to heart. Don't get mad, get even. You are certainly smart enough to know when this applies."

"Yes Mom."

Sandra said, "I never saw Angel angry, not once. She always acted like - an angel when she was around us."

Jeff said, "When Angel gets angry things start to happen. It causes her to clamp down on her emotions. When she was attacked it wasn't only Judo that saved her. She has powers that are still developing and I think Barbara was warning her to keep a tight rein on her emotions."

Mom said, "Angel, is that true?"

"I've never lost control, not completely anyway. I don't think I'll have any problem."

The next afternoon we were back in Kansas City and I got to see firsthand the changes in my little sister. Grandmother Powers said, "I didn't have much of a problem with Elizabeth. She can't run as fast as I can walk, but the little dickens tries her best. She's so smart I bet you can start her potty training now."

I picked up Elizabeth and said, "Wow, you weigh a ton."

Elizabeth hugged my neck and gave me a wet kiss on the cheek. I asked Dad to toss me the soft toy I had packed inside my luggage. I caught the toy and showed it to my sister, whose eyes widened in surprise and wonder and held out her hands for it. I set her on the floor and watched her play with it, while my parents took their luggage into their bedroom.

I showed Grandmother pictures mother had taken of Jeff and me at the our graduation. I told her how I made Valedictorian, and that Jeff and I both received honor diplomas. "Oh honey, you have done so well and it won't be long before you will be a doctor. I'm so proud of you, and this little tyke is probably going to follow in your footsteps."

While Grandmother stayed with us I slept on the couch. Jeff

and I only had until after the New Year before we had to return to new duties as interns at Johns Hopkins. Before we left we had received notice of which department we were going to begin with. Jeff would be with anesthesia, and me at medicine. The first year we would normally rotate between departments every three months.

As I waited for sleep to overtake me I wondered if I could shortcut this procedure somehow. The next thing I knew Elizabeth was looking at me when I opened my eyes. I said, "Elizabeth, what are you doing up and about?"

She smiled at me and tottered over to Mom, who was sitting nearby. I sat up and asked, "What's up?"

"I thought you might want to eat breakfast with us. Your grandmother is about to start on it. Do you want to help her?"

"Do you think she'll let me?"

"You, she might. Besides you need to get some tips on cooking before you get married. You probably won't have many opportunities to cook for Jeff, but you should know how to fix one or two meals he would like. Ask Sandra what he likes best and concentrate on those."

"Okay, I'm on it." I said as I hurried to the bathroom.

CHAPTER TWENTY-SIX

I had just finished orientation for my second intern assignment with the Anesthesia Department at Johns Hopkins. My first assignment with the Medicine Department was completed and I was ready for something different. Jeff had just left the Anesthesia Department and was now assigned to Emergency Medicine.

Dr. Janice Wiener headed the Anesthesia Department and made sure that any task assigned to an intern was double checked for accuracy. Preparation of dosage and types of anesthesia for surgery was very important and correct labeling was critical. One of my fellow interns seemed distracted as he was preparing an order for a surgery planned for later that day. He was not following protocol which resulted in a mistake in labeling.

Before he continued I said, "Mr. Williams you should stop what you're doing. You've made a mistake in labeling that bag."

He turned to me in surprise, but once he recognized me he asked, "Okay Angel, what did I screw up?"

I retraced his steps for him and showed him what he had done wrong. His face turned white as he realized he could have caused someone's death.

"What should I do?"

"First, set that incorrectly labeled bag aside after marking a red X over the label. Next, start over and do it according to protocol. Last, take the mislabeled bag and explain what happened to the supervisor."

Williams swallowed back a negative response to that last part, but seeing my resolve he agreed. After he had returned to his tasks I felt a presence behind me. Turning I found Dr. Jackson standing there. He crooked his finger at me to follow him and we left the room. I followed him down the hall to his office, where he shut the door.

"Take a seat. Ms. Pearson isn't it?"

"Yes sir. Have I done something wrong?"

"No. In fact you did everything correctly. I watched you and Williams and you seemed to have a gift of getting other people to do what you want. He didn't even complain when you told him to report his mistake to the supervisor. Oh, he didn't want to, but your force of personality convinced him to do it. I think it's called leadership ability."

"He had something personal that was bothering him which caused a lapse in his concentration. I'm sure his attention is on the job at hand now."

"You're wasted here. Which department would you like to go next?"

"Pathology, if that's possible."

"I'll give Dr. Grant a call and see if she will take you. Wait outside until I call you back."

Thirty minutes later I was sitting in her office. Dr. Julia Grant was a small woman, only standing as tall as my shoulder. Her piercing dark eyes missed nothing and I sat quietly waiting on her to speak.

"Ms. Pearson, what interests you in my department?"

"I'm interested in keeping people alive, to cure or repair what's causing them to die. Maybe by learning what the cause of death is I can learn how to beat it."

"My! You're not shy about touting your ability. Do you really think you can do this?"

"Dr. Grant I used to be able to cure anybody of anything simply by touching them. Now I have to use my head to do what my hands used to do. It's taking longer than I like, but I'm making progress."

"So, it's true. You are the same Angel Pearson who was a

healer."

"There's not that many of us. Surely you've heard rumors of what I've done since starting medical school."

"Rumors are not reliable. Seeing is believing, show me what you can do."

I followed her to an autopsy room where a body lay under a white sheet. She turned to me and asked, "What do you intend to do?"

"I've had experience in removing an appendix without surgery. Once I'm finished, you can cut to the location and verify that the appendix is gone."

"This man died of heart failure. Do you think you can repair the damage?"

"I don't know. Do you have scans so that I can view the damage?"

She said, "Follow me and we'll look at them together."

"I see three arteries completely blocked and a tear in the heart wall. Do you agree?"

I said, "No wonder he died. I can clear the blockage, but the tear is uncertain. May I check for other problems?"

Once gowned up, and donning protective gloves I studied the scan for several minutes. "This man had several critical problems, including emphysema, probably caused by long term smoking. Most likely the cause of his heart condition. I also see a blood clout in the right upper leg. I would like to see if I can repair the heart damage for my own edification."

Dr. Grant appraised me with a critical eye. "Good, let's see if you can do it. I'll get scrubbed and gowned to check your repair job. I'll be back shortly."

A Pathologist was called in to stand by with Dr. Grant as I touched the corpse's chest and felt my way to the heart. Quickly clearing the blockages, I felt my way to the tear in the heart muscle. I don't know if I could have done this repair if the heart was pumping, but lying still it turned out to be an easy task.

"I'm finished. How long did it take?"

Dr. Grant looked at the clock on the wall. "Less than five minutes. Dr. Phelps let's see how well she did."

Dr. Phelps did the Y cut and opened the chest cavity, removing the heart and attached arteries. After carefully examining the arteries for blockage, he declared them clear. Checking for a tear in the heart muscle, all he found was a discoloration where there was once a tear.

Dr. Grant looked at me in wonder for a moment, then she told Dr. Phelps to go ahead with the examination and to send a copy to her. "Ms. Pearson we need to talk some more about your stay with us."

Back into her office she leaned back into her chair and stared at me considering her options. "I see what you wanted here. A chance to experiment without risk to a live person. Okay, I'm going to allow it, but I want complete documentation. Like today, show what the scans show for the obvious cause of death. If it's not obvious, you and the pathologist reflect your best guess. You perform a fix on whatever is wrong shown by the scans. Detail what you intend to do and verify the results with the pathologist. Would you agree to a six month stay here, rather than the typical three?"

"Yes, only if this is cleared with your supervisors so that neither one of us gets into trouble."

"Who are you most concerned about?"

"President Smithson and Dr. Jacobson."

"Whoa! You've got big sponsors. No wonder you were concerned. I'll contact Dr. Jacobson and get his approval. President Smithson I'd rather not bother."

I smiled at her. "He's really a nice person to get to know. Of course, we met in unusual circumstances."

Recollection flooded her eyes. "You were the student that one of the staff tried to have killed."

"It didn't work out well for the killers or him. Greed is a false God to worship. Whether you'd rather stay off his radar or not, he keeps a close watch on my activities. Don't be surprised if he calls you in to get your opinion on me."

"Maybe you'll bring me good luck, and a pay raise." She winked.

My last three months was with Emergency Medicine headed by Dr. Julia Song. Dr. Brad Lowry was in charge of the interns. There were six of us lined up before him in alphabetical order, with me fifth in line. Dr. Lowry was connecting faces with names and when he got to me started saying, "Your name is Angel..."

He quickly looked up at me and smiled. "Well, we finally got you back with us. Students, this young lady is Angel Pearson who on her last visit here probably saved the life of one of your classmates. Angel, what should they know before we get started?"

"Don't be here if you faint at the sight of blood!"

Dr. Song appeared at that moment and I blushed thinking she may have overheard my flippant remark.

"Ms. Pearson! It's good to see you again. I hope you pick us when you select your residency department. Students, in case you didn't already know it she has a big advantage over the rest of you. She can touch a patient and immediately know what's wrong with them. At her last visit one of our students fainted at the sight of blood and hit his head on the way to the floor. Ms. Pearson immediately took action and put gauze over the head wound. She also informed Dr. Lowry that the student had a depressed skull fracture, which was not apparent from looking at him. He's fine now, but lost a semester recovering from his injury. However, if we hadn't acted quickly he might have suffered brain trauma or even have died."

Dr. Lowry said, "Show of hands, does anyone faint at the sight of blood."

No one held up their hands. "Alright! Follow me and let's see if I can get someone to throw up."

Interns work twelve hours on, with twelve hours off. Sometime we have to work eighteen hours. If this happens they give us a two or three hour break, and if we're lucky we can get a short nap. I'm one of the lucky few who can fall asleep as soon as my head hits the pillow.

I was awakened by a struggle taking place in a bed a few feet away. A female intern was fighting off a male attacker who was apparently trying to rape her. Grabbing him by the scuff of his neck I threw him across the room where he hit the wall with a loud bang. He swore profanely and started toward me. Since I had no room to properly use my Judo training, I used my new powers to slam him back against the wall. When he started to slide down I grabbed an arm and leg and tossed him against the door, which collapsed off its hinges into the hallway.

The intended victim, Mary O'Dell, and I used a bed sheet to hog tie the intruder. We were the only people in the sleeping room, which must have made a tempting target for the would be rapist. Ignoring our captive I checked Mary for injuries. I found bruises and a few scratches, but otherwise she appeared fine. Apparently someone had heard the noise of our fight, because security soon arrived. Mary and I told our stories while our captive remained unconscious.

The would-be attacker was taken to the emergency room in restraints for treatment. Mary and I still had almost three hours before we were due to return to duty. I put my arm around Mary's shoulders and walked her back into the sleeping room. Sitting on a bed together, she broke down and cried in my arms.

She was cried out and asleep on another bed when Dr. Song entered. I quickly stood and motioned for us to leave the room.

Dr. Song asked, "How is she coping?"

"She talked and cried until she fell asleep. Physically she appears to be fine. I think she needs to see a shrink before coming back to work though."

"What did you do to that guy? He's got a broken shoulder and left arm, three broken ribs, and a concussion."

"He must of gotten all that when I threw him through the door. He seemed okay when I threw him into the wall twice, but he still wanted to play, so he went out the door."

"Angel, that guy weighed almost three hundred pounds and you just tossed him around like he was a beach ball."

"When I was home last, I was warned that I should watch my temper. I guess I now know what they were talking about. I was really angry to wake up and find him trying to rape Mary. However, I know I didn't completely lose it because I debated each move."

"I'll make sure Mary gets psych approval before returning, but you are off for twenty-four hours. Go home, get some sleep, food, and a hug from your boyfriend."

Jeff and I shared a apartment, but we hardly ever were off at the same time. It was almost like living alone. I took a long hot shower and then headed for the bed where I slept without dreams for at least eight hours. I was awakened by the front door closing. Getting out of bed quickly I looked down the hall where I saw Jeff looking though our snail mail.

I said, "Hello stranger."

Jeff dropped the mail and hurried to give me a hug and a kiss on my neck, which got my emotional engine purring, but didn't give either of us a burning sensation. He led me back to the kitchen, where he made coffee for us.

"What happened? You're not due for a break until next week."

"Someone tried to rape Mary O'Dell in the sleeping room right next to me. I bounced him around the room and then through the door. Mary seems fine, but needs to be evaluated before she comes back. Me, they gave twenty-four hours off. Now down to sixteen."

"Well, I'm just starting my twenty-four. I can sleep after we do something together. What would you like to do?"

"I want to cuddle with my fiancé and make passionate love, but I'll settle for holding you in my arms. Let's test the burn before we do anything else."

Jeff took me in his arms and kissed me on the lips softly at first, then more passionately. After we broke apart, I touched my burning lips. "No, it's still not the time. However, I'd like another kiss here." I said as I touched my neck, just below my ear lobe.

CHAPTER TWENTY-SEVEN

The first year of our internship came to a close and it was time for us to select a department for our residency. Jeff picked Surgery and I stayed in Emergency Medicine. Instead of assisting, I was now tasked with performing duties under supervision. Jeff's move was more gradual as he gained experience in surgery.

Mary O'Dell somehow became my shadow. Apparently, she convinced Dr. Song that she and I worked better as a team. Her dependency on me stemmed from the near-attack of her would-be rapist. Mary was good at her job and I went out of my way to compliment her when I could. I considered her to be a good friend.

The other residents seemed in awe of my gift and my ability to defend myself. One afternoon, I had just finished clearing a patient into the hospital for treatment, when a resident called me over for a consult on his patient.

"Angel, this young patient has confusing symptoms, would you touch her and confirm what's wrong?"

"Peter, I could, but you are here to learn. What do you think is wrong from her symptoms?"

"It could be her appendix or she could have gas."

"Peter, think! Check her throat for swelling, check her blood, touch her stomach area for tenderness. Ask her questions; what has she eaten recently. What did her parents say when she was brought in? Go through the list as if I wasn't here at all."

"They said she was crying with a stomach ache. I sent her blood in, but haven't got a reply yet." I leaned over and smelled the three-year olds breath. I asked Peter to move her clothing out of the way so I could view her skin color. "

"God save me! It could be nothing or something serious. I'd better check." I said as I touched her arm.

"She's swallowed something toxic. Pump her stomach and try to find out what it was she took. Ask her parents if there was anything at home she can reach, pills, bleach, anything. We'll go from there."

Peter hurried to comply and I moved to my next patient, an motorcycle rider not using a helmet. I looked at the eighteen year old male who had a compound fracture of the right tibia. The leathers he was wearing were shredded as if he had slid through rocks.

"Was there anyone else with you when this happened?"

"Helen, but she didn't make it. She hit a tree."

"Was she wearing a helmet?"

"No, that's for pussies."

"Maybe, but she might be alive today if she'd been wearing one. That's on you, friend. You were lucky with only the loss of some skin and a broken leg. She's not coming home."

"It wasn't my fault, we got run off the road."

"Who convinced her not to wear a helmet?"

He stared at me in realization. "Helen, Helen, what did I do?"

I checked his body for further injuries, then cleared him for leg surgery after wrapping the leg in gauze and putting an inflatable splint in place.

Later, when we had a break from new patients, I asked Peter about the little girl who swallowed something toxic. "We pumped her stomach and later found out from her parents that she had drank some vinegar. We gave her a counter agent and should be fine."

"Peter I'm sorry I was short with you, but I thought you were using me for a crutch. When I realized you were concerned about the patient because of the delay in getting lab results and what that delay might mean for the patient, I did as you asked. As it turned out the delay in getting lab results would have had no adverse effect on the patient. If this happens again don't hesitate to ask for help. I may give you a hard time, but I'll listen to you."

I took a bathroom break and was washing my hands when Dr. Song entered. She looked under the stalls making sure we were alone, then said, "Angel, I watched you with Peter. I was afraid the other residents would use you for a crutch, but if they had that on their minds, that won't happen now. You're a great teacher and as you gain experience you're going to be a great ER doctor. Keep up the good work."

A year later I was the lead resident of my shift. Dr. Lowry checked on me from time to time and I caught Dr. Song watching from a distance at least once each shift. Mary O'Dell had progressed as well. She was an excellent ER resident, but best of all she no longer needed my presence to feel safe. On our down times I had instructed her in some basic self defense Judo moves.

Mary was treating a male patient arriving with an apparent drug overdose. He was not restrained when he arrived because he was unconscious. When she started to examine him he came awake and grabbed her forearm.

I yelled for security, while she used her other hand to pinch the nerve pressure point on the wrist holding her arm, causing him to release her. She and I each grabbed a flailing arm and secured them to the gurney, while two others secured his legs.

"Mary, are you alright?"

"Sure, piece of cake. Thanks for the assist. I can handle it from here."

I smiled at her and walked over to Dr. Lowry. "Would it be possible to have all unconscious patients secured to the gurney before they arrive here?"

"I know. I saw what happened. I'll check with Dr. Song and see what can be done."

Later during the shift Dr. Song found Mary and me in the break room. She sat down with us and said, "Mary, what happened when that drug overdose came in?"

"He was unconscious and unrestrained. I was just getting ready to check his eyes when he grabbed my arm. See." She said as she showed a purple bruise on her underarm.

"I used my other hand to press on his nerve pressure point until he released me. Then Angel and I secured his arms and a couple of others helped with his legs."

"I bet Angel taught you where that nerve point was."

"Yes, and a few other self defense moves. Did you know she's a black belt in Judo?"

"Yes, Angel is a woman who can take care of herself. Now, it looks like you can too. I want to move you to the other shift as lead resident. Do you think you can handle it?"

Mary looked at me for confirmation. "Angel, what about it. Can you get along without me?"

I grimaced. "Dr. Song, you're taking my best resident."

I stood and pulled Mary into a hug. "I'm going to miss you, you know that don't you?"

Tears ran down Mary's cheeks. "Me too. It's time I leave you before I become too dependent."

Dr. Song said, "On the matter of restraints, until we get approval it will be up to staff to determine if restraints are necessary."

Mary and I were pleased with this. I said, "I think that's clear. May we use security to apply restraints?"

"I'll advise security to follow your instructions. Angel, who are you going to take under your wing once Mary leaves."

"My shift is in good shape. Is there someone on the other shift needing attention?"

"I should send you one from there in any case, the weakest they have. Good luck, both of you."

Another year has passed and Jeff and I are in Kansas City for a long weekend. Dr. Song told me that I'm ready to take my Boards and gave me a week to prepare for the tests. Jeff has at least another year before he will be ready for his Boards with a Surgery Specialty.

Elizabeth was almost three and I decided to have an early birthday party for her because I wasn't going to be home on her birthday. In Elizabeth's mind she was going to have two parties. She was finally starting to look and act like a little adult. Mother showed me a picture of me at the same age and Elizabeth and I could be twins, except Elizabeth's hair was not as white as mine.

Mother hired a nanny for my sister so that she could return to work, and she made sure that the new nanny could teach her as well, similar to what I had when I was little. Mom and Dad wanted

Elizabeth to thrive as I had.

I asked Elizabeth, "Do you know what I am training myself for?"

"Mama says you're going to be a doctor. Barbara tells me I'm going to help you when I get bigger. Am I going to be a doctor too?"

"Do you talk to Barbara often? What do you talk about?"

"Barbara talks to me mostly in my dreams because Mrs. Mulroney is with me during the day. She tells me stories about you growing up here and how much she loves us."

"Barbara is mother's sister, like I'm your sister. Barbara died long before you or I were born, but I think she feels we are her children, by extension if nothing else. She is our angel sent to guide us through life. When I was eight God gave me a great gift, and it's possible that you may receive a similar gift when you are ten. After all, we are sisters and we share many things. I'm going to return to Kansas City in a few years and we are going to be very close like sisters should be. Would you like that?"

"Yes. I've missed you. I wish I could talk to you more often."

"Maybe Barbara can help us to do that in our dreams. Would you like that?"

Elizabeth climbed into my lap and hugged me. "Yeah! Cool!"

I took her back to the dining room where mom and dad had finished decorating for a birthday party. Later, while Elizabeth was playing with her new toys I asked, "Has the firm had any contact from Johns Hopkins?"

They both looked at me in surprise. Mom said, "How would you know that?"

"Because two years ago I talked to senior management where I expressed a desire that Johns Hopkins establish a satellite hospital here in Kansas City. I told them of my plans and that my sister would be a healer when she was ten. They agreed, but needed board approval. If my proposal was approved, then about now they should be looking for a location. I gave your firm as the ideal place to start because of their experience with me."

Dad said, "I'm glad you didn't tell us this might happen. We have had contact and he seemed surprised we didn't already know of their plans, now I know why. Actually, he was very happy we didn't know, since he could now trust our recommendations without reservation."

"Have you found a site yet?"

"It's down to three sites, but I believe they are leaning toward purchasing an existing hospital north of the Missouri River in Gladstone. It's the right size and doesn't require too much to rehabilitate. Best of all, it doesn't require a needs authorization."

"That was one of the options mentioned when we discussed possible sites. How far a drive is it from our apartment?"

"Not far, maybe twenty to thirty minutes depending on the time of day."

"Good. My tentative plan is for Elizabeth to come to the hospital for a hour or two each day she is needed. A limo would pick her and the nanny up and later return her to the apartment."

Mom asked, "So, you don't expect a huge demand on her time?"

I explained my three-tiered approach. "Conventional treatment that would include Jeff's talent, unconventional treatment headed by me, and the hopeless for Elizabeth. The healing picture should continue to work until Elizabeth comes into her own powers."

"What if the demand proves greater than you anticipate?" Mom said.

"God will provide an answer or solution. I'm not going to worry about that until there's an actual problem."

Dad asked, "Who's going to manage the Kansas City hospital?"

"Not me. I expect to have some say in the operation, but management is beyond me. I'm sure they will send people they need from Baltimore."

Mom looked at me and shook her head. "Angel, they wouldn't be here without you. They are going to want substantial input from you, beginning with the hospital layout. So resolve yourself to that fact. You're going to be a doctor, administrator, and educator. Johns Hopkins is going to send doctors here to be trained by you."

This was something I hadn't considered and it made me stop to think, *why did I miss this*?

Jeff and I were sitting together on our flight back to Baltimore. He seemed a little down, so I placed my hand over his and asked, "What's wrong?"

"Surgery is taking so long, and you're already getting ready to take your Boards. I guess I'm jealous you're moving ahead faster than me."

I raised the armrest between us and put my head against his shoulder. "Jeff, it won't be much longer than another year or two. We've almost finished with the hard part. Give me a kiss. He smiled at me and then pulled me over into his lap and kissed me. When he finished he was ready to release me, but I squeezed closer to him and kissed him with so much passion that he gasped for air when I released him.

"I take it that you didn't get a burn that time."

"No Babe. I think it's time we started planning our marriage. Well, just as soon as I pass my Boards."

Two weeks later I finished my Boards and was waiting on the results, which were due out today. I was going to check the results as soon as my shift ended. However, I was somewhat startled when Doctors Song and Lowry arrived together in the ER causing a stir from the residents and interns. I headed toward Dr. Song before she saw me. She clapped her hands together, causing everyone to look her way.

"Attention everyone! Angel passed her Boards and is now on full salary. Stop by the break room and share the cake and ice cream that she paid for."

Dr. Song hugged me and then said, "Dr. Pearson as of now you are on an eight hour shift beginning at one a.m. tomorrow. So eat cake and then get some rest."

CHAPTER TWENTY-EIGHT

Six months later I received a message to report to President Smithson's office at the end of shift. It was a warm spring morning as I walked the campus sidewalk toward my meeting. I stopped and admired the flower gardens with their variety of colors and scents, before continuing on. Later, after arriving at President Smithson's office, I was shown in.

Once inside I found several others present besides President Smithson. I shook hands with Doctors Jacobson, Ellsworth, and Holmes. In addition, I was introduced to Robert Wiley, an architect.

President Smithson pointed to a large conference table, covered with drawings and blueprints. "We want your input before we make any final decisions regarding the design of the Kansas City hospital."

The drawing showed a ten-story glass enclosed building with a large Johns Hopkins logo at its top. I asked, "How many beds?"

Wiley responded, "536 depending on how we decide to allocate the rooms."

I nodded my head looking at the plans. "I think the terminal patients should have private rooms, but they are going to be quick turnovers, so twenty should be enough initially. We can adjust that after we have some history. I think they should be on the first floor if possible, but in any case grouped together no matter where they are placed in the hospital. The long term conventional patients should be placed on the top floors, with my nonconventional patients between. Where were you going to place the surgery suites?"

"Dr. Holmes suggested between the conventional and nonconventional patients. Plans are for six suites."

I asked, "Dr. Holmes, how many patients will those suites serve in a twelve-hour day?"

"Normally, we try for an eight-hour day which would handle up to fifteen patients. Twelve-hour day would be twenty-one, assuming we have the surgeons to handle that work load."

"Mr. Wiley, is there room to expand the surgery suites if needed?"

"Yes, three more can be added. Any more than that would have to be on another floor."

I asked, "If we made all the patient rooms private we would quickly run out of room. Has there been any discussion about building an addition if it becomes necessary?"

Dr. Jacobson said, "A all private room hospital would be a tremendous draw on its own. Other hospitals have tried it to prevent infectious disease from spreading with success. I predict that with two patients per room we will be out of room in six to nine months. I think we need another 600 rooms now."

I said, "I recommend that we add another wing with at least as many rooms as the original building, perhaps the new wing should be private rooms for those patients who need to be isolated from other patients. I assume we have room to add additional wings if the need arises?"

President Smithson asked, "I hope someone is taking notes. Mr. Wiley is there enough land for future expansions?"

"Yes, it won't look pretty, more like a big H. Parking is going to be a problem, so we need to buy adjacent land immediately."

I asked, "I assume the ER is on the ground floor. How big will it be and what will the numbers be?"

Mr. Wiley showed me the past and future plans. It looked like about half the size of where I worked now. "Dr. Jacobson, this may be small for the area the hospital serves. All the other hospitals are south of the Missouri River, which means we will get most of the activity north of the river. I think it should be as big as what we have here."

I considered other things as I viewed the number and placement of elevators, nurse stations, break rooms, and pharmacy. "Dr. Ellsworth, how about staffing. I assume we are closing down the hospital for construction. What is going to happen to them in the meantime?"

"Normally, they are hired by other hospitals or move to other cities for employment."

"Why not check the personnel records and keep those you would like to hire back on three-quarter pay. Work out a deal that you will get that money back over a period of time, or just write it off. You will probably have to offer a bonus when you start hiring people from the other hospitals and it would be helpful to have a core already in place. What's the construction time going to be on the original structure?"

Wiley said, "Six months and another eighteen months on the first wing."

"I would recommend that you keep your supervisors and other key personnel at a minimum. Make a list and add as many more as you can afford."

President Smithson looked at the others and gave them a rueful smile. "I guess that's all we can absorb now. Dr. Pearson thank you for your thoughts and insight. I'm sure we will want to talk to you again once we have reviewed your recommendations."

* * *

After Dr. Pearson left, President Smithson said, "That's why I wanted her insight. All that was just off the top of her head. She hasn't been working three months trying to get this to come together like we have. Did anyone even think about our personnel problem. Let's make these changes and have her back later for some more ideas."

* * *

I headed back to my apartment as I still had to work on my upcoming wedding this weekend. Reverend Jacob Black from our

Kansas City church was going to officiate. When I was ten I healed him from terminal cancer before our church congregation. I still attended church as often as I could, considering my school demands.

Reverend Black told me once that he considered me his direct link to God and would be happy to help me in any capacity. When I asked him to officiate at my wedding, he smiled and kissed me on the forehead, saying, "When do you want to schedule it?"

That was it. I was expecting more before getting married, but upon reflection it makes sense. He's known me since I was a child, and my history with healing him and a visit from an angel he must figure God had already placed his blessing on the marriage. My grandparents and family from Coffeyville and Baxter Springs would be there. Barbara Messing from Coffeyville was going to be one of my brides-maids and promised me another painting. My two roomies from medical school were coming from Atlanta as brides-maids. They said that they were close to taking their Boards. My sister, Elizabeth, was my flower girl. Lilly and Robert Cox, and both my and Jeff's parents, and his siblings rounded out the guest list.

I finally made a decision regarding my Maid of Honor and called Barbara Messing. "Barbara, I know I'm late calling you, but would you do me the honor of being my Maid of Honor?"

I heard a gasp and a sob. "Barbara, you are as close to being family as you can get without a blood tie. Besides, my parents and I feel you have a spiritual relationship with us. The title means you get the other girls together and throw me a tame party. What do you say?"

I could hear Barbara blow her nose in the background. "I don't know what came over me. I didn't realize that you thought of me like that. Of course I'll be your Maid of Honor. When do the other girls arrive?"

"Friday evening at six and there are only two, my old roommates from medical school. They know about the other Barbara and have spoken to her."

"Well, this should be interesting. Do they know my history with the family?"

"I'm not sure, Barbara may have told them something, but I don't think so."

"What about this guy you're marrying, I assume he knows your history."

"Yes, poor Jeff. We've been together for about seven years and the most we've done is kiss because we were told to wait until near the end of our residency. They enforced that ban by making his kisses burn me."

"Wow! What about my history. How much does he know?"

"Pretty much all of it, including that you're a famous painter now. You're not married are you?"

"Me? As soon as a man gets too close to me they get scared and run off. What's up with that?"

"Barbara, you haven't met the right one yet. I sense God's hand in this, so don't give up."

"Okay, but I'm beginning to think it's not going to happen. What time are you going to arrive?"

"About noon on Friday. I'm wearing mom's wedding dress and I need to make sure it will fit. She says it will fit like a glove or she's going to have a word with her sister."

"I wish I had a sister, even a dead angel sister like Barbara."

"I didn't have one until Elizabeth showed up. I know what you mean. I think you'll like Elizabeth, even now she looks like me."

"Like you? I bet she's going to be another you when she grows up."

"You're right. When she turns ten she will have healing powers."

"Angel, what does God have in store for your family?"

"I have an inkling, but it all depends on what happens in the next ten to twenty years. Random acts disturb what God has planned for us. Case in point, Barbara died before her time and her sister took her place as my mother."

"Okay. I get your point. I'll keep looking for my mate. See you Friday."

On our flight to Kansas City, Jeff told me he had gotten Bob Peterson to be his best man and Bob would arrive this afternoon. Jeff would pick him up and take him home with him where he would stay until he left Sunday. Bob had taken his Boards and was working in Dallas. I told him about Barbara Messing as my maid of honor, and that she was depressed because she hasn't found a man.

"Hey, maybe your guy and my girl will hit it off."

"She's a little older than Bob isn't she."

"Yes, but she's exotic, you know like me."

"Yeah, you're definitely that." He said, then laughed.

"You know, it just might work. When we first met you he said you were weird, but a good weird. We'll see if it works out."

We shared a cab to my parents apartment where we split up and he continued on to his house. When I entered the apartment I yelled, "I'm home," whereupon Elizabeth ran to meet me, yelling "Angel's here," several times before I picked her up and hugged her.

Mother came into the room looking harried and said, "Come back here and try on this dress before I have a nervous breakdown."

I looked at Elizabeth and she shrugged her shoulders. "I think mommy's stressed."

I smiled at her and asked, "What's stressed mean?"

"Look at her, that's stressed. You better get in there before she gets mad."

I set her down and said, "Alright, but you better stay out of the way."

I quickly undressed and mother helped me into the dress. She zipped me up and turned me toward a mirror. I adjusted the bodice shifting my boobs in the built in bra until it felt right. "Mother, this dress is beautiful and it fits me perfectly."

"I'm pissed! You look better in it than I did, but I did get to wear it twice. Turn around, I want to see it from all angles."

Mom went to her jewelry box and brought back a diamond necklace and hung it around my neck. "How does this look?"

"Mom it looked great on you, but it's not me. Besides, I want my husband to dangle something like that around my neck."

"Oh dear. You're right of course. How did he afford your wedding ring."

"I think he borrowed money from his father. Once we're both working we'll be fine, but right now I'm the sole provider. By the way, you were right about management wanting my input on the Kansas City hospital. I can't believe the things they overlooked and they've been at it for several months."

"How did they take it?"

"I'm not sure. Most of them had their mouths open when I left, but President Smithson said he wanted to see me again after they worked on the things I mentioned."

Elizabeth said, "Angel, you look like a real angel in that dress."

Mom took Elizabeth and they sat on the bed looking at me. "Elizabeth, I think you're right. She does look like a angel."

"Mother, will I ever look as pretty as you and Angel?"

"Honey, you already do. Besides, you look just like Angel did when she was your age."

CHAPTER TWENTY-NINE

Barbara Messing arrived to pick me up at the apartment and then drove us to the airport to pick-up the other brides maids. They were waiting at the curb when we pulled up to the loading zone. I quickly made introductions and we were on our way to the hotel where Barbara made reservations for them.

After everyone was checked in we went downstairs to the bar where Lillie Cox was waiting for us. I explained that Lillie was going to be an honorary brides maid, because she was married, and then told Barbara and the others of Lillie's and my past history together as roommates when we attended MU together. Julie and Robin told Barbara stories of all the excitement they had while rooming with me.

Barbara looked over at me as the stories kept getting more outrageous. "Angel, did your parents ever tell you about the number of times Olivia got them out of hot water? I grew up on those stories from Mother Powers. Why, the day they got married Olivia took out an assassin."

Robin looked at me in awe. "Angel, your whole family has been under attack so many times! I guess that's why you have a guardian angel."

Barbara said, "Don't forget about her Aunt Barbara, she's an angel too."

Julie laughed. "The first time Robin and I saw Barbara, I about wet myself. I miss not having that picture in the common room. She gave us some good advice, but guys were scared to come over with her there."

I said, "Aunt Barbara and Barbara are well acquainted. Barbara showed up at my parents' law office when she was seven. Aunt Barbara spoke through her telling my parents what was going on with her aunt dying leaving her a orphan. Mom's parents eventually raised Barbara. Barbara is the spitting image of Aunt Barbara, haven't you noticed."

Julie, Robin, and Lilly looked at Barbara in surprise, then Robin said, "It must be your hair style that threw us. You did look familiar, but I didn't make the connection."

I said, "She's a famous painter too. You remember my healing picture. Barbara did that."

Julie gushed, "Oh my gosh, you're that Barbara. You're famous, I mean real famous. Are you going to do another one of Elizabeth?"

"I don't know. I would like to do another family portrait."

I said, "Oh Barbara, I almost forgot. Jeff's best man, Bob Peterson, might be the guy we were talking about before. He works in Dallas right now, but that can change."

"Hey, what about us. We're single too. You owe us for having your Aunt Barbara scare off our boyfriends."

"Jeff told me he's into weird women, like Barbara and me."

Barbara laughed. "It's kind of funny if I get introduced to my soul mate by a self-confessed weird woman. I guess I am a little weird."

I said, "Barbara, we are both a lot weird. I was lucky to find Jeff and maybe now it's your turn."

Barbara looked upwards. "God, please make him the right one."

Julie said to Robin. "We don't stand a chance if she's calling on God for help. I need a drink, anyone else?"

Neither Barbara or I drank much, but we ordered a glass of wine to be sociable with the other three. However, it was three hours later before I left the drinkers to Barbara's care and took a taxi home.

When I entered the apartment, Dad asked, "Did you have a good time?"

"Barbara and Lilly stayed to pour them into bed. My old roommates are the drinkers. Mom, is there anything I need to do tonight?"

"No dear. You look all in, so go change and sit with us."

I awoke to the smell of frying bacon and Elizabeth was standing over me with a big smile on her face. "Elizabeth, what is it that I smell?"

"Bacon! Get up! Daddy is making pancakes too."

Later, when we were all sitting at the table, I pointed at mother's plate. "Mom, what's going on? You have two pieces of bacon!"

"Oh Poo. It's my first daughter's wedding and I'm treating myself. I probably won't do it again until Elizabeth gets married."

Elizabeth said, "Momma, when's that going to be?"

"Probably when you are thirty. Oh my gosh, how old will I be then."

"I said, "Ancient!"

Mother threw a biscuit at me in response, which I caught one-handed. Elizabeth started laughing and picked up her biscuit, which I quickly snatched out of her hand. "Eat, not throw. These are too good to waste, so eat up. I'll go over your duties as the flower girl after breakfast."

An hour later the Powers family arrived with Grandmother Pearson. They hadn't had breakfast, so she volunteered. The men went into the living room while all the other woman went towards the master bedroom to see the wedding dress. Grandmother Alice Powers and mother spread the dress out on top of the bed.

Alice said, "Oh, the dress is still as beautiful as the day you wore it at your wedding."

"Wait until you see it on Angel. It will take your breath away. My Angel looks like an angel in it."

Ben's wife, Judy, said, "I saw you wear it on your first wedding anniversary and you looked fabulous."

Mother said, "I wonder if Elizabeth will want to wear it when it's her turn?"

When the women turned to Elizabeth, she grimaced as a reply.

There was general laughter as the women looked at the dress wistfully. Grandmother Pearson called, "Soups on!" Which emptied the room except for mother, Elizabeth and me. Mom hugged us to her breast and thanked God for her blessings.

We all left to join Dad to wait until the others finished breakfast. Grandmother Pearson cooked a big breakfast and I quickly stole a small piece of ham off the platter, eating it while asking Uncle Ben about his kids. He and Judy now had four, two of each sex, with the youngest four and the oldest twelve.

Judy said, "Lisa's at the age where it's not cool to have parents. We're worried she may get into trouble."

"Do you want me to send Ben's sister Barbara to speak to her? I'm sure she would listen to an angel. In fact if she agrees, have all your kids together with you when she visits. Introduce Barbara as their Aunt, who is now an angel."

Ben and Judy looked at each other, relieved. "As soon as I finish breakfast, Judy and I will ask her."

I went into the living room to talk to Aunt Barbara. "Well, it's finally my wedding day. A day that was a long time coming, but I'm marrying a good man that I love very much. I hope he is now under Olivia's protection because I don't think I could survive losing him. The Kansas City project is moving along and Jeff and I expect to move here within three years. Put in a good word for Barbara Messing. She's very lonely and needs a good mate. She's my maid of honor and will be here soon, so say hello. We still love you, so watch over us. Ben's oldest daughter is giving him trouble, so hear what he has to say."

I then went and sat with my family, watching as Ben and Judy talked to Aunt Barbara. Barbara stepped out of the painting and hugged Ben, then listened as he explained what he wanted from her. Barbara and my other brides-maids arrived while Aunt Barbara was still talking to Ben.

Aunt Barbara looked up at them, then motioned for them to enter and pointed where she wanted them. All four of my brides-maids were pale and uncertain of what was to come. After Ben and Judy left, Aunt Barbara walked over to them.

"I understand that you three primary brides maids feel I may have had some part in your inability to find a mate. Barbara, I have not been very observant of your problem. You will meet a suitable man today, but it will be up to you two to make it happen."

Barbara looked at me and I winked. Aunt Barbara continued, "You two are young beautiful women and soon to be successful doctors. There should be no reason why you can't find someone to love. I'll give you a hint, if you look at a man and feel a spark, go after him before he gets away. If he felt a spark too, he'll let you know."

Aunt Barbara turned to me. "Angel, come here."

I quickly hurried to stand beside my brides-maids. "Angel, Jeff is under the protection of Olivia and has been for two years. In five years you and Jeff will have a daughter. She will become very powerful and will help mankind with you and your sister."

Aunt Barbara then disappeared into her painting and everyone crowded around me. Mother hugged me and softly said, "Now you know how I felt when I was told I was having another child."

"I'm going to have a daughter, a very powerful daughter. I guess Elizabeth and I are going to be kept busy."

Grandmother Pearson said, "It seems the woman of this family have been chosen to carry the banner for God."

Later, as I walked down the aisle toward Jeff, I saw his eyes widen as I approached with my hand on dad's arm. When I finally stood beside Jeff he whispered, "you look like an angel."

After we said our vows, our kiss seemed to last forever. We broke apart to thundering applause of our guests. The waiting was finally over for us. My lips felt tender - not burned. Outside, we ran for the limo through a cloud of thrown rice, that was to take us back to my parents apartment for the reception.

Jeff and I did the usual things; cut the cake, posed for photos, and looked dreamy eyed at each other. I saw that Barbara and Bob Peterson standing close together at the back of the room talking. I hoped for Barbara's sake that they would connect.

It was time for me to throw the bridal bouquet. All the single women were grouped together, then I turned my back and threw the bouquet over my shoulder. I heard a mad scramble and a triumphant yell before I turned to find Barbara holding it above her head. I gave her a thumbs up sign, then turned and kissed my husband.

We quickly changed into our travel clothes, said goodbye to our guests and left for the airport for our return flight to Baltimore. We would spend our wedding night together in our apartment. Since Jeff had to return to his surgical residency the next day, I was wistful about not having a honeymoon . I was not due back on my job until Monday evening, but that was the life we had chosen for ourselves.

We arrived at our apartment in Baltimore in late afternoon. Since Jeff was carrying our luggage I started to open our door, when Jeff said, "Wait a moment. I want to carry you over the threshold on the day of our wedding."

When he sat me down inside we kissed passionately as a married couple. Jeff quickly brought our luggage inside while I hurried into the bedroom preparing myself for our wedding night. Neither of us were shy about disrobing in front of the other and we could tell from our mates eyes how much we hungered for the others touch.

When Jeff left the apartment for his shift the next day he walked with a small spring in his step. I lay in bed smiling recalling our memorable first night together. I wondered if we would ever get to the point of taking each other for granted. No, I would make sure Jeff would always want to come back to my passionate embrace.

I hadn't told him yet of Aunt Barbara's message about our daughter's birth in five years. No, I'd wait awhile before I dropped that bomb on him.

CHAPTER THIRTY

About two weeks later I received another message to meet President Smithson at his office after my shift ended. It was unseasonably warm as I walked to his office and I basked in its warmth after the cold ER. I sat for five minutes taking in the smells of spring and watching as others like me were enjoying the beautiful day.

When I entered President Smithson's office, the same individuals were present as before. President Smithson said, "I want to congratulate you on your recent marriage and it seems to agree with you. You're glowing."

I blushed a little and thanked him. "What have you got for me?"

"Not much. The tentative opening date for Phase I is ten months from next week. We want you there at least a month before that to help with staffing and operations. The hospital Administrator and CEO is going to be Dr. Ellsworth."

I asked Dr. Jacobson, "Do you have an estimate on when Jeff will be ready for his Boards?"

"Dr. Holmes will be coming to Kansas City as chief surgeon and he has asked for your husband as his lead resident. Dr. Holmes estimates that Jeff has another year before he's ready for his Boards and that's early for his specialty."

"Great. This is working out perfect time wise. My sister has about five or six years before she comes into her powers. That gives us time to get the hospital staffed and the new wing completed."

Dr. Ellsworth said, "I've arranged for you to be certified by the state of Missouri, so that you can practice in Kansas City when the hospital opens. I'm going to give you a listing of staff that have volunteered to transfer to Kansas City, along with what I anticipate our needs are going to be. Please check these and give me your thoughts. Based upon your previous advice we retained a core staff of old employees, so it's not going to be as bad as it could have been."

I thought a moment before replying. "To avoid problems we should soon hire an experienced local person to run our human resource office. We need him or her in place as soon as we arrive on the scene. Let that person hire additional help as needed for that department. Hopefully, all we would need to do is hire the best people for the open positions. I do know that if you don't already have it, we need a large security presence there 24/7 until the hospital opens for business, then security can be scaled back as needed. A hospital construction site is a tempting target."

Jeff was not due for another shift break for another four days, so I voice mailed him a message to his phone, telling him about his move with me to Kansas City in about nine months. I then called my parents about my move and asked them to start looking for a suitable apartment for us.

Mom asked, "Do you want one on the north side of the river?"

"Yes, a nice one not too far from the hospital. Jeff will still have about a year of residency left, so he won't be home much at first, but later a short commute will be nice."

"Honey, it will be great to have you close by again and I'm sure Sandra will be happy to have Jeff close too. Can I tell her?"

"Sure, why not. I'm sure Jeff will call soon too, but his next break is another four days. Maybe between the two of you you'll find us the perfect apartment."

Nine months later Dr. Ellsworth and I were at the Johns Hopkins Hospital in Kansas City interviewing applicants for the nursing staff. Helping us were the nurse supervisors that we had retained from the old hospital. Actually, they interviewed and we supervised. I didn't realize until then how smart I'd been to suggest they stay on at three quarter pay until we were ready to use them again.

We also needed doctors and Dr. Holmes would be here next week to supervise hiring his surgical staff. Dr. Ellsworth already obtained eleven doctors from the John Hopkins system that had volunteered to move to Kansas City. These doctors were in various specialties, that were sufficient to get us started, but we would need more as our patient level increased.

Lilly and Bob Cox were the first nurses hired and were now with Human Resources filling out their paperwork so that could start getting the emergency room ready for operation. When I called them and gave them the expected opening date of the new Johns Hopkins Hospital, they were ecstatic.

"You and I are going to be the ones to set up the ER, so look around where you now work and put your thinking caps on. What changes would you make, and what would stay the same. I want to hear your idea's when you see our ER, but at first you will be alone. I'll send you help, hopefully trained ER staff, and I will be there as soon as I can get free."

When Lilly and Bob finished their paperwork I escorted them to the Emergency Room. It was filled with boxes of equipment and medical supplies, and I let them take in the scene for a few silent minutes. "It looks different now, but this is where we're going to be working soon."

Lilly went to the sliding entrance doors, then turned and looked back into the ER. "We need empty gurneys stashed here for use. Somebody did good by having those high intensity lights installed above each station, and there are eight stations. We need two nurses assigned to each one. How many ER doctors do we have so far?"

"You are looking at her."

That drew a laugh from both Lilly and Bob. Bob said, "I assume we are the only ER nurses so far."

Lilly said, "We can start pulling these boxes apart and setting up the machines, but it would be nice to have some help."

"I'll send them as we get them hired. We need to hire food service personnel too. Even after we get everything up and running, we need to pass certification before we can open. At noon, come up for me and I'll take you to lunch."

When I returned to the interview room I pulled Dr. Ellsworth aside and said, "We need to hire copious numbers of nurses aids for the grunt work. We can hire them off the street and eventually keep the ones we like. I think a newspaper ad would get all we need."

She looked at me and said, "Do it."

I went into the Human Resources office and talked to its head, Joyce Brewster. "Joyce, I've just gotten Dr. Ellsworth's okay for you to put an ad in the *Star* for Nurses Aids. We need fifty, so run background checks and do blood tests for drugs on them for now, we'll cull them later after we get this rush over."

"Got you. I'll get them to where you need them as soon as I can."

Dr. Ellsworth ate lunch with us and learned my history with Lilly. "So Angel counseled both of you to come to Kansas City and become ER nurses, and this was what - two, three years ago."

Lilly said, "Almost four years now. You have to realize, we were like sisters the three years we were together at MU. She would have been my maid of honor when I married Bob, if she could have arranged it. So what she asked was no big deal for me or Bob. Besides, it's about the best paying nurses job there is."

"That's not my point. Angel was making plans for coming here that far back. She didn't approach us until about eighteen months ago."

"Didn't Angel tell you that she's been getting instructions from God through her dead Aunt Barbara, the angel?"

"Yes, but that's a little hard to get your mind around. It was easier to believe she's just a genius of a medical student and now a doctor."

"Well, she's that too. People who haven't actually talked to her Aunt Barbara don't realize how much backing she has from God. She even has a guardian angel for protection in addition to her Aunt Barbara."

I finally broke in. "It's nice to hear all these accolades, but we have work to do and right now hiring the right people is our job. The ER needs nurses and doctors. To be fully staffed we need sixteen nurses for each eight hour shift. We can get by with one doctor per shift, and we can call more from within the hospital on need. I would like three on duty at all times, but until we get fully staffed, that's not going to happen."

The following week Dr. Jacob Holmes arrived with two surgical residents from the Baltimore hospital. I was surprised when Jeff walked into the interview room, pulled me into his arms and kissed me. His kiss left me a little weak and I leaned on him for support.

"Oh, that was nice. Did you just get here?"

"Yeah, Dr. Holmes sent me to ask for help on the surgical floor. We need three nurses now."

I asked the lead nurse interviewer, "He needs three surgical nurses, what can we give him?"

"One trained surgical nurse and two nurses aids."

"That's all we have for now, but we'll send more as we hire them. We have extra aids if that's any help."

"Give us an extra aid for now, we have a whole floor to cover. I'll see you later when we go home together. Dr. Holmes said that today is going to be a short day for us."

Two hours later Jeff was back asking for more nurses aids. We gave him three male aids and he left happy as he now had strong backs to help him. The top patient floors were the first to be started, now the surgical floor was in process. When those floors were finished, then the next two floors containing the unconventional medicine rooms would be completed. The private rooms on the ground floor would be the last finished as there was no pressing need for them yet.

Lilly and Bob had help now in the ER, with two nurses and three nurses aids assisting them. The hospital had a no smoking ban anywhere inside, but during our second week the fire alarm went off. Dr. Ellsworth had set the alarms at their most sensitive to detect people smoking and quickly shut them off. All the staff were told to exit the hospital and when everyone was gathered, Dr. Ellsworth used a bullhorn to inform them that the next time anyone was caught smoking inside they would be terminated, no excuses.

Three weeks later the hospital was eighty percent staffed and had passed all inspections. The formal opening was set for next Saturday, in three days, with TV and newspaper coverage. The ER was open and all medical agencies were notified in case of an emergency.

Jeff and I were having a quiet night together after returning to the apartment after eating out. We were sitting together on the couch watching TV, when a news bulletin broke in about a big traffic pile up on Interstate 35 north of the Missouri River. I called the ER on my cell and alerted them to prepare for business soon. We might not get anyone, but I wanted to be prepared. I then called Dr. Ellsworth and told her we may need to call in another shift if the accident was bad. She gave me approval and Jeff and I headed to the hospital.

We got out of our car just as the first ambulance arrived at the ER. Jeff and I changed to scrubs and he followed me offering help as I requested. Both Lilly and Bob soon arrived and pitched in. After the fourth ambulance arrived I called in the next shift early and Jeff called Dr. Holmes for surgical help. We soon had three ER doctors and sixteen nurses working the patients as they arrived.

I called Dr. Ellsworth for a shift of nurses and aids to handle the patients being admitted. "How many do you have to be admitted?"

"Twelve and we're starting to run low on gurneys. Patients are still arriving by ambulance and our eight stations are full."

"Fine, you have the new shift of nurses to open the patient floor and I'm coming down there to help."

I soon lost Jeff when he went to the surgical floor with Dr. Holmes. I called the ambulance dispatcher and requested only critical cases come to us now as we were swamped. He acknowledged my request, but said, "The south lane of the bridge to KC is closed because of another accident."

"Never mind, we'll handle it then."

I thought to myself, *well Angel, let's see just how good you are*.

I began with my first patient, a woman with broken ribs and deep cuts. Using my powers I quickly repaired the ribs and sealed the cuts. I took her chart and noted the damage repaired and asked for follow-up x-rays. Next was a young boy with a head wound. Finding no other injury I sealed the head cut and noted the action taken. I continued on until I reached a young woman whose leg was so seriously damaged that normally it would have to be amputated. She suffered no other injuries except small cuts. I used my powers to connect arteries, major veins, and torn tissue and then checked if there was more I could do for the leg. It looked good, so I sealed all her cuts and noted what I repaired on her chart.

Eventually I looked up for the next patient and found no one waiting. I took a deep breath and looked back into the ER where everyone else had finished and they rushed towards me congratulating me on what we had accomplished. Lilly hugged me and I leaned on her heavily until Bob helped his wife get me to a gurney where I stretched out and sighed in relief.

I must of passed out for a few minutes, because when I opened my eyes Dr. Ellsworth's face was smiling down at me. "Feeling better now?"

I sat up. "I guess I overdid it. How are the patients?"

"No one died after getting here. Six had to have surgery and are doing fine in ICU. The last eight that you worked on were all released, except for the one whose leg you saved. She's weak from blood loss and residual trauma to the leg."

"I should check on her, maybe I can do something more for the leg."

"Not tonight. As soon as Jeff gets down here he's going to take you home and I don't want to see you back here until after lunch. You really drained your reserves. Go home. Rest. Cuddle with Jeff, but no sex until tomorrow."

"Yeah, like I'm up for that the way I feel now."

I made it back to the hospital at one p.m. after sleeping ten hours straight. I felt refreshed as I entered the interview room and sat down next to Dr. Ellsworth. I asked, "How many patients went through our ER last night?"

"Twenty-eight, eighteen were admitted, and the remainder were treated and released. All but one of the last eight you worked on were released. Dr. Holmes took x-rays and ultrasounds of the leg you saved on that young woman and can't believe how well you did putting it together again. Lindsey Scott, the woman you worked on, wants to talk to you. Do you want me to come with you?"

"No, that's alright, I feel fine now. What's her room number?"

"1012. She has it to herself. You can probably release her after you see her."

It seemed strange to visit a patient of mine in her hospital room. I bumped into a nurse who had just left Lindsey's room and held up my hand to stop him. "I'm Doctor Pearson-Blake. How is she doing?"

"I had her up walking this morning and she was experiencing some mild pain, but was walking without a limp. Great work doctor."

I smiled at him and entered Lindsey's room. She was a pretty brunette appearing to be in her early twenties. "Lindsey, I'm Dr. Pearson-Blake. I worked on your leg last night. Are you feeling any pain or discomfort?"

Lindsey tearfully said, "I saw my leg when they wheeled me into the emergency room and fully expected to lose it. When you approached me it was like looking at an angel. You had a glow about you and when you touched me the pain stopped. I saw you look at my leg as a project to fix, not to cut off, and it gave me hope that I might keep it. You probably didn't realize it, but I watched you repair my leg starting with the arteries and working up through the muscle tissue and finally sealing the tear in my skin. Look at it now, it's just a faint pink line. I've got you to thank for this miracle."

"Lindsey, what do you intend to do with your life?"

"I'm a physical therapist and I can continue to do that thanks to your efforts."

"Do you work near here?"

"No, I just lost my job when the business I worked for went bankrupt."

"Is anyone going to pick you up when you're dismissed today?"

"No, I live alone. I guess I'll call a cab."

"Your clothes were ruined. Wait a moment and I'll get you some scrubs to wear when you leave here."

I went to the nurses' station and asked for some scrubs my size for the patient in 1012. I signed her release and took the scrubs to Lindsey. After changing she looked at me questioningly.

"If you follow me I'll take you to the hospitals interview room. They are hiring for a variety of positions. Are you game?"

"Lead on. I need a job in the worst way. My car was totaled and I need a job. It's been a bad month!"

I took her to the human resources office and told them to hire her if they had a use for her. Lindsey looked at me in awe and sat down with the manager.

I sat down beside Dr. Ellsworth and said, "That girl has a good heart. I hope we hire her."

CHAPTER THIRTY-ONE

At the grand opening ceremony, the Mayor of North Kansas City gave a speech extolling how the new Johns Hopkins Hospital of Kansas City was going to add to the safety and health of the city. President Raymond Smithson followed the mayor and stood on the podium for a moment looking at the news cameras and reporters waiting to record what he was going to say for their next edition.

"I want to tell you a story that involves one of your own. A ten-year old girl by the name of Angel Pearson who could heal people by touch. I'm sure that you remember her even though she hasn't been in the news for years. When Angel was fifteen she no longer could heal even though her pictures continued to heal people around the world. Instead, she was given other powers, including the ability to diagnose illness and injury by touch. She was told by an angel that she needed medical training to make better use of this ability. She entered Missouri University at fifteen. You might think this was a little early to enter college, but she already had a year's worth of credits when she started. Three years later she started at Johns Hopkins Medical School when she was only eighteen. Three and a half years later she graduated as her class Valedictorian, something never accomplished before in the school's history. She completed her internship and residency requirements at Johns Hopkins Hospital and is now on staff at this hospital as head of the Emergency Medicine Department. Last Wednesday night the only part of the hospital open for business was the ER when that horrific traffic accident occurred on Interstate 35, and another on the southbound lane of the bridge across the Missouri River. Dr. Angel Pearson-Blake heard about the accidents on TV and immediately made preparations at her ER in case we received any of the patients. She was present when twenty-eight patients arrived at her untried ER. She and the extra called in staff treated all those who entered with no loss of life from any who arrived alive. Eight were treated and released and twenty were admitted, even though we were not officially open. I want to introduce you again to one of your own, Dr. Angel Pearson-Blake."

I wasn't expecting this high praise from the President of Johns Hopkins, but this was an opportunity for free publicity. I smiled into the camera and said, "Hello again. I'm happy to be back in Kansas City after my long absence. You've heard how I've kept busy and I want to assure everyone that Johns Hopkins Hospital is going to be known as one of the best in the Midwest. As you can see we are already expanding our operation by adding another 600 bed wing to hopefully be ready in another year. Does anyone have questions for any of our staff?"

A woman with a press pass held up her hand, and I acknowledged her. "I'm Jody Rader from the *Kansas City Star*. Dr. Pearson-Blake, several of us in the press have heard rumors about the extraordinary treatment they received in your ER, many of the treatments were performed by you personally."

"I have other powers than just the ability to diagnose and I used some of them Wednesday night. I hope my patients are not complaining about their treatment."

"On the contrary. They are ecstatic about leaving the hospital with little evidence of their injuries, some were reported to be quite severe."

"We at Johns Hopkins are happy to serve the public. Any other questions?"

After several more questions along the same line, President Smithson took the podium and turned it over to Dr. Ellsworth as the Hospital Administrator, who said, "Members of the press if you feel you need additional information about our operation I have arranged a panel discussion between yourselves and my staff this Monday night at six at the Channel 7 studio."

At the conclusion of the opening ceremony and everyone was leaving, I looked at Dr. Ellsworth with a raised eyebrow. She shrugged her shoulders and said, "When I heard that President Smithson was going to tell your story I knew we would get this reaction, so I arranged with Channel 7 to have this live in-depth interview. Besides it's great advertising for the hospital."

"What kind of format is it going to be?"

"No format, they ask and we answer. I'll try to field questions to the department heads that should answer the question."

"Why do I feel that most of the questions are going to be to me?"

"Angel, you wanted this, so suck it up and let's get the show on the road."

I hugged her and said, "I'm going to check on my department, then head home to my husband."

Dr. Ellsworth had everyone wear our white hospital coats with the Johns Hopkins logo to the interview. Not every department had separate heads. I was the head of Emergency Medicine, Medicine, and Orthopedics. Dr. Holmes was the head of Surgery and Anesthesia. Besides Dr. Ellsworth, there were six department heads sitting at the table. Facing us were newsmen from both Channel 7 and newspapers.

At the appointed time the interview started with the first question to Dr. Ellsworth from Jody Rader, the *Kansas City Star* reporter. "Dr. Ellsworth you are a long time staff member of the Johns Hopkins University. What can you tell us about Dr. Angel Pearson-Blake as a student?"

"She was an outstanding student. She has a genius IQ and an eidetic memory, so she usually attained the highest score among her peers. Upon our request, she started a self defense class for the students and later for staff members. She has a black belt in Judo, which she used to protect herself and other students when her class was attacked by several men. During her final two years at the University she was encouraged to enter our College Olympics, where she helped her team win both contests. By the time she graduated there was not a student who didn't know her personally or by reputation."

"Was she well liked?"

"Yes, when she left medical school there was a huge vacuum where she had been."

Channel 7 news anchor Jason Byrd asked, "We have talked to several of Dr. Pearson-Blake patients from the recent Interstate 35 accident and it's apparent that she used something different in treating her patients. As an example, look at this picture of a head wound that has healed to nothing but a faint pink line in less than five days time. This picture was taken two days ago and here is another taken this morning. Even the faint line has disappeared."

Dr. Ellsworth asked, "Is there a question in that statement?"

"Yes, can you give us an explanation?"

"Dr. Pearson-Blake you're up."

"You know I used to heal people by touch? Why is this procedure so hard to understand. I was given special powers that I'm still learning how to use. After repairing disfiguring injuries I saw no reason to leave a scar, so I used my powers to seal the wound that left no scar."

Jody Rader asked, "I've heard rumors that you repaired a woman's leg that normally would have to be amputated. Is that true?"

"Yes, her name is Lindsey Scott and she has been hired here as a physical therapist. You'll have to ask her what I did. She was awake during the whole procedure."

"She's able to walk and function as a physical therapist?"

"Yes, I released her from the hospital Thursday."

I was done with further questions and Dr. Ellsworth answered the majority of the other questions. Later, at home, the late TV news showed almost all my responses to questions put to me. Jeff said I looked professional, whatever that means. I called mother and asked if she had seen me on the news?

"Honey, I watched the original live show. You did well and I'm so happy that you were able to save that girl's leg. Is this what you're planning on doing in the future?"

"It's not set in stone yet. I'm going to consult with the chief of surgery and see if we can work out something we both can live with."

"Oh my. I wish you luck, turf battles are never easy. Dad says hi. Talk to you later."

The next day I asked Dr. Ellsworth if I should go through her in my discussions with Dr. Holmes regarding who would head up surgeries. She looked at me for a moment, then said, "I think whatever agreements are made should be part of hospital policy. So, I better be part of the discussion. How much time do you have today?"

After a call to Dr. Holmes we agreed to meet this afternoon in the Administrator's Office. When we were all together Dr. Ellsworth said, "Angel suggested we arrive at an agreement between her and you on what types of work she does."

Dr. Holmes asked, "Angel, is there anything you can't do?"

"I don't think so, but my time is limited. I would like to try to save people's limbs, once it's deemed hopeless. If after your surgery a large scar is going to occur, especially when it can be seen when wearing summer clothes, I want to seal the wound. Most wounds I find in the ER are minor and we will handle those. Unless you want my help I'll leave the other surgeries to your department. Is that satisfactory?"

"Angel, I really wish you would work full time in my department. No one can do the work you do, including your husband, and he's good. Okay, it's agreed. But I'm going to be calling on you from time to time."

Dr. Ellsworth sighed in relief. "Well, that was easy. I'll put this into final form and make a copy for each of you."

After we left Dr. Ellsworths office he said, "When you told me Jeff was a natural surgeon, you were right. I'm going to put him up for his Boards next month."

"Wow. Have you told Jeff yet?"

"Not yet, do you want to tell him?"

I thought a moment before replying. "Yes. I'll make it a special night for him."

I made a pass through the ER before returning to my office. Being the head of two departments required a lot of time; paperwork, paperwork, it never seems to end. I heard a knock on my door and looked up to see Lindsey Scott standing there.

"Come in Lindsey. What can I do for you?"

"I've got my work area squared away, but I haven't got any patients yet. I hate doing nothing. Is there somewhere you can put me where I can be of use?"

"How are you on paperwork? Look at my desk, we've killed a lot of trees for this much paper."

Lindsey smiled at me. "Give me a couple of hours and come back. I might be able to help you."

I looked at her with a raised eyebrow, but not wanting to look a gift horse in the mouth, I said, "Have at it. I'll see you later."

I almost ran from the office as I made the rounds of my departments and patients. Eventually, I found Lilly and Bob in the ER break room and joined them. I sat down with a cup of hot coffee and asked, "What's up?"

Lilly said, "Nothing right now. We have a good staff, except for the shortage of ER doctors. I understand we need numbers to justify more, but I feel uneasy."

"Me too. However, we did alright during that traffic pileup, and since then we've only been averaging five patients a day."

"We did alright during that jam up because of your efforts. What if you're not here and it happens again?"

"What if is a big scare term and nothing more. Every day we're open, our numbers get better and we hire more staff. ER will get our share I promise you. Anything besides staff I can help you with?"

Lilly looked at me and smiled. "Yes, give me a hug and make all my doubts go away."

We stood and hugged. I looked at Bob and asked, "What about you?"

He looked at us and shook his head. "I'll get my hug from Lilly. Don't worry about us, we'll make do."

My phone rang. Dr. Holmes wanted to see me in his office and when I arrived two black suited people were also present. "Dr. Pearson-Blake, these are Secret Service Agents Jackson Bourne and Beverly Graham. They are part of the advance team for the White House protection detail. If something happens and hospital treatment is necessary they want the best available."

Agent Bourne said, "Dr. Pearson-Blake, recent TV news coverage indicates that you have special abilities in the medical field, some say you are a miracle worker. I'm going to give you a what if example. Let's say a member of the first family is shot in the head and survives to reach this hospital. What procedures would you take?"

"Assuming the patient comes to the ER and not directly to Dr. Holmes, I would ascertain what the damage is to the brain and surrounding tissue by touch. Assuming the patient is not brain dead, I would begin immediate treatment. However, if the patient goes directly to the surgery suite, then I would wait for Dr. Holmes to ask for my assistance. You see, I'm not on the surgery staff, I'm the ER Department Head."

Agent Graham asked, "Assuming the patient came to the ER and you attempted to repair the brain trauma, what would be the odds for recovery?"

"That depends on the brain damage, but in the majority of injuries I've studied I believe I could save the patient's life. However, depending on the injury, there may be temporary or lasting disability."

Agent Bourne asked, "How many brain injuries have you worked on?"

"None."

Dr. Holmes spoke, "She recently repaired a leg injury that I wouldn't even have attempted. She hadn't done that before either."

Agent Graham asked, "When you were young, between ten and fifteen, you could heal people by touch. You then went to MU and then Johns Hopkins Medical School because you wanted to make the best use of the ability to diagnose illness or injury by touch. Apparently, you have developed additional abilities that you are still learning how to use. Is this true?"

"Mostly. I believe I can do any kind of repair on the human body that is not already dead."

"That's a big claim. How come you aren't on the surgical staff?"

Dr. Holmes said, "That's not because I haven't tried. She has other projects and duties, but has agreed to help me on call."

"My husband, Surgical Resident Jeff Blake, is going to be the designated surgeon in our family."

Agent Graham asked, "He's not a qualified doctor yet?"

Dr. Holmes said, "No, but he's taking his Boards next month."

Agent Graham said, "Just how good a surgeon is he?"

"As good as me and will probably be better in another year."

"But not as good as Dr. Pearson-Blake?"

"Nobody is as good as she is. She doesn't need a scalpel. She goes in with her mind and makes the repairs. In injuries where the outer skin is cut, she seals the wound in such a fashion that in a few days you can't determine where it was."

Agent Bourne said, "Are any of those patients still in the hospital? I would like to see this first hand."

I said, "Lindsey Scott, the leg patient, is working in my office. When we finish here I can take you there to observe her wound, if she doesn't mind."

Agent Graham said, "I think we're about done here Dr. Holmes. If we need additional information we'll contact you. Dr. Pearson-Blake lead on and we'll follow."

When we entered my office I saw that Lindsey had arranged all my papers in stacks, from which she was inputting data into my computer. She immediately stood and moved from behind my desk to greet me. "Lindsey, these are Secret Service Agents Bourne and Graham. If you don't mind, would you show them your leg that I repaired?"

Lindsey was wearing scrubs that had loose pants legs that were fairly easy to pull up past the area where the injury occurred. "You can't see anything now. Before, there was a faint pink line, but it's gone now."

Agent Graham asked, "There's no ill effects, soreness or a limp?"

Lindsey said, "No problems now. The first two days it was a little sore and I walk fine, see!" Lindsey walked around the office in a normal stride.

Agent Bourne said, "Can you show us your ER before we leave?"

CHAPTER THIRTY-TWO

After the Secret Service Agents had left I returned to my office to check on what Lindsey was up to. She was behind my desk still working on transferring data to my computer. I asked, "Would you explain what you're doing?"

"Your computer already had a software program for what you were trying to do by hand. Step over here and I'll show you what I'm doing."

When Lindsey finished explaining I said, "That's been there all this time? Am I the only department head that didn't know this?"

Lindsey said, "You're the only department head without a administrative assistant. I can do this for you until you hire one of your own."

"Go ahead and finish what you started. I'm going to look for an assistant. This job is looking better with a little help with the paperwork."

A year later the new wing was completed, making the Johns Hopkins Hospital appear to have an L shape. A medical helicopter landing area had been designed on the roof of the new wing for incoming emergency patients for their ER. There was room for three helicopters on the roof landing area, but so far the hospital had no immediate plans for a helicopter of their own.

The new wing was designed for single patient rooms to combat infectious diseases from spreading, but it was the privacy afforded that made it so popular. Patients were transferred from the old building to the new addition as fast as new staff hires made it possible.

The ER and other departments were now fully staffed with qualified personnel. Jeff and I moved from our old apartment to a larger condo within a mile of the hospital. I was now only the department head of Emergency Medicine, and Jeff was the lead surgeon under Dr. Holmes. I was called in by Dr. Holmes for difficult procedures if the patient's condition was critical, but usually I supervised and occasionally helped in the ER.

My sister, Elizabeth, was six and attending first grade at the primary school I attended when I was her age. Mother had her IQ tested, which showed she was a high genius much like me at that age. She was taking computer courses to keep her from being bored, but mother wanted to keep her in school as long as she could for the social interaction.

One Saturday I took Elizabeth with me on a tour of my ER. I had her covered in a splatter gown, mask, and cap while we observed a doctor and nurses working on stemming the flow of blood from a patient involved in an automobile crash. I asked, "Elizabeth, does the sight and smell of blood bother you?"

"No Angel. Can we move closer so I can hear what is being said?"

I put my hand on her shoulder and moved us closer so she could hear. The young woman patient had a compound fracture of the left tibia about half way between the knee and ankle. Elizabeth pulled on my hand getting my attention. She whispered, "Why don't they fix that bone sticking out of her skin?"

"They will, but first they are checking her to see if she has other injuries that might be more serious."

"She has something sticking out of her back that shouldn't be there."

"Did you see it or did you sense it?"

"Silly, I couldn't see it, it's on her back."

I said, "Dr. Brock, my sister tells me the patient has an object penetrating her back, turn her over gingerly and check it please."

Dr. Brock looked at me and then down at Elizabeth in

surprise, but he had been with me long enough that he wasn't surprised by anything I did. The nurses turned her enough that they could see a small metal object protruding from her back.

"Let me check to see if we can remove it before we do anything else."

I touched her arm for about fifteen seconds, then said, "It's only penetrating into the muscle an inch. If someone would hand me some forceps I'll remove it."

Soon we all were looking at what appeared to be the inside knob of a door lock. "She doesn't have any other injuries, so you can start on the fracture."

I looked down at Elizabeth and asked, "Do you sense any other injuries?"

"No, but she appears to have something growing in her lower stomach area."

"Dr. Brock you should also know that the patient is about six weeks pregnant, so take what precautions are necessary."

After we left the ER and cleaned up in the scrub room, Elizabeth asked, "What is pregnant?"

"It means she is growing a child in her body. That's the growth you sensed."

"Oh. How does that happen?"

"When you are a little older, mother will tell you the facts of life. I better not or she'll be mad at me, that's a mother duty."

When I took Elizabeth home I sat with mom in the kitchen drinking tea while Elizabeth was taking a class on her computer. I described Elizabeth's reactions in the ER and her apparent ability to sense the patient's physical condition. "Sorry, I told Elizabeth that you would explain the facts of life to her about how a person gets pregnant."

"What! Angel, she's only six. Why now?"

"Mom, she has access to the internet. I bet she's already searching for the answer. Satisfy her curiosity by telling her enough to answer her question. You can go into the moral reasons against recreational sex at a later time."

"Okay, but you started this and I want you with me when I talk to her."

I went to check on Elizabeth and asked her, "Save what you're doing and come into the kitchen with me. Mom wants to talk to you."

Mom looked at her young daughter with admiration and a little exasperation. "Angel told me about your trip to her ER today and your question about how a woman gets pregnant."

She then told her how the biological function worked. Elizabeth response was, "Yuck! Mom that's gross! Can I go back to my course now?"

After Elizabeth left, mom looked at me and asked, "Is that a normal reaction for a girl her age?"

"I found out when I was seven from one of my girlfriends. My reaction was about the same as hers. Of course when I had my first period I thought I was dying. You were a little slow on the facts of life speech to me. Does Elizabeth have an eidetic memory too?"

"I'm not sure, but it appears that she does. Why don't you give her a little informal memory test."

About an hour later Elizabeth came into the kitchen where we were still talking and asked for a juice drink. After she was settled and finished her first sip I asked, "Elizabeth, what computer course did you last finish?"

She responded with the answer and I asked, "Can you remember the first line of the course introduction?"

Without hesitation she gave me what the first line said. "How about on page 126, line four. What did it say?"

"Are you trying to determine if I have an eidetic memory like you?"

"Yep. Do you?"

"Yes. I was wondering why my friends can't remember anything, so I googled memory and found what an eidetic memory is. Then I did more research and found that you had it too. I also found out that we are both considered geniuses."

I said, "It's best if you don't brag about your memory or how smart you are to your friends. They'll think you have a big head who thinks you are better than they are. Keep a low profile and be your normal friendly self. Help your friends if they ask for it. They will know how smart you are without you telling them."

I returned to my apartment when Jeff arrived from his shift at the hospital. I met him at the door and kissed him. "I'm pooped. Let's order delivery, I'm so tired that I could eat anything."

While he was taking a shower I leafed through all the take-out menus we had accumulated and settled on Chinese. Jeff and I were watching TV when the food arrived. I didn't realize how hungry I was until I opened the first container and the smell of sweet and sour chicken hit me. We ate quickly and eventually ended up back on the couch in each other's arms.

Later, mother called me, "honey brace yourself I've just heard from my mother that Grandmother Pearson has died. Apparently, she died in her sleep last night and we'll let you know about the funeral arrangements later."

The news hit me hard and as I turned to Jeff to tell him what happened I broke down and cried into his chest. He just held me close until I was able to tell him the news.

We all traveled together in Mom and Dad's SUV to Baxter Springs, Kansas for the funeral. We met other family members at the Baptist Church where Grandmother attended.

I was a little surprised when we entered to find it was standing room only. I guess she touched other people the same as her family.

Mother and Father were both emotionally broken up. However, Grandmother Powers appeared even more distraught because she lost her best friend.

After the service, our family returned to the Powers home in nearby Coffeyville. We comforted each other by telling stories about Grandmother.

Grandmother Powers said, "Elizabeth gave me her apple pie recipe just a week before she died. She told me to bake Jack his favorite pie so he will remember her every time he eats a piece."

Mom embraced Dad as they both shook with silent sobs. My sister Elizabeth and I joined them as we all had an emotional melt down. Later, we sat down to a piece of Grandmother Pearson's apple pie to honor her memory. She was in a better place.

* * *

I couldn't believe it had been three years since Grandmother Pearson's passing. I still missed her and I was sure the rest of the family did, too. Jeff and I were visiting my parents, and I saw the strange look my sister Elizabeth was giving me then I hear a smile in her voice.

"Angel, you're glowing." Her smile broadened. "Yes! You're pregnant. Did you know that?"

Of course I did. I rubbed my abdomen and looked at Jeff. "It's true. I'm almost four weeks." Mom and Dad hugged me.

Jeff shook his head in wonder. "The prophesy of you having a baby girl in four years is coming true." He took me in his arms and kissed me.

I welcomed the safety of his embrace. "We're going to have a baby girl." I looked toward my sister. "Elizabeth, how strong of a reading did I put out? Was I hard to read?"

"No. My senses seem to be expanding the closer I get to my tenth birthday. For example, I can feel the energy from my niece. She is strong even now."

Mom said, "Okay, I think it's time we brought this topic up. Your father and I want to gift you the penthouse apartment that we're presently using to mail out the healing pictures of you. According to Barbara that miracle is going to stop when Elizabeth reaches her tenth birthday and comes into her own healing powers. The apartment needs to be refurbished, but we should be able to have it remodeled well before your due date."

I said, "I suppose we should consider additional security for Elizabeth, and my daughter."

Dad said, "Remember the crazy people who tried to attack us when you first became known as the healer. Some of those people have been reminded of who you are by the recent publicity about the new Johns Hopkins Hospital, and it will get worse when Elizabeth starts going to the hospital to heal."

"Okay, I get your point. Jeff, how do you feel about all this?"

"Your parents have thought this through, which is something I haven't done. I know my parents will like us closer to them and mother would make a great babysitter. The larger apartment is a real plus in addition to the security aspect. I'm all for it."

I hugged Jeff and said, "We're in, but I don't want to move here until I start my maternity leave in about seven months. Do you think it'll be ready by then?"

Mother said, "We'll make sure it is. I'll talk to Sandra after Jeff breaks the news of the baby to her, and between the two of us it's going to get done."

I said, "I wish Grandmother Pearson was alive to see another of her grandchildren. I miss her a lot these past few years."

Elizabeth, her namesake, said, "Me too. I talked to her on the phone a while before she died and she told me that Angel would show me the way. If I had a question about anything, Angel would know as she's already experienced it, and if she wasn't handy just ask Barbara because she's a real angel."

The next work day I stopped by Dr. Ellsworth's office and gave her the good news of my pregnancy and expected due date. She gave me a slow smile and then laughed. "You've been expecting this for years now, which means Elizabeth's tenth birth date is coming soon. I've gotten the press releases ready and last week I had the private rooms cleared and prepared for her use. We're ready when she is."

THE END OF THE MIDDLE

ABOUT THE AUTHOR

Hugh A. Flowers retired after almost thirty years with the Federal Deposit Insurance Corporation as a bank examiner. He now spends his time reading and writing novels and short stories and traveling the world.

Angel's Triumph is the second book of the spiritual trilogy Salvation. Salvation being the first and the third will be coming soon. You won't want to miss all the publications in this trilogy.

Other publications by Hugh are Salvation, Oklahoma Tomboy, Fountainhead, and Project Inception.

www.ingramcontent.com/pod-product-compliance
Lightning Source LLC
Chambersburg PA
CBHW051435170626
46809CB00006B/2468